Terms

Terms

Ben Lyle

Hookline Books

Published by Hookline Books
Bookline & Thinker Ltd
#231, 405 King's Road
London SW10 0BB
Tel: 0845 116 1476
www.hooklinebooks.com

The right of Ben Lyle to be identified as the author of this work has been asserted in accordance with the Copyright, Designs and Patents Act 1988.

A CIP catalogue for this book is available from the British Library.

This book is a work of fiction. Names, characters, places and incidents are either a product of the author's imagination or are used fictitiously.
ISBN: 9780993287428

Cover design by Gee Mac.
Printed and bound by Lightning Source UK

For Sally and David

Part 1

'The Government's purpose... is to secure for children a happier childhood...'
Introduction to the White Paper on Educational Reconstruction, 1943

'Education is what survives when what has been learnt has been forgotten.'
BF Skinner

1

'Wait,' I shouted, slapping my hand against the side of the coach. I ran to the doors and looked up through the glass at the driver. Fat, pale and middle-aged, he sat at the wheel like a man drinking alone in a pub. He rolled his shoulders and eyed me for a second.

I heaved myself up the steps sideways, making room for my backpack, 'Thanks,' I said. 'A return to Dungowan, please.'

'We should've left by now.' He looked down in disappointment at the small payment tray. 'I've got no change.'

I threw down some coins. 'The train out of Carlisle was delayed,' I said.

'I didn't ask for your life story.' The dash-mounted machine ticker-taped out a skimpy receipt. 'This is the last bus,' he added.

'Thanks for the tip,' I said. I hadn't been to Scotland since childhood but I was glad the welcome was as cheery as ever. Exactly what I needed after six hours on the train.

My rucksack was too bulky for the narrow gangway and I bumped a couple of heads as I inched to a free pair of seats near the back. The coach was half-full of people on their way home from work, but everyone sat on their own and guarded the adjacent seat with handbags or coats or cold glances.

It was a relief to finally uncouple myself from my bag. The air-con nozzle above me responded to my fiddling with a weak hiss, and cooled only the palm of my upraised hand while releasing a faint smell of petrol. My shirt was wet with sweat where my backpack had pressed against me. It made me feel hot and cold all at the same time.

The coach nudged through the outskirts of town, pebble-dashed bungalows stood among solid-looking houses made from a pinkish stone the colour of clouds just after a summer sunset. Windows still had posters up from the election. Most of them were the bright red and yellow of the New Labour government, a month into their first term in eighteen years – almost the exact duration of my education.

I tried reading the novel I had with me, but closed it on page two. Since I'd finished my finals I couldn't read anything for too long. I unfolded the crossword but couldn't concentrate. On the way up from London I'd managed five clues in total. Often, forgetting about a clue for a while helps make the solution become clear, as if you knew it all along – your brain doing the work without you noticing. But my mind couldn't rest. A graduate, I was in a limbo state between the completion of a degree and the public acknowledgement of the fact. Now that I was free to think about whatever I wanted, I couldn't settle on a single thing. My education was complete, my head empty.

Education is the big buzzword, ever since Blair's speech in Blackpool. It meant so much, he said it three times. I stood at the back of the Winter Gardens and cheered and clapped with the other student delegates. Older party members grinned at us. I wish I was your age, you've got it all ahead of you, they said, we'll be in power for years. And now we'd won. I saw Peter Mandelson striding through the conference centre, the star behind the star – only with too many skeletons to make it to the top job.

Now I found myself coming back to my old school. I had a spare month before graduation, I wanted a spot in one of the New Labour think tanks and I knew my educational past gave me an edge. Visiting Bannock House again might round out my CV nicely. At least, that's what I told myself when I boarded the train at Euston six hours earlier. I tried not to think of my own skeletons.

We picked up speed and cut through a hillocked countryside, criss-crossed by the uneven grey lines of dry stone dykes. Cars buzzed by in concussive bursts. I fidgeted with the ashtray jutting from the seat in front, now only a depository for used chewing gum. The girl on the other side of the aisle tutted loudly, so I stopped. She stared fixedly out of the window, her face angled away from me, but a couple of times she brushed white-blonde hair out of her eyes. A dark birthmark coloured the point of her jaw and I wondered if she plucked its hairs. She was about my age but wore a shop uniform of a white blouse and black polyester skirt, the kind that made people seem forty. Her cheek raged red and I could tell she sensed me looking at her. She smoothed her skirt over her legs but didn't glance my way again.

The coach pulled into Kirkmichael, about halfway to my destination. I stretched to see the driver, but the steps to the exit were out of view. A couple of shaven-headed teenagers in tracksuits appeared and bundled up the aisle, sniggering at something. Their eyes snared on the girl.

'Alright hen?' the first boy said. His taller friend behind grinned then flicked his eyes at me, challenging.

Her head barely twitched. 'Fuck off,' she said.

'Easy,' he laughed. The lad behind pushed his mate and they collapsed into the middle of the back bench. 'Just trying to be friendly,' he said. 'You look like you could do with a shag.'

I craned my head.

'Got a problem pal?' the tall one said. I swivelled back and looked aslant at the girl. She shot me a quick smile.

'Leave her Jinxy,' the tall one continued to his friend. 'She's a fucking lezza.'

The girl carried on staring out of the window. 'I'm no' a lezza,' she said calmly. 'I just wouldnae shag a wain like you.'

I didn't notice straightaway but someone else had got on at Kirkmichael. At first, I could only see the back of his head, a few seats behind the driver. A rising crinkled corona of dark hair, dust motes swirling above. It made me think of a bonfire. An old lady shuffled to the front, away from him and I soon realised why. The man's smell crept down the coach, a faint but persistent odour of rank neglect, like a long blocked drain.

3

People started coughing and muttering. The girl opposite put her hand to her face.

'Christ that's reekin,' someone said.

I glanced back at the two boys. The tall one sharpened his face for a moment then nudged his mate. 'It's giro day, so it is.' His friend laughed.

We turned off the main road and began a twisting ascent into the Bannock Hills. The shallow valley to the left looked less grand than I remembered; a few fields marked by dark gashes of dried mud, the river a shrunken trickle. I held my nose – there was something oddly familiar about the tramp's smell that I couldn't quite place. The coach's engine struggled against the incline and, as we bent around corners, I could see the dark black flowers of smoke blooming from the exhaust, fading into the air.

'Frumious, I say!' The tramp thrust an arm into the air and shouted. 'Frandship, frangible.' He swung onto his feet, gabbling and turned towards the back of the bus. His face was a mass of knotted black hair — like a caveman in a cartoon. He wore an ill-fitting suit over a filthy grey T-shirt. Rake-thin, he looked possessed, eyes cavorting as he lurched up and down the aisle gripping each seat for balance. He was rancid drunk.

'Fuck sake, it's the missing link,' one of boys behind me cried.

'No,' the other corrected him. 'It's the weirdo from Dalry.'

'I know that, ya bampot,' the first boy said. 'It's a joke.'

'Get away with ya, the fucking fairy,' the tall boy called out.

'Shocking,' a middle-aged man in front of me muttered. He then shouted suddenly. 'You stink.' Nervous sniggers broke out.

The tramp bowed to the coach and flourished his free arm, the other cradling a large bottle. The girl grasped a hanky to her mouth, her eyes wide, her birthmark stretched.

4

I saw the old woman who had moved to the front hunch forward and speak to the driver. 'It's no' right,' she said in a loud voice. 'He shouldnae be allowed on. I cannae breathe.'

A couple of other passengers added to the complaints but no one spoke directly to the hairy man. An exclusion zone now marked out his space in the coach. My thighs scratched against the coarse upholstery.

'He's paid his fare,' the driver called over his shoulder. 'Jesus.'

Oblivious to the noise around him, the tramp brought the heavy bottle to his lips.

'This guy's toxic,' the angry man shouted. 'Get him off.'

The birthmarked girl glanced at me but I avoided her eye. I held my breath, waiting to see what the tramp would do next. The bus lurched around a tight uphill corner and he stumbled onto his knees. His bottle clunked to the floor and wheeled along the aisle. 'Aw fuck sake,' a voice boomed. The bottle rested against the seat in front of me, a sad dribble of cider spilling from its neck.

One of the boys behind me laughed. The tramp rose and stumbled after his prize. With him washed the stench of undressed sores. I picked up the bottle to hand it to him as he scrabbled on the floor, muttering to himself in unknown words. Around us, the condemnation continued. *Get off, ya dirty bastard you. Away to yer bath.*

The tramp's face bobbed up inches from my own. His dancing eyes suddenly stilled and sharpened as he looked at me. I turned my head aside, the smell deeper and more cloying close up.

'Bastard!' he cried and launched his head into my nose. 'Satan's son. Beelzebub.'

I fell to the floor, holding my face, as he punched away – bottle forgotten, a whirl of wiry fury. A girl screamed. His fists struck me on the head then on the body.

'Liar,' he said over and over. 'Liar, liar, liar!'

I felt the bus slow to a stop. 'Get inta him,' one of the boys screamed and in seconds he and his friend where kicking

5

over my head. 'Fucking nutter.' A middle-aged man grabbed the tramp's suit and hauled him backwards. Like a writhing many-armed beast, the man and the two boys bundled the tramp towards the door. The drunken man's eyes went wild once more.

Blood ran from my nose and my shirt was drenched with cider, broken glass strewn around me.

'You alright son?' An old lady held out a paper tissue. 'Keep the packet,' she said.

I levered myself onto the seat.

The boys, my knights in shining shell-suits, shouted obscenities at the tramp as they kicked him clear of the doors. Everyone on the bus craned to the right-hand side to catch sight of him.

'What was all that about?' the birthmarked girl asked, pulling her fringe aside.

'God knows. I have no idea who he is,' I lied.

It's always a shock, the first time you see your teachers in a different setting from the classroom. When you're a child, they bestride the school like gods, all-powerful, all knowing, a species of philosopher-kings. Then you see them walking down the high street with their shopping bags, or hooting their horn in frustration in a traffic jam and you realise they are just like everybody else. I remember seeing my first primary teacher, Miss Giddens, sobbing into a napkin in a burger bar one day and realizing the world wasn't quite what it seemed.

Physically, the tramp looked all of sixty-years-old, but I knew he couldn't be more than forty-five. He had been in his mid-thirties when he first taught me. I used to be a mouthy twelve-year-old with a comeback for everything, but I couldn't think of anything to say now as my old maths teacher, Mervyn, stood on the grass verge. He made crazy shapes in the air with his hands and juiced his lips at the people on the bus. Then he mooed, like a Tex Avery cartoon character, and took an exaggerated bow, his anger forgotten. The passengers stared back, hard-eyed and embarrassed, and urged the driver on.

I caught the flash of the top of his head as we began to pull away. The driver crunched the gears and cursed. I twisted in my seat and looked back at Mervyn's bedraggled figure disappearing in the bus's rear window.

It was through a window that I first saw him.

*

My best friend Charlie and I sat in the school library on the Sunday before the first day of term. As boarders, we'd arrived at the weekend to settle in and we soon found ourselves alone at work. We shared a large drop-leaf table, its wooden edges striped by the marks of penknives. Charlie had been tutored in science over the holidays and took me through some basic physics. He scrabbled around for his proper calculator – the silly one on his Casio wristwatch useless for anything but tiny addition. I turned to the window and gazed out over the gravel, past the sloping football pitch towards the meadow. Grey, green, greener and then again grey — the low dark grey of the troubled Scottish sky.

At that moment a fast-moving figure stalked across the gravel in front of me, his face determined and serious. I watched through the window as he moved around our flank with swift, precise strides. He had wild, shoulder-length hair that rippled in the wind. His beard reached from his nose to the top of his chest and stretched from ear-to-ear unchecked. He came close to the building and I saw amid the inky bushes of his face two ale-dark eyes and a swollen red nose. He looked like an escapee from *The Muppets*.

'It's the yeti!' Charlie giggled.

'More like Rasputin,' I said as we scrambled to the next window.

The stranger bobbed away from us towards the South Gate. 'Who is he?' Charlie asked.

A Canadian voice answered from behind us, sounding American but not. 'That's Mervyn, the new math teacher.' Fran, the part-time cook and sometime politics teacher stood by

7

the open door. The teachers often doubled up jobs; Bannock House was that kind of school, everything a bit vague around the edges. You never quite knew where you were. 'What are you two boys doing in here?' she said.

'Nothing,' I muttered just as Charlie blurted out, 'Physics.' He tugged at one of the ginger curls framing his face and glanced at me in apology. 'My physics homework. From home.'

'Physics!' Fran barked. As she pushed chairs around, her fringed purple poncho swished in time with the clacking of her clogs. 'You're only twelve. You kids should be running around or something.'

'There's nothing wrong with science,' I said, suddenly feeling bad for Charlie. He always trusted people with his thoughts. 'It's the truth.'

'You majoring in pomposity now?' She shook her head and turned to Charlie. 'I can't believe your dad's got you studying in the holidays. It's crazy.'

'Leave him alone,' I said. 'All we want is an education.'

She dipped her chin and looked at me through round rimless glasses, her eyebrows raised. 'Not now, James.'

'If this was a proper school,' I went on. 'You'd be…'

'I'd be telling you what to do and you'd have to obey, or face a caning,' she said. 'If this was a *proper* school.' She leant forward on the table, her ringless fingers splayed, elbows bent. 'Now please, can you guys move out? The staff meditation session is about to begin.'

I opened my mouth to speak but Charlie touched me on the arm. 'Let's go,' he tapped his watch theatrically. 'We can finish this later.'

Outside, Charlie pointed in the direction we'd seen Mervyn go. I followed his gaze past the wooden tripod-shaped climbing frame and beyond a bristling bank of rhododendrons. 'You know, I think that new teacher was wearing a tie. Did you see it?' he said in excitement.

'I'm not sure.'

'Let's take a look,' Charlie said. 'I'll race you.'

We chased after Mervyn. It felt good to run with someone again. I'd spent the summer holidays pretty much on my own, which was nothing new, and had forgotten what it was like to run wherever you wanted, to take off without worrying about the traffic, or strangers, or coming home to an empty house. Charlie made it all seem normal and not stupid or childish or anything. It didn't really matter where we were going; I sprinted, listening to Charlie's panting as he tried to keep up.

'Ooomph!' he cried. I turned to see him stretched out, face in the stone-studded path. 'I tripped.' He showed a scuffed palm, flecked red.

'Dipstick,' I said. 'I told you to get a belt.' I hauled him up by his elbow. A sunbeam burst through the heavy clouds, dappling his face for a second.

'It wasn't my trousers.' He pretended to be angry. 'Know-it-all.' He dusted himself down and all the energy of our chase seeped away. I looked back towards the Big House. I didn't know when it had been built but it felt too old. It was made from dirty, unbrushed stones of different sizes with only a window here and there. It swallowed the sun. Round about it, trees bubbled like gigantic broccoli. The building looked like an overgrown gravestone in mourning for itself.

Through the nearest window, I saw Fran moving around in the library before she reached up and shut the curtains, banning the light. 'We've lost him now,' I said.

'Let's cut through the Tangle.' Charlie hiked his loose jeans, folding the empty belt-band over itself. 'If he's going to Dungowan we'll see him on the road,' he went on, cheerfully. The clouds shuttered, sending a shadow racing back toward the house. I glanced at Charlie. I'd almost forgotten what it was like to have someone smiling full in your face, as if it were you that made them happy.

We struck off the path. The Tangle was a huge triangle of overgrown land off the track that led to the lodge and the South Gate. It stretched to the river on one side and the road to the nearest village on the other. I'd only ever been in there once, in my first term, but never explored it properly. A couple of times

Charlie suggested we take a look but I'd never seen the point before.

Trees, bushes and long grass grew together like a complex sci-fi monster. When you pulled one branch out of your face, something else rustled yards away. The ground was wet underfoot, the kind of damp that could never be dry, even if the sun shone for a hundred years. Every footstep squelched and slid. Charlie chattered on about his holiday, about his irritating little sister and the granny with blue hair and too many hairs on her upper lip. I liked hearing about his family.

'I don't know why you bother arguing with Fran,' he said after a while. 'You two disagree about everything.'

A branch snapped in my hand. 'I can't lie,' I said.

'Saying nothing isn't the same as lying.'

We walked on. It was hard work slashing through the Tangle and we quickly realised Mervyn would be long gone, even if he had been going to the village. Besides, we'd see him soon enough. He was a teacher, not a visitor. Following him through the Tangle was the kind of idea that made sense on the spur of the moment but didn't stand up when you thought about it. Not when you find yourself cold and damp and dark and not quite sure of the way. We decided to try to get to the road all the same, to see if we could do it. I crawled under a low cross branch, urging Charlie to follow. In the distance we heard cars arriving at the Big House, girls screaming their reunions. It wouldn't be much fun back there. I could never think of the right thing to say, not without Charlie to smooth things over.

As we carried on deeper into the Tangle the sound of other people faded. I squeezed through a briar and came across a small, cobbled together wooden hut. The older kids often made huts out of cheap timber that the school bought for fuel. Little huts were all over the grounds, mostly in trees, private places for cigarettes, beer and snogging. I'd only ever been in one once before. When Charlie had an invite on Midsummer's Eve, he took me with him. But I didn't expect to find one in the Tangle. It seemed strange to drag the wood here in the first place, let alone having to cut your way through to it every time. 'Charlie,' I shouted. 'Over here!'

From outside the hut looked ramshackle and abandoned. It was about four feet high and sat on small stilts at the bottom of a shallow dip in the ground. Long grass wisped around its base and moss mottled the front deck. A piece of white plastic sheeting flapped from the side of the roof. Wicker matting lay fallen from the front wall, its edges twisted and frayed. I grasped the door handle, only to find it had been lathe-turned. That's not so odd in a school that specialised in craft but still, I didn't know of any of the older kids who would go to so much trouble about a hut. It felt eerie, like a derelict church.

'Charlie?' I shouted again. Something about that smooth ball of a door handle made me hesitate. I didn't want to go in alone.

'James?' Charlie cried, uncertain. 'James?' he called again, in a rising tone.

I stepped away from the hut, surprised how faint Charlie sounded, how far I had come. Following his voice through the moist undergrowth, I finally found him, snarled in a blackberry bush. His baggy blue sweatshirt was trapped in the thorns, his left foot shoeless. He hung there, smiling an anxious smile, looking like the last fat berry of the summer.

'Can we go back now?' he said.

'Fuck off!' a deep Scottish voice boomed across the grounds. 'English poof.'

As I rounded the corner of the Big House the next day I saw Keith, a boy of about fifteen with a pierced eyebrow and acne, gesturing at the log cabin which housed Mervyn's classroom. He swept back his long girlish hair and picked up a rock from the rough path. 'You can shove your fucking equations right up your arse.' He threw the missile at the cabin and cast around for another.

'Don't bother Keith,' Lone grabbed his arm. She was a Danish girl, about his age, with Timotei hair and perfect

English. 'He shan't last long. The committee will never stand for such behaviour.'

'It's a fucking outrage, is what it is.' He shrugged her away but stopped looking for another stone. 'He shouldnae talk me like that. Cunt.' The two of them walked away from the cabin, towards me. As they did so a breathless Charlie ran up by my side. 'You two got Maths?' Keith jabbed a finger in our direction. I nodded. 'You tell that hairy fucking cunt that I'll give him the heid next time I see him. Alright?' He swept past with Lone, or 'loan-AH' as Keith called her. She spoke softly in his ear, through the red-brown hair that fanned over his heavy leather jacket. The coat had M A I D E N studded across the shoulders in small nickel tacks. He'd done it himself in metalwork. They joined a gang of older kids and wandered across the gravel. Bannock House didn't have a dress code. We were encouraged to express our individuality, which meant we all had knotted hair, jeans, colourful T-shirts, scruffy jumpers – it was as effective as any school uniform.

'The heid?' Charlie said.

'It's Scottish for head. He wants to head butt Mervyn.'

'Wow. That's a bit unfriendly for the first day.' He plucked at my sleeve. 'Come on, let's go.'

Mervyn took his lessons in a large log cabin on the edge of the Tangle. It hadn't been used the year before but over the summer Murdo, the one-eyed caretaker, had cleaned it out and it was now the maths room. Windowless on three sides, the cabin was made from round logs like telegraph poles, topped by an inverted wide-angle 'V' of an asphalt roof that reached almost to the ground. Brambles and bushes licked and clung to the cabin's corners. From far way, it looked like it had no doors. It straddled two ridges and under the cabin the ground had been hollowed away even more, almost making a bridge. Charlie and I scrambled beneath the cabin and then up the thick wooden ladder, through the trap door in the floor. I was small enough not to crouch but I imagined Mervyn bent double every time he came and went.

Inside, the sloping roof made it feel like an attic. A watery light came from behind us as we sat, casting faint shadows when the sun penetrated the ever-scudding clouds. The windows were small panes each the size of a shoebox lid, separated by steel frames. A couple were cracked and one was taped up with cardboard. None of them seemed to open.

Mervyn stood by the far wall and adjusted the freestanding blackboard. A small wood-burning stove hissed inadequately and the threadbare carpet didn't even reach the walls.

'I feel like Anne Frank,' I said, getting up to close the trapdoor on Mervyn's mute instruction. Everybody ignored my joke. 'Anne Frank?' I tried again, looking at the blank faces around me. Charlie smiled but I knew he didn't understand. Lex, a small boy my age with insect-big eyes, lank black hair and clenched fists only glared while the two girls ignored me.

Mervyn tossed each of us an exercise book and began scratching something out on the board, his back to us. Lex picked up a pencil and pulled it back to his ear, like a dart, ready to throw it at me.

'Put. That. Down,' Mervyn said. Lex stared open-mouthed at Mervyn's back. The whole class looked around, amazed, for Mervyn had been focussed on the blackboard yet had somehow seen or felt what was going on behind him.

'How could you...' Lex began.

'Silence.' Mervyn didn't raise his voice but the word shocked me all the same, coming from a Bannock House teacher. He turned and pointed his chalk-scarred hand at the diagram he'd just drawn. 'Does anyone know what this is?' He stretched out the vowels when he spoke, like my cousins from Bristol that I hardly ever saw.

I sat rapt as he led us through the basics of Pythagoras' theorem. Mervyn explained the diagram he'd drawn, the theory and why it worked. Lex kept fiddling with his pencil, opening his mouth to speak but then saying nothing. Eventually, he tapped the pencil repeatedly against the edge of his desk. Mervyn carried on speaking but paced over to Lex, took the pencil out of his hand and set it back down on the desk. He fixed him with a glowering stare and then went back to Pythagoras. Lex cast his eyes down, too disorientated to offer any resistance. It was weird.

Everything that Mervyn said made perfect sense to me. There was no room for argument – it was correct, and obviously right. Charlie fidgeted next to me though, like he didn't understand.

'You already know what the length is.' Charlie pointed at the blackboard 'It says it's z. Look.'

'Z's an unknown.' Mervyn tapped at the board on each letter. 'X, y and z – they're all unknowns.'

'But if they're all unknown how do you find them out,' Charlie said. He wiped his snub nose, adding to the silver spindles on his sweat-shirted forearm.

'Look again at the rectangle,' Mervyn said. 'The right-angled triangle is always half a rectangle.'

'I get it, I get it.' Charlie's face lit up. 'It doesn't matter about the length, it's the angle that counts.'

'Exactly so. Well done.'

As the lesson continued, Mervyn prowled behind our desks, examining our work. We were arrayed in a tight horseshoe facing the blackboard, with the windows at our backs. I straightened as he came past me, allowing him a clear view, but he singled out a mole-speckled girl called Jenny and pointed to her doodles.

'The exercise books are for mathematics,' he handed her a rubber. 'Not flowers. Erase them please.'

He stooped over Lex, peering at his scrawl. 'You need to make the two smaller, so it sits on the x's shoulder – that's right. It means multiplied by itself not by two.' As he straightened, he rested his hand on Lex's back for a moment.

The bell rang. Everybody started to pack up.

'What are you doing?' Mervyn said. 'I haven't said you can go.'

Jenny looked up, surprised. 'But that's the bell.'

'I have fully functioning eardrums, thank you very much Jennifer,' Mervyn replied. He stepped back and flipped over the blackboard, like a magic trick. 'Here are the set questions for next week.'

'You mean, we have to answer all those?' I said, as I began to copy them down.

'Brilliant. You're obviously the brains of the class.'

'I have to work in my own time?'

'That's why it's called homework, now clear off.' He wiped the board clean as everyone clambered out of the trapdoor.

I lingered. 'But it's a boarding school. I won't be going home for weeks.'

He turned and examined me closely for the first time. Bending his head forward, his eyes rose over an invisible pair of glasses, struggling to focus. His left eyeball had a small red splash in its corner, like blood in a raw egg. I looked quickly at a cobweb strung between the chimney and the ceiling. It quivered in a draught. Mervyn fumbled at his tie knot. He held a piece of chalk in his hand and rolled it slowly between finger and thumb. A dying fly tapped uselessly against the window, snaring Mervyn's attention. Then he blinked three times and looked at me clear-eyed. 'Don't be smart,' he said.

'If I'm not smart, how do you expect me to do the sums?'

'They are not *sums*,' he said, severe. 'They are *equations*.' He pursed his lips, his dark eyes set and probing. Something about his stare made me cold for a second, like when the sun goes behind a cloud all of a sudden. I grabbed my bag and scrambled through the trapdoor, eager to catch up with the others.

The gang walked past the Big House, straggled together and talking about the class. As I drew level with Charlie, I heard Jenny complaining. She'd set hard and high the chin of her moon-shaped face, something she always did when she wanted to appear mature.

'I can't believe he told me off for drawing a flower,' she said. 'I'm telling Moira.'

15

Fat Moira taught art. Most people loved the art classes because they could do what they wanted. Jenny had threaded red cotton through her dark ponytail that morning and been given high praise.

Lex kicked at the ground, sending a pebble skimming across the gravel. 'Maths is boring,' he said. 'I hate Mervyn.'

They chuntered on in the same way – even Charlie had some doubts but I didn't care what they said. None of it mattered to me. I knew how to calculate the distance of the hypotenuse of a right-angled triangle. Of *any* right-angled triangle, ever. No-one could tell me any different, no-one could argue. Mervyn had taught us something that we didn't need a meeting to confirm.

That term Charlie and I were still Sparrows – the youngest of boarders. The kids were divided into three rough age groups for the purposes of accommodation: Sparrows, Kestrels and Eagles. Although we sometimes had lessons with older pupils, we shared our living space with kids of a similar age. This meant Charlie and I still lived on the top landing of the Big House's north wing, in the same dorm as the year before.

Painted a dark, oily orange, our room had inexplicable stains on the ceiling and an icy lino floor. Ivy clung to the sills, and the sash windows rattled in the wind. We never got truly warm, partly because the electric heater could only be turned on if you were in the room at the time. (The school wasn't strict about anything except money.) The best thing about the dorm – apart from not having to share with anyone else – was its position, perched on a high corner of the Big House. One window opened out on the front gravel and the football pitch. From the other window, we could see the muddy path that led to the meeting hut called the Octagon, its curved grey roof visible through the trees. Beyond the Octagon and set on a small hill stood the craft building.

A dusty drive ran beneath the dorm's side window and opposite loomed a tall tree with hand-size leaves. Thick twisted rope hung from one of its branches with a tractor tyre dangling from its end. Every now and then, one of the girls would lie in the innards half-hidden by the rubber walls. On the other side of the tree, obscured by summer leaves but visible through the bare branches of winter, lay two converted train carriages where the Eagles slept. Years ago, the school had bought the old sleeping cars from the railways. Instead of steaming back and forth from London to Edinburgh behind the flying Scotsman, they idled in a marshy dip out past the farm buildings.

I used to sit by myself at the window, like a cabin boy sent up to the crow's nest, watching the ebb and flow of the school go about its business. During his first few weeks, Mervyn would stride past the football pitch in the late afternoon and head off out of the main gates. He walked with quick, jerky movements that sliced through the air, always alone.

One day, about a month into term, I saw him jolting down the drive with the neat oblong of the folded newspaper held out in front of him. He'd kept himself to himself since he'd arrived and didn't even pass the time of day with us outside the classroom. I didn't know whether he was trying to create an air of mystery or whether he simply didn't like children. It didn't stop me wanting to know about him, to see if he knew as much about other things as he did about maths. I rushed from my room to intercept him.

Mervyn was already well up the driveway when I made it outside. He didn't seem to hear me running and I slowed, suddenly embarrassed by my obvious pursuit. 'Can you teach me how to do those,' I called out, pointing at the newspaper as I did so. Mervyn had been staring at the crossword puzzle as he walked.

He turned, surprised. 'I'm here to teach you mathematics.' He looked some way over my head – as if reciting the words from memory. Then he twitched his shoulders to one side and swivelled on his heel towards the gate.

I followed his nervy movements. 'Go on, give us one clue at least,' I said.

He inclined his head towards me but didn't stop walking. 'I don't encourage fraternization,' he said.

'Is that the clue?' I hurried to keep up with him. 'It sounds like gobbledegook.'

'It is not gobbledegook.' He laughed and looked directly at me for the first time since I'd caught up with him. 'Nor is it a clue.' His face sharpened for an instant, like an illustrated stoat or weasel from my copy of *The Wind in The Willows*. 'Good word though,' he continued. 'So much better than poppycock.' He blinked repeatedly, and then fixed me in his sights. 'Now leave me alone.'

I followed him up the drive, past the woodshed and picked up a cricket bat-sized shard of timber as we passed. Down to the left of the drive I could see Fran kneeling in the vegetable patch and tugging at something. She didn't seem to notice us.

'Maybe I'll bring you up,' I said as I swung the piece of wood in my hand.

He stopped short of the gate. 'What the hell do you mean by that?'

'In the meeting,' I said. 'I could bring you up in the school meeting for being uncooperative or unfriendly or something like that. It happens all the time.'

He angled towards me, his back to the road. 'To the teachers?' His eyes widened in his bushy face, like bird's eggs in a nest.

'Don't worry, I won't with you,' I said, surprised at how scared he seemed.

'You're not another like Keith are you?' he said. 'I had you down as different.'

'No, no. I was only joking. I'm not like Keith.'

He made a deep cawing sound in the back of his throat and stepped out into the road.

As I walked back, Fran trudged up beside me, her muddied hands cradling bunches of green vegetables. She held

18

them like a baby. 'Hey James,' she said. 'What was that all about?'

'Nothing.'

'It didn't look like nothing.'

I sighed. 'We talked about the crossword. Okay?'

'Okay.'

We walked side by side for a moment. The green leaves in her arms rustled and she smelt of fresh earth and sweat. 'Where was he going, do you think?'

'I don't know,' I said. 'I didn't ask.'

Getting to know Mervyn wasn't easy. When he did put in an appearance outside the classroom, he never stayed still long enough to share more than a grunted word or two. But about a week before half term, I arrived late for lunch and saw a spot next to him on one of the benches. He rarely ate in public, so I leapt at the chance to sit beside him. The rest of the table, five or six adults and a couple of kids, were talking in loud voices so I slipped into the seat unnoticed and helped myself to tomato soup from the large communal bowl. Mervyn kept his eyes on the food and didn't seem interested in conversation. I hadn't seen him utter a single word to an adult in the whole month he'd been at the school.

I listened to the others. Fran, Fat Moira and Raymond, a young teacher from San Francisco, were talking politics. Moira shook a tuft of bread at Fran. 'Listen to me,' she said, in a squeaky voice that belied her size. 'This is the political battleground; this is where it's at. Bugger the local education authority – there are bigger issues at stake.' Politics at the table was nothing new – Kinnock's 'outrageous lurch to the right' was one of Moira's favourite moans – but more often than not it was about running the school along correct lines. They seemed to think it mattered to the kids.

Fran's tone was flat and careful. 'Are you saying it's imperative we do something about the gender imbalance?'

I turned to Mervyn. 'What college did you go to?'

'*Which* college,' he said, pumping salt into his bowl. 'Maudlin. Spelt M-a-g-d-a-l-e-n-e. Oxford has a college with the same name but without the final E. After Mary Magdalene.'

'Who's she?'

He spluttered. 'Mary Magdalene? She's in the Bible!' He looked at me for a moment then slurped up the spilt soup from his beard. 'Haven't they taught you anything here?'

'This school's not religious,' I said. 'Unless you count blind faith.' I gestured around us. Mervyn chuckled. It was the kind of joke that ninety-five percent of the school wouldn't have laughed at.

Moira's voice grew louder. 'I still think we should look at massage lessons for the boys and martial arts for the girls.'

'I'm not sure if that'll go down too well with the Inspectorate,' Fran said, her spoon hanging halfway between her bowl and mouth. 'Maybe we should concentrate on some maintenance issues first. And the syllabus, too. If we're not careful…'

Moira slapped her hand on the table. 'Bourgeois,' she said through a mouth full of bread. 'And the inspectors aren't due this year anyway. Show some ambition.'

'That's so right,' Raymond said, tucking curly black hair under his headband. He wore a different coloured one every day, depending on his mood. 'I'm not sure about martial arts for the girls, though,' he went on. 'That's not so peace loving is it? How about something more outdoorsy, you know? Woodcraft maybe?'

Moira closed her eyes and breathed in, one hand clasped around her fleshy neck. 'Don't be so American,' she said after a moment. 'Remember, you're new here.'

'Maybe now's not the time,' Fran tapped a spoon on the side of her plate. She glanced at the kids around the table before addressing Moira. 'We can discuss this in senior committee.'

Mervyn hadn't said anything throughout the conversation, even though the other teachers looked at him every now and then. Not talking made you a bit of a weirdo at Bannock

House. Especially when you're dressed in a shirt and tie and everyone else looks like they've tumbled out of a VW camper van circa 1976.

Charlie came over and put his hand on my shoulder. 'We should get changed,' he said. 'Raymond's taking football this afternoon. Except he calls it soccer.'

Raymond looked over at the mention of his name. 'You got it,' he cried. 'Soccer's on me.'

Mervyn collected his cutlery, ready to leave. Everybody had to clean up their dirty plates, even Sparrows. It taught us self-sufficiency and a commitment to the community. As if kids in the rest of the country couldn't clean up after themselves.

'Will you show me how to do the crossword?' I asked him.

He stood up. 'No.'

Charlie still had his hand on my shoulder. 'What is it with you and crosswords?'

'Please?' I looked up at Mervyn. 'You know so much more than everyone else here.' I didn't say this loudly but I didn't care if any of the other teachers heard me. They already knew I didn't respect them.

He fingered his moustache with his free hand. 'It's not a good idea, it really isn't.' But he didn't move. 'Look James,' he said, at last. I liked it when he used my name. 'A cryptic clue usually has a straight definition either at the beginning or the end of it. The other parts of the clue help you to decode the synonym. But beware, the setters are skilled at misdirection. They want you to think of irrelevant things, to take your mind down blind and arid alleys.' He paused, perhaps uncomfortable about speaking so much. 'If you are serious about cryptics, it's best to start with the quick crossword. Now I must go.'

'You should watch us play football,' I said, but he'd already turned towards the door. I watched him dump his cutlery at the head table and leave. He didn't look back. Charlie tugged at my shirt and I saw Fran's eyes follow after Mervyn. When she noticed me she ducked her head and took off her glasses to polish them on her sleeve. It made her seem smaller and older at the same time.

Charlie and I changed into football kit in our dorm. The school didn't have dedicated dressing rooms for games. It didn't really have much money or facilities for anything other than woodwork, art and pottery.

I pulled my mud-caked boots out from under the bed. Charlie unwound himself from his various layers of clothing. 'We're going to the Lake District for half term,' he said. 'There's not much to do there but I suppose it will be alright.' I pulled crusty socks over my Bryan Robson shin-pads. Charlie tied his flag-sized shorts with a big bow and slipped on a T-shirt. 'My grandma's coming too – she farts all the time but my mum says we're not allowed to laugh. She says it's best to pretend it never happened, because it upsets my dad. He worries, that's why he sleeps a lot. Are your parents coming up for half term or are you going home?'

'It's raining,' I said.

'Oh god, it is too. Another mud bath. I hope it doesn't rain in the Lake District – my sister gets carsick. Why did you ask Mervyn to watch?'

I said nothing as we clattered down the stairs. Normally, I liked Charlie talking about his family but I didn't want to get into a conversation about holidays, or mention the postcard my father had sent me from New York. That's where he'd be when I went home for half term. The card made no reference to my mother. She'd probably be out at dinner parties for most of the holiday week, boasting about my idyllic education in the Scottish Highlands and how happy the school made me. Bannock House wasn't even in the Highlands.

We trudged through the rain to the pitch. Everybody called it the 'football pitch' but it wasn't even rectangular. It sloped from one wing to the other but also rose sharply into a goal mouth and tapered at one end. The splintering goalposts creaked in the wind and we had to collect the ball through gaping holes in the nets.

'Get a move on Dessie, it's fucking freezing,' someone called out.

'My name is not Des,' Raymond shouted. 'For crying out loud.'

'Sorry, *Raymond*.' Keith laughed.

When he first arrived from America, the summer before, a rumour sprung up that Raymond was the secret love child of Charles Manson. He had the same dark, staring eyes and flailing hippy hair, so it made sense. I don't know who started it, but the story stuck for a while until Raymond finally had enough and produced a pale Polaroid of two frumpy square-headed WASPS. He pinned it to the noticeboard with a scrawled note: 'Raymond's Mom and Pop. Lifetime residents of Des Moines, Iowa.' The upshot of this for Raymond, though, was that the kids started calling him 'Dessie', 'Des' (as in Desmond) or even 'Square Des,' which annoyed him even more than the whole Charles Manson thing. He would stamp his foot in frustration and shout: 'You're not even saying it right. It's *day moin, day moin*.'

There were about sixteen players in total, made up of all ages with the Eagles such as Keith shared between the two sides. Like most Bannock House classes, it was run in as haphazard a way as possible. The teacher hardly needed to be there at all. I wondered why the teachers bothered to turn up to classes sometimes, never mind the kids. Raymond towered over all of us. He wore a baggy green T-shirt and his enormous tracksuit trousers billowed around sockless ankles.

'Come on guys, let's go for it,' he screamed, bouncing on the balls of his feet. 'Soccer, YES!' He slapped the back of Paddy, a skin and bones Kestrel with a bowl cut. Paddy coughed. We all looked down at the ground. 'Go team,' Raymond said, more quietly, once he realised no one was going to say anything.

His curly hair held in check by a wide, white headband, he reminded me of John McEnroe. Except that Raymond was a total stranger to physical grace. He played the game as if controlled by a drunken puppeteer, arms and legs flailing

23

uselessly as opponents charged past him. The one time he did get the ball I slid in and tackled him to the ground before he'd gone far.

'Time out, time out,' he cried, making a T-sign with his hands. 'This game is getting way too aggressive.'

Keith picked up the ball. 'You don't have time outs in football,' he said. 'And we're not even timing it.'

'Whatever.' Raymond took the ball. 'I'm taking a free hit here.'

'But it wasn't a foul,' Keith said, hauling me up from where I lay after the tackle.

'And it's a free *kick*, not hit,' Charlie added.

'Look guys,' Raymond said too loudly. He stopped, took a deep breath and began again. 'Let's keep things fair. Peace and love, right? Soccer's not a contact sport – so let's cut out the rough stuff.'

'You mean tackling?' I said.

'Right!'

We carried on but Raymond stopped the game after every tackle. It wasn't much fun after that. A couple of kids even gave up completely and took to diving in the mud slick that had formed in the bottom goalmouth. I kicked the ball as hard as I could every time I got it, it didn't matter in which direction. Once the rules had been tampered with, the game felt pointless.

'Over here,' Charlie called from the wing and for once I tried to pass it accurately. As I did so, I noticed Mervyn patrolling the edge of the pitch. He followed the game, I could see, but I didn't know how long he'd been there. He didn't have a raincoat or umbrella and the rain made his head look like a black mop. Charlie went for the ball but Keith grabbed him around the waist with both arms and held him back, laughing.

'Stop it,' Charlie squealed.

I ran over and grabbed Keith's arm. 'Leave him alone.'

'Easy, wee man,' he said. 'It's only a joke.'

Charlie smiled.

Mervyn stood close by, his hands thrust deep into his pockets, oblivious to the rain darkening his jumper. But his eyes shone and his tongue flashed purple through his beard. He half-stepped forward, as if ready to uncoil. Then he saw me looking at him and turned his face away.

'Play on,' Raymond cried, free on goal for the first time in the match. He'd taken the chance to slip clear. We all watched as he bore down on the goalkeeper. He drew back his right leg to strike but as he did so his standing foot accidentally tapped the ball away. His boot swung viciously at thin air, trouser leg flapping, and he overbalanced, falling into the goalmouth puddle.

'That. Is. It.' He shouted. 'I'm through.' He pushed himself up from the ground, mud-soaked. The kids cackled in unison as Raymond, looking like some lagoon creature, stomped about. 'Game over.' He sliced his hands in a crossing motion. 'You guys are totally, totally…'

He picked up the ball and then yelled at us again. 'This is so uncool.' He swept away towards the Big House, the school's only good football lodged under his arm.

'That is sooo sooo, totally, like uncool man,' Paddy said in an American accent and everyone laughed and mimicked Raymond's voice.

As we started back to our dorms, I heard Mervyn say 'Buffoon.' I turned back, wanting to know what he meant, but he was already striding towards his rooms. In that one afternoon, though, I'd learnt more about Mervyn than the whole of the preceding term. I couldn't forget the life in his eyes when he saw Keith and Charlie tussle, couldn't forget how quickly he turned away when he saw I'd noticed. He definitely liked games.

While classes at Bannock House were often optional, when it came to eating you had to be there on the dot or you were liable to miss out. Not long after half term, and maybe three weeks after Raymond had stormed out of football, I had forgotten about supper one night and hurried down from the library to make sure I wasn't too late. As Sparrows, we took the last meal of the day at eight every evening – an hour before designated 'lights out'. We always had the same thing: tea and thick slices of toast spread with St Ivel Gold and honey. Unlike the other meals, we ate it in the school's huge kitchen. It had two entrances, the main one leading from the hallway and a second one that connected to a scullery out the back.

As I hurried through the scullery, I heard all the usual suppertime noises, the clanking of teacups and the card game calls. In the kitchen proper, the rest of the Sparrows – Jenny, Charlie, Lex and a couple of others – sat playing cards, ringed around the far end of the broad Formica-topped table that dominated the room. Three bright lights hung low over the white surface giving it the feel of a bleached snooker table. A black and yellow Aga stretched along the length of one of the walls, for about twenty feet, like a 1950s vision of the future with shiny round hotplate covers, and curved panels on the oven doors. I was about to sit when I stopped short, surprised to see Mervyn leaning against the large oven.

Fran appeared from the walk-in larder and saw me hesitate. 'Mervyn's helping out tonight,' she said. 'Moira's had to visit her mother.' Moira and Fran shared the job of house-parents. Each of the age groups had two members of staff who made supper and put the kids to bed. The idea was to create a home away from home for children, though who among us had two mothers and no father, I don't know. If they'd wanted to recreate my home life accurately, they should have left a note.

'Her mother's ill,' Fran said.

I took a stool at the head of the table. 'Fat Moira's got a mother?'

The ancient kettle on the Aga steamed hot fog into the room but Mervyn looked unsure of how to pick it up. He half-turned towards the hotplate, and then cast around for guidance. Fran stepped past him with the teapot in her hand. 'You need to bring the pot over,' she said in a soft voice. 'And pour like this.' She emptied the kettle with hands swaddled by oven gloves. 'James, you shouldn't call Moira fat. It's not nice.' She heaved the steel teapot to the table. It looked like the head of the Tin Man.

A card slapped down. 'Shithead!' Lex cried, pointing to the loser of the hand. 'Your deal.'

Charlie turned from the game. 'She really is fat,' he said to Fran. 'I'm sorry.'

'She's so fat, she looks like she's in bed,' I said. Mervyn laughed and Fran frowned. Mervyn stopped laughing.

I poured myself a cup of tea and watched the play, though it didn't interest me. The point of the game was to lose all your cards as quickly as possible but with no real skill involved, only luck. Mervyn twitched and I looked at him out of the corner of my eye. He didn't know where to put his hands and kept glancing at Fran as she moved about the kitchen. 'Did you complete the crossword today?' I asked him.

'Of course,' Mervyn said with pride.

I hadn't seen Mervyn outside class since before half term, and so hadn't got far in my quest to learn the secrets of the cryptic crossword. I pulled the school's *Guardian* towards me and started the quick crossword.

'Shithead!' Jenny screamed.

'Hey Mervyn,' Fran called from the walk-in larder. 'Could you cut some more bread?'

He shot forward from the Aga. 'Certainly,' he said. His hand on the bread knife reminded me of an over-cooked chicken wing, all bone and stretched papery skin. He hacked at a heavy brown loaf but his first effort sheered off halfway down and he had to begin again.

'What's a buffoon?' I said as if to no one in particular. Mervyn struggled with a second slice. 'Try starting an inch in,' I suggested.

'How many letters?' he replied. That caught me off guard. I watched as he prised a saggy piece of bread from the loaf. His hand shook for a moment, then I realised he expected a reply.

'It's not a clue,' I said. 'I was just wondering, that's all.'

The phone rang. Fran moved around the table and out into the hall. 'Can you put those slices on to toast, please Mervyn?' she called over her shoulder.

The telephone had its own cupboard, off the hallway. It had an old-fashioned dial with letters under each number and a small lock on the 'two'. You had to borrow the key from the member of staff on duty and then write down how long your call took on a clipboard hanging on the door. The cost was added to your parents' bill at the end of each term.

Fran walked back into the kitchen from the hall. 'Charlie, it's your pa.'

Parents tended to call at supper – they knew their kids would be by the school's only phone at that time. Charlie ambled through to the hall. It was no big deal for him.

'Don't be long,' Jenny said. 'My mum's calling tonight.'

'I'm ringing home too,' someone else said.

Fran picked up her knitting and sat next to me. 'Trying to call tonight?' she asked. I shook my head. In my first year, I used to ring home often but it was never a convenient time of day for my mother and father. Either they were out or heading out whenever I called. It had taken me a while to understand that sending me to boarding school freed up my mother's social life. Once she realised she could do what she wanted while I was away, that stretched into the rest of her life. Her idea of maternal care now involved asking the housekeeper to sew nametags onto all my clothes.

Jenny turned her attention from the game for a second. 'Why does no one call you?' she said, tossing hair from her eyes.

'Shut the fuck up, melon head,' I shot back. 'Nobody asked you.'

'I was only asking.'

'We're not all motormouths, okay. Satisfied?'

The cards flopped down on the table and for a moment everyone became quiet, listening to Charlie's muffled chatter from the phone cupboard and the rhythmic clacking of Fran's needles. 'I hear Raymond didn't have too much fun at games the other week?' she said after a pause.

I looked down at the tight whorls of wool spooling from her hands, hypnotised.

'James?' she said again.

'Football's too aggressive according to Raymond,' I said. 'We dance now instead. It's non-competitive.'

'Is that the American?' Mervyn asked, placing a couple of bent slices of bread on the griddle. Fran nodded. He chuckled to himself and shook his shaggy head.

The smell of toast, like wholemeal caramel, filled the kitchen. 'Shithead!' Lex called out, and Jenny dashed down her cards. 'Your deal,' he said rapping his knuckles against the tabletop. He looked along the table at me with his big bug eyes. 'Don't you want to play Shithead, shit head?'

I ignored him and tried to concentrate on the crossword.

'Know much about soccer, Mervyn?' Fran ventured.

'Yessss!' Lex said in a parody of pleasure at the cards he'd been dealt.

'Blast,' Mervyn cried, clattering the griddle to the floor as he tried to pull it out of the oven. He stepped back, flicking his burnt fingers rapidly and rushed into the scullery. Over the running tap he called out. 'I used to referee.' I kept my head down but I could sense Fran's interest in my reaction.

She walked around to the griddle and picked it up with an oven glove, still talking to Mervyn through the doorway. 'Maybe you should give a helping hand in games,' she said. 'I'm sure the kids would appreciate someone who knew the rules.' I looked up at the scullery door, waiting for Mervyn's reply.

He appeared, sucking his finger. 'I don't know,' he said at last, looking across at Fran. Framed in the doorway, indecisive, caught between yes and no. Fran faced him, about six feet away, and they stared at each other without moving. Although Mervyn was a tall and hairy adult, in that moment he reminded me of myself as a nine-year-old standing in front of my mother and not quite knowing how to please her. I looked at Fran. She

29

had one hand on the side of the Aga, where she'd laid the griddle down, and the other held on her hip, a pose that made her look thinner yet rounder all at the same time.

'Jenny, it's your turn,' Charlie hollered from the hallway. 'I'll play your hand.'

I seized my chance. 'Mervyn's going to take football next week,' I said to Charlie.

'Great.' Charlie looked up at Mervyn. 'Raymond doesn't have a clue.'

'Unless you want to express anger through the medium of dance,' I added.

Fran stretched her arms out to Charlie and me in an odd gesture, palms facing up and rising. She addressed Mervyn. 'Looks like you're hired.' She smiled.

Mervyn hesitated. 'I suppose I'd better find a whistle.'

After supper it was my turn to do the washing up at the scullery sinks. In the kitchen, I heard Fran thank Mervyn. 'It's good of you to take on the soccer match. I think the kids'll appreciate it.'

'Right, yes,' Mervyn said. 'Of course.'

'You know, it gets pretty cold here in winter.' I heard one of them shut the larder door and lock it. 'I could knit you some kind of sweater if you like?'

Mervyn stumbled over his reply. 'Well, no, I mean, I couldn't possibly. Your time?'

'Nonsense,' Fran said, brushing away his reticence. 'I can knock you one out in a couple of committee meetings, right?' She laughed in a way I'd never heard from her before, light and floaty as if nothing weighed very much at all.

'Um, I suppose…no. I really couldn't ask you to put yourself out.'

'Well, if you change your mind. Now let's get these damn kids to bed.' She came through the scullery door. 'Oh God, James,' she said startled, her hand rising to her heart. 'You scared me. I thought you'd gone upstairs.'

'I didn't hear anything,' I said. 'I was drying up.'

She clapped her hands twice. 'Get to bed now.' I saw Mervyn's face appear behind her shoulder and he looked a bit put out, as if I'd done something wrong. I went up the stairs and heard Fran say to him: 'Lex normally needs a bit of extra help. Do you want to take him or shall I?'

'Oh, I'll do the others. You do Lex.' Hearing that made me feel better. I didn't think Lex deserved extra time with Mervyn just because he couldn't brush his teeth properly.

At lights out, Mervyn poked his head around our door with his hand on the light switch. 'Ready?' he said. Charlie and I, duvets pinned beneath our chins, chimed goodnight in unison.

'Oh, by the way,' Mervyn flicked the switch, leaving only the crinkled over-sized silhouette of his head against the hall lights. 'A buffoon is a jester, an ass or a fool.'

Mervyn began taking football every week. He didn't play himself, never even kicked a ball, and wore his usual clothes with the addition of a big silver whistle around his neck. Instead of simply playing a match straightaway, he made us warm up first. We jogged around the outside of the pitch twice while he stood in the centre circle shouting at the laggards to keep up. Then we had drills. He found traffic cones from somewhere and we had to dribble through them. We formed passing triangles. We ran shuttles. Only then were we allowed to play a game, which Mervyn refereed.

At first, some people grumbled and said they didn't turn up to football just to run around but the complaints soon stopped. For the routines made the whole thing more enjoyable. We began to trap the ball better, we ran faster and we started passing to each other rather than always trying to run and shoot ourselves. Even the kids who hated Mervyn's maths classes loved his football sessions. Beforehand, everybody would swarm around the ball like it was some kind of powerful magnet, but Mervyn taught us to play with discipline. It felt like we were playing a version of the real

31

thing. We kept 'our shape' tactically, stayed in position so our teammates could pass to us.

He was also a strict referee. Although he praised tackling as much as anything else – he'd mutter 'tackle' or 'shot' and so on every time we did something good – he wouldn't hesitate to pierce the air with his gleaming whistle if someone fouled.

One day in November, we turned out to play even though the ground was still hard from the frost the night before. We shivered through the warm ups and Charlie's bright white thighs went as red as his hair. During the game, I played a one-two with Keith and was through on goal when Lex blatantly tripped me, sending me sprawling on my front. Mervyn's whistle went and I turned to see him running over.

'I never touched him,' Lex said. 'He dived. I was nowhere near.'

Mervyn's brow knitted and his moustache quivered. 'Do not lie to me,' he said. 'I had been planning to caution you for the patent foul challenge. But lying compounds the offence.'

'What are you talking about?' Lex pouted.

'A red card.'

'A red card?' Lex still couldn't quite understand.

'Foul play and then ungentlemanly conduct. Two yellows make a red. Obviously, I don't actually have any cards but you get the idea. Off you go. I'm sending you off.' He pointed towards the Big House in dramatic style.

'That's fucking rubbish,' Lex shouted, but he didn't stick around. We watched as he walked off screaming and swearing. 'I'm not playing again,' he cried.

Mervyn placed the ball for the free kick. 'He'll be back next week,' he said and blew to restart.

Once the match finished, I went to help him carry the cones and the ball back to the sports cupboard. Everyone else jogged off to get inside to the warmth. Mervyn didn't often talk a lot but something about the incident with Lex made me think he'd talk to me at that moment. It was almost as if he enjoyed the action of sending someone off and I sensed his heightened energy, his excitement. Like the first time he watched us play. I thought again of his dark purple tongue.

'Why don't you play?' I asked him.

He stacked the red and white striped cones. 'Never been any good at football,' he said. 'Cricket's my game.'

'Let's play that,' I said. 'You can teach us.'

'It's the bleak midwinter,' he said. 'Cricket's for the summer. Good game though. Like life.' Hot air plumed from his mouth in the cold. It reminded me of the smoke from my father's cigars.

'Like life?'

'Do you ever stop asking questions?' he said.

I stayed silent. 'Oh yes, I see, very clever,' he went on. 'Cricket's like life because from the outside it seems to be a team game, similar to football, eleven against eleven. Family, colleagues and so forth. But actually, you're on your own. When you bat, it's you against the bowler and vice versa. Excellent training for life – no-one can help, you've got to rely on yourself. Can't trust the other chap not to nick one to slip, it's you alone against eleven others, trying their hardest to defeat you. Statistically one can measure exactly an individual player's performance. Tough game, being out there not knowing what's coming next, bouncer, beamer, yorker, no one to help. It's lonely.' His voice tailed off and we walked to the southern end of the courtyard in silence. He coughed. 'Actually, football only became popular in public schools because the Victorians thought it a good way to sublimate the, er, sexual urges of young boys. Did you know that?'

'No, I didn't,' I said, unsure what sublimate meant. And what he meant, too.

Mervyn coughed again. He carried the cones while I had the ball. 'What do the other teachers say about your style?' I said.

'My style?'

'Teaching style,' I said. 'You know, telling us what to do and stuff. You're not like the others.'

'I haven't the faintest idea what they think of my teaching,' he said. 'Nor do I care.'

I couldn't believe he didn't know. In a school the size of Bannock House, it was hard to hide anything. The other teachers had made the occasional sly remark: *'This isn't Mervyn's class,'* or *'You can do what you want here, you know.'* I assumed he would have realised. But he genuinely didn't have any idea and, more thrillingly, he really didn't seem to care about what they thought. 'Don't they talk about it in the staff meeting?'

'How dare you imply that I listen to the committee?' He pulled the cupboard key from his pocket. 'I make it a point of honour to ignore every word of the theoretical piffle spoken there.' He struggled to put the key in the lock and then spoke again, almost to himself. 'Do you know, the other day someone seriously suggested playing touch rugby instead of football on the grounds that handling skills are more creative? Risible hebetude!' He flourished these last words.

'Where did you teach before here?' I asked. I wanted to ask him what risible hebetude meant but it might have made him feel bad, spoiling an effect he so obviously enjoyed.

He scratched and fiddled at the lock, the key clinking. 'Hold these,' he said, handing me the cones. He couldn't manage with the key at all. 'Blast, this bloody thing never opens.'

I put the cones on the floor. 'Let me,' I said taking the key from him. I held it as gently as I could, like an injured bird, and the lock eased open. 'It's all in the wrist,' I said.

He stowed the cones. 'That's it for today. Go away and stop annoying me. The school day is over. The sun has dipped below the yardarm. Goodbye.' He sprang from the storeroom and he hurried off in the direction of his rooms.

When I got back to the dorm, I found Charlie lying in his bed. He'd taken his boots off, but I saw he still had on his football shirt. His arms were flat out over the covers. 'I'm knackered,' he said through heavy breaths. The rawness of his cheeks, glowing red outside, had paled.

I sat down with my back to him and pulled at my football boots. 'Can you believe Mervyn?' I said. 'Sending Lex off like that?'

'Did you dive?' Charlie asked quietly.

I kept my back to him. 'Of course not,' I said. 'What's wrong?'

His breathing gradually slowed. 'Maybe I'm not fit enough for football Mervyn style,' he said.

I pulled the woven tartan blanket from my bed. 'You're just feeling the cold.' I stepped over and added it to the pile of covers on his bed and said: 'I think Mervyn likes me.'

2

'He really didn't like you, did he?'

I blinked open my eyes. 'What?'

'The weirdo. Didn't like you at all.' The girl with the birthmark and the white blonde hair stood over me. She ducked her head to the front of the bus. 'This is the stop for Dungowan, by the way.'

Dried blood crackled in my nose.

'You're for Dungowan right?' she challenged, flicking at her fringe. 'I heard you ask for your ticket, that's all.'

'Hey big man,' one of the boys at the back called. 'Looks like you've pulled.'

'Fuck off, Bambi,' she snapped.

I pulled my rucksack on and followed her down the aisle. A few of the passengers looked at me with bored but unashamed curiosity and I felt again the blood caked on my top lip, my cider-stained shirt. We were the only two getting off. The girl waited at the bus stop, her chin turned slightly into her shoulder – the ghost of a childhood movement still visible in her early twenties and one, perhaps, she would carry with her forever, like the birthmark on her jaw.

'Dungowan's up there,' she pointed towards the dark shape of the village, set back from the main road. The bus pulled away from the shallow lay-by where we stood. 'Where're you staying? I mean, you're a right mess. Sorry. I'm just trying to, you know. No, you're right. Shut up Janice, you're talking shite. Again.'

'It's okay.' My head was thick with sleep and memories. 'I've got a tent.' I followed her as she stepped off the road onto a footpath through a dusty, unused field. Her polyester skirt scrunched against her thighs as she walked.

'If you need to have a wash, or anything, I live in the village. But I guess you know that already. God,' she muttered. 'And actually, I don't know. You know? It should be okay. I'll have to check.'

'Check?'

'My dad. But he should be in the pub by seven.'

'It's fine, really,' I said. 'It's nice of you to even offer. You're the first person that's talked to me for days.'

She smiled, quick and sharp, one front tooth a little askew and larger than the rest. But my confession stalled the conversation so we went on across the field in silence, my mind swinging back and forth between the bus and Bannock House, the smell of cider still clinging to my nostrils.

After a few minutes Janice started talking again but it filled my ears like the noise of a big fat fly too close. I hadn't thought of Charlie in years.

*

When I first arrived at Bannock House, the moment on the front gravel was the worst. Left there, on your own, watching everybody else's excitement. Kids threaded between knots of adults, shouts and laughter. Parents stood by their cars, holding coats and bags in arms like branches. Even the newer children seemed to know each other, somehow. My mother said she had to get the five-fifteen and left, using the same cab in which we'd come.

'You must be James.' Fran said, though I didn't know her name then. 'Where's your mom?'

'She had to catch the train back to London,' I said. 'We're busy people.'

'Right.' She looked round for a second and then offered her hand. 'I'm Fran.'

A stray drop of rain splashed onto my too-new raincoat. I flicked up the hood and looked down. Fran shouted to someone over my head and wandered off.

'Hello,' said the owner of a pair of white Nike trainers with the red tick. 'I'm Charlie.' I peered at a chubby pale face, splashed with freckles. Charlie's light ginger hair sprang from his head untamed, and I was grateful that he was my height. 'I think we're sharing a room. Come on, it's this way,' he said.

I followed him across the gravel as he pushed through a thicket of excited people towards a side door of the Big House. Charlie called to a few of the kids as we passed and I heard a couple of them shout out to him good-naturedly.

'We're on the top landing of the north wing,' he went on as we shuffled along a gloomy corridor. Dull light spilled in through half-opened doors and Charlie's voice echoed into the unseen depths of the house. 'Our room's pretty big – bigger than the others, anyway.' We climbed steel-capped stairs and crossed a large square landing with five doors leading off it. My feet stuck to the black and white chessboard lino. 'You can have whichever bed you want, I don't mind. I hope you don't snore. Where are you from? Do you grind your teeth?'

'What?' I said, bringing my hand up to my jaw, worried that it showed.

'Oh good, you speak,' he threw my bag on a single bed by the window. 'So you grind your teeth? I'm only asking because my dad's a dentist. Look, don't be shy – if you do, it's cool. We're sharing, so you may as well tell me.'

'How long have you been here?' I asked.

'About an hour,' he said looking at his watch. 'It's got a calculator,' he added, holding up his wrist to illustrate the chunky black timepiece.

'An hour? But I thought…'

'Everyone's really friendly here,' he said, struggling with the sash window. 'Considering it's my first day at the school. God, this thing's really stuck.'

I stepped over, flipped the catch and lifted the sash in one swift movement.

'Oh great.' He smiled with a mouth full of braces, like a good dentist's son. 'We're a team.'

So it proved. I did everything with Charlie that first year. We explored the grounds, from the hillocks past the carriages to the small farm (where we saw a pig slaughtered), to the overgrown grass tennis court, guarded by a Lebanese cedar that touched the lowering sky and where, on sunny days, the older boys would climb using a fixed rope and call out in triumph from the top. We'd run from one dreadful class to the next: from the Big House, where most of the dorms were and where we ate, to the arts buildings set on top a hill in one corner of the grounds, to the squat ex-stables with peeling white paint and rickety doors that housed the other classrooms. We complained about the lack of a science teacher and the poor facilities, we took it upon ourselves to study alone in the library. We even shared the bath on wash night. Of course, everybody liked Charlie but he chose me to be his best friend. Sharing a room with someone makes it hard not to get close to them and maybe Charlie liked me because I said the unfriendly things that he couldn't, or could think quicker or run faster.

I thought, then, that we'd look after each other if not for all time then at least until the end of our school days – which is as good as all time when you're twelve. An eternal carousel of classrooms, term ends, holidays; of teachers, subjects, friendships made and broken; of boredom unrestrained, of gossip, nicknames and revelation – I thought we'd look after each other through it all, and beyond.

*

'Paedo.' Janice's Achilles tendons strained against the tight black, false leather of her flats. I could pick out the nicks and cracks of everyday work, of accelerated aging. Paedo. It was easier to follow her than do anything else, my mind awash with indecision.

'What was that? Paedo?' I said at last, snagged on the one word I could make out.

'Aye, paedo. Your best pal on the bus. Giant Haystacks' wee brother. They say he's a paedo – as in kiddie-fiddler.'

Pink light from the dipping sun kissed the handrails. He touched me here, here and here. And then he made me touch him too.

'I know,' I said, bringing Janice to a halt in front of me.

She flipped around, eyes oval in surprise. 'How? I thought you said you didn't know him?'

I looked at Janice and felt the resistance and deceit ebb away from me, setting with the sun after a long day's travel. 'I mean,' I sighed. 'I know that's what they say about him. He was my teacher.'

*

Mervyn didn't talk to me much after football. Every time I approached him he'd increase his choppy strides and veer away. He never talked to the other kids as far as I could tell and no one seemed interested in him. I wasn't so easily put off, though. Whenever I went to maths, I'd pass some remark about one of the other teachers or Moira's latest crazy idea. He never replied but I could tell when he was amused because the filaments of his beard would twitch.

A week before the end of the autumn term, I scrambled into the maths cabin and made him laugh out loud. 'We've just come from a session in elementary astrology,' I said. 'Fat Moira's taken us through the basics. If you tell me where and when you were born, I can tell you why you ended up in this dump.'

Mervyn spluttered, unable to hide his laughter.

Pleased, I went on. 'I know, it's totally risible.'

He coughed, put his hand to his mouth and straightened up. 'Right, quiet now.'

It was the final period of the day and so cold in the cabin that almost without thinking we scrunched ourselves together. The wood-burning stove bubbled and cracked but didn't release much heat. Mervyn appeared oblivious to the conditions. While the rest of us kept our coats and scarves on, he wore only a thin jumper over his usual shirt, frayed at the cuffs.

Lex's teeth chattered audibly, like a joke.

Mervyn stopped scratching on the board. 'Are you cold?' he said, pivoting to face us.

Jenny pointed to the bright purple pudding on her head and puffed out her mole-speckled, crab apple cheeks. 'You think I like bobble hats? I had to borrow this from Fran.'

'I'm really, really cold,' Lex said. Mervyn eyed him for a moment, then bent down and opened the door to the stove.

'Better? I'll be as quick as possible,' he said as he moved back to the board.

Despite the cold it was one of the best classes, a recap of all the work we'd done over the previous term. Mervyn underlined mathematical expressions, got us to redraw diagrams and asked us questions about what we'd learnt. Charlie, squeezed beside me in a ripped ski-jacket, nudged my arm and gestured towards his exercise book. He'd written: 'Haven't we done this already?' and I nodded in excitement. I'd already guessed what Mervyn had planned.

'Right, that's everything,' Mervyn said. He put the chalk down and brushed his hands together. 'You should be prepared.'

'Prepared for what?' Charlie asked.

'The end of term test,' Mervyn said.

'Test!' Everyone sang out aloud, apart from me.

'But we don't have tests,' Jenny said. 'Not at Bannock House.'

'Well now you do,' Mervyn said. 'I need to know which of you requires extra help and what to tell your parents. Now clear off, if you're all so cold.'

Charlie and the girls poured themselves down the ladder but I waited at the trapdoor, hoping to walk back with Mervyn. I wanted to ask him about the test. As the class had gone on, the sky outside had darkened and most of the light came from the single suspended bulb. Lex had also remained in his seat. At some point during the class, he must have worked free one of his shoes because he was hunched down trying to re-tie his shoelaces and failing. Charlie often had to tie them for him before we all went down to breakfast.

Mervyn had his back to me as we both looked at Lex. I don't think he knew I was there because he stepped forwards and knelt in front of Lex, just as I was about to speak. He pulled apart the tangled double knot and retied the laces before pausing. Then he took hold of Lex's calf in his left hand while the right rested behind his heel. It reminded me of the times when my father regarded a new bottle he'd pulled from the wine rack. The two of them stayed silent for a moment. Mervyn's narrow shoulders heaved noiselessly, like the errant wings of a large bird perching, unable to keep quite still despite his unmoving head. Lex held his eyes down and waited.

A trio of sparks spilled from the open stove in front of me. 'Do you think astrology's stupid then?' I said, jerked out of my reverie.

Mervyn let go of Lex's leg and pushed himself upright all in the same movement. Surprise, confusion and something I couldn't read flashed across his face as he turned towards me. He looked as if suddenly reminded of an unpleasant memory.

'Astrology, yes,' he said flatly. 'Astronomy, no.' He stepped to the sideboard and ruffled paper. 'Get along now,' he grunted. 'I've got work to do.'

Lex and I shuffled away from the cabin, I put my hand to his back, intending to shove him to the ground but stopped myself. It would have given him too much satisfaction.

As we emerged into the open Charlie ran over. 'It's settling,' he said in excitement. 'It's settling.' It was only then that I noticed the snow, swirling down in fat flakes from a charcoal sky, like ash blown from a burnt out bonfire. I held my hand flat and felt the coolness dissolve on my palm, gone in an instant but replenished almost immediately.

'Fights tomorrow,' Lex said as he and Charlie peeled away to the Big House steps. I stood alone and watched the snow resting easily on the hard, welcoming earth around me.

Lex was right about fights. The next day, a Friday, kids swarmed the grounds flinging snowballs at each other. Afternoon classes were abandoned to let people play outside – Moira even organised a snow sculpture party. As monstrously deformed snowmen rose from the football pitch, I sat looking out of my dorm window every now and then and listened to the calls, laughs and occasional cries of the battle.

'You put a stone in that one,' someone shouted.

'Did not!' I recognised Lex's voice. 'Wimp.'

Charlie kept racing in to the dorm to report back the action, a running commentary of injuries and great shots. He urged me to join in a couple of times but I shook my head. 'I'm trying to revise for the maths test,' I said after he came in for a third time. It was at least partially true. I loved the idea of being tested, especially at an objective subject like maths. I'd probably come top of our class but I wanted to get the highest mark possible, I wanted to show Mervyn what I'd learned.

'It's a snowball fight,' he said, as if that were explanation enough. 'The test isn't until next week.' He stood with his hand resting against the open door.

'I want to do well,' I said.

He let his free arm drop to his thigh in a rare gesture of frustration. 'It doesn't matter. It's only for Mervyn.'

'It matters to me,' I said, looking away.

'You're obsessed.'

'It's alright for you,' I replied, sharply. 'I don't have an army of tutors teaching me in the holidays, making sure I keep up with the outside world. I'm on my own.' At that moment a snowball thudded into the window beside my head, making me flinch.

I looked down to see Lex flicking me a fat, gloved finger before running away across the gravel.

Charlie approached the window. 'I think it's cracked.' He pointed to a dark asterisk in the corner of the pane. His breathing sounded short and painful. 'I knew he was putting stones in his snowballs.' He walked hurriedly across the room and swung through the door without saying another word. Our two tired dressing gowns, hung on the door's hook, fluttered together for a second after he left and then settled.

It annoyed me that Charlie didn't understand. It wasn't only that I wanted to work on the test so much as I couldn't see the fun of a snowball fight. There were no rules, anyone could do anything, which meant nothing really mattered.

We didn't mention our argument that night but the next morning I woke with an uneasy feeling in my stomach. Charlie and I often had minor disagreements but I'd never once held his circumstances at home against him – it wasn't his fault his parents chose to take an interest in his life.

I faced the wall while I heard him get dressed for breakfast.

'Are you coming or what?' he said finally.

Pretending to be sleep-groggy, I mumbled. 'Hmm?' When I turned, I saw Charlie smiling his normal smile. He simply wasn't the type to hold a grudge and, as usual, he made sure I couldn't either – at least, not against him.

The dining room sang with the chirruping of snow-drunk children. As we entered, I noticed Mervyn sitting at a far table with Fran and a couple of Eagles. I automatically went to join them but suddenly thought of Charlie and how that might look. Instead I followed him to a table on our left. At the weekends, we were allowed cereal as some kind of treat – only at Bannock House could Rice Crispies be thought of as a luxury. The rest of the week we ate thick porridge the colour of old underwear.

I looked over at Mervyn. He held his head down and angled towards Fran, his face a picture of total concentration. I couldn't make out what she was saying but something odd struck me about Mervyn, or rather something different.

An argument had started on my own table about the relative merits of organising a snowball fight into competing teams or carrying on with the total free-for-all that had taken place the day before. As usual, everybody was happy to espouse an opinion, though no one suggested that they shouldn't be playing in the snow. I tuned out.

'You okay?' Charlie asked.

Then I got it. Mervyn wore a new jumper. That's what was so different about him. A rippling creamy Aran thing, with lines of bobbles striped down its front. Perhaps I hadn't noticed it initially because he sat by the window, the wool blending into the whiteout scenery behind him. I wondered where it had come from. It didn't fit in with his previous style at all, and I couldn't believe he'd gone up to town to buy it, at least not in the last week. He didn't drive. I knew Mervyn walked to Dungowan most Saturday lunch times, I wasn't sure why, but the village had no clothes shops.

'James?' Charlie persisted.

'What? Oh, yeah. Do you see?' I started to point to Mervyn but stopped myself. Charlie probably didn't want to know about Mervyn's new clothes, at least not just then. 'Should we hike out later?' I turned back to Charlie. 'See what the valley looks like in the snow?'

'The valley?' he said surprised.

'We could go up to Dungowan,' I went on. 'Just the two of us.'

He agreed, happily enough, and later that morning we wrapped up in our warmest gear. As I watched Charlie weave his ludicrously long scarf around his neck (he said it was his dad's from university), I felt strangled by my own mixture of feelings. It was great to be doing something with Charlie after our argument, and I felt especially pleased that it had been my idea – I had offered up the token of peace first. But some part of me thought we might also get a look at Mervyn, see why he went on those mid-day jaunts to Dungowan. He always waved me away when I asked about his Saturday walks, refusing to tell me anything. I thought perhaps he hid a friend there. I didn't tell Charlie this, though, and it was the first time I'd kept my motives truly hidden. It was this that troubled me most.

The school had a funny attitude to leaving the grounds. It wasn't prohibited as such, it was more that no one tended to do it. Everyone seemed to think the school was sufficient unto itself. Even the staff rarely left, except Mervyn. When Charlie and I made our way to the South Gate, I felt a nervous thrill as we stepped out of the school grounds and took a left towards the village. It had stopped snowing sometime in the night but the sky remained low and heavy. We crunched towards the humped bridge in the distance, the first staging post on our journey. One lane of tyre marks striped away from us through the snow and we each took a track, silent for a moment, wondering wide-eyed at the bleak whiteness.

Charlie scooped up a handful of snow and flung it at a low hanging branch. Bricks of snow cascaded to the ground, a mini-avalanche. 'We haven't done this for ages,' he said.

I looked at him for any signs of reproach in this remark but could detect none. I grunted in reply, not wanting to discuss what else I might have been doing instead of hanging out with him. He knew I'd been spending more time in the library, but he didn't seem to hold it against me or ask why.

'Hey look,' he said, undeterred by my silence. 'The river's frozen.' We'd reached the bridge and Charlie pointed over its low stone wall, his lime green ski mitts the only colour against the dark, dense grey of the ice, visible through a thin scattering of snow. We threw stones and watched them bounce and skittle along the ice of the river, frozen solid.

'Let's get on,' I said. 'Check out the view from the village.' I glanced back along the straight road to the school, eager to head up the twisting hill in front of us.

Charlie exclaimed every so often at the landscape. 'It's so, I don't know, white!' he said. Vocabulary was never his strong point. I agreed when necessary but left him to chatter on in his own friendly way. After thirty minutes or so, as the road curved up, I stopped to look back down the hill behind us. The bridge was clearly visible from our high vantage point and I made out a small figure moving towards it, as I hoped he would, picking his way along one of the tyre tracks just as we'd done beforehand. His new Aran jumper disappeared into the snowy background, making his hairy head look like a dark smudge bouncing through the landscape. A bodyless Mervyn, head floating in the snow. I almost called out to Charlie, to make some joke, but instead hurried to catch up with him.

As we crested the hill, a raw wind slapped us in the face. I pulled up my collar and caught a whiff of dampness from my scarf – a smell that pervaded most of the clothes at Bannock House come winter. The road flattened out and we could see Dungowan laid before us. Little more than an extended crossroads, from our spot the village looked like a dark, elongated crucifix scored out of the white surrounds. Most of the houses were made of heavy grey stone, strung along in squat terraces. Away to one side stood a small estate of boxish, newer houses, out of which ribboned thin streams of smoke.

'What now?' Charlie said, before we even reached the edge of the village. 'Maybe we should head back for lunch? It's almost twelve.' He sounded tired and disappointed, the vision of Dungowan in the snow wasn't quite as spectacular as he'd expected.

I looked over my shoulder. 'Why don't we check out the churchyard?' I replied. 'The snow must be a foot thick there.' The truth was I didn't want to encounter Mervyn on the way back down the road. We had to kill enough time for him to get into the village, if I was going to find out where he went. Charlie put his head on one side, puzzled, but said nothing and we entered the graveyard. It stood close to the near side of the crossroads and gave a decent view of the whole village.

'Are you going to bring up Lex for cracking the window?' Charlie said, suddenly, as we stomped between snow-capped headstones.

'Why not?' I said. 'If I don't, we'll have to fix it ourselves. And the cost of the glass will come out of our pocket money.' The school had a policy that if you broke anything, you had to fix it yourself – some hippy crap about taking responsibility for your actions, as if that had anything to do with a good education.

'No one needs to know,' Charlie said. 'It's only a crack.'

'I don't see why,' I began but broke off. Away to our left, Mervyn's head appeared. This time, the high stone dyke of the graveyard obscured his body. I watched as he drifted through the village. The wind blew hard in my ears, so I couldn't hear, but it looked to me as if he were whistling.

'We could say we found it like that,' Charlie went on unaware. 'I don't think Lex can afford it. And I'm sure he didn't mean to break the window.'

I stumbled forward as Mervyn passed. The snow was thick in the lee of the dry stone wall but I reached it in time to see him turn left at the crossroads and duck into a house with an unusually large frosted window on the ground floor.

'Where are you going?' Charlie called after me. 'James?'

'Sorry.' I made my way back to him. 'I thought I saw something.' He looked at with me with his mouth open but I didn't want to explain so I simply said. 'Okay. I won't grass on Lex.'

'Let's go back,' Charlie said. 'This place is a dump.'

'Can we just swing through the village?' I said. We walked over the crossroads and instead of taking the way we'd come we went past the small house Mervyn had entered. Charlie relaxed and began chattering again. I craned to get a look through the window but the frosting extended above my height. Stencilled across it were the letters M c E W A N S. It was a pub, but unlike any I'd seen in London. This one looked exactly like the houses around it apart from the large window and a small sign above the door that stated who owned the licence. Charlie carried on ahead but I stood staring at the pub. Suddenly the door crashed open and an old man stumbled out, releasing from within the sound of loud conversation and the smell of trapped smoke. The man, clad in a heavy black coat with leather patches on the shoulders, glanced up with bloodshot eyes, as if blaming me for his misstep. I hurried away.

Charlie had reached the far side of the village and I could see he'd stepped into the ditch that ran along the verge. He scrabbled around in a hedgerow, presumably looking for somewhere to take a piss. I saw a flash of green as he tossed his mitts to the ground.

'Hey yous,' someone shouted from behind me in a high-pitched local accent.

I turned around and saw a girl running up to me. She stopped short when she reached ten feet or so away. Her hair was scraped back against her head and she had a puffy pink jacket on. The pale skin around her mouth was chapped and puckered and two sharp creases pinched the space between her eyebrows. She was dressed like an adult but must have been a young teen, maybe even my age. Beyond her, I could see a collection of teenagers emerging from the estate. Unlike the kids from Bannock House, the boys all had super-short hair, tight clothes and an air of organisation about them, as if they'd act as one. They looked bored, restless and ready.

'You're from the hippy school, right?' the girl went on. 'What's it like? Do the kids sleep with the teachers and that?' Her head reminded me of a bird's, darting, nervous and piercing.

I finally found my voice. 'Fuck off,' I said and ran towards Charlie. I heard the girl call back to her friends, and a deeper male voice shout. 'What the? Let's get the bikes, the cheeky bastards.'

'Run,' I called out to Charlie as I approached. He looked around, startled, just as I bundled him through the tangled hedgerow. 'They're going to kill us,' I yelled.

Charlie and I tore across the open field, our feet breaking through the untouched snow. I heard him mutter. 'My mitts.' But he didn't stop. We could hear the distant cries of the village kids from the road. I didn't dare look around as I headed to a tight copse of fir trees, with Charlie at my shoulder. For a terrible moment I feared we'd be overrun, end up beaten and robbed by a gang of poor teenagers with nothing better to do on a Saturday than terrorise a couple of posh kids. I thought that's how they worked. We scrambled over a dyke and then, running, panting, stumbling we rolled another twenty yards down a steep, icy hill. The trees loomed large on our left and,

49

once we stopped, we realised that the village kids hadn't followed us cross-country.

'They must have stayed on the road,' I said, slapping the snow from my legs.

Charlie wheezed before eventually catching his breath. 'What was all that about?'

'There was a gang of kids,' I said. 'They attacked me.'

'Really, why? Was it the locals?'

'Of course it was the locals,' I snapped. 'Loads of them.' My heart trilled against my shirt, exertion taking over from fear. 'We can't go back that way.'

'What about my gloves?' Charlie looked down at his bare hands.

'We'll still make lunch,' I said, lifting my voice. 'We can follow the trees down this side and rejoin the road at the bottom of the hill. It's like the two perpendicular lines of a triangle – it's longer than taking the diagonal but we'll get there.' Charlie didn't look convinced but our mad rush had taken the wind out of him, so he nodded silently.

The trouble with the countryside is that it's not set out as neatly as a chalk diagram on a blackboard. After about an hour's walking, we realised we were no nearer the road, or rather, we didn't really know where the road lay. The rolling humps and broken fields of our descent had been rendered almost identical by the thick covering of snow. Eventually, I reasoned, we would get somewhere near the school if we kept following the gradient down but Charlie was suffering increasingly from the cold. We stopped often and I gave him my own gloves after I noticed his hands shaking.

At one of the breaks, Charlie sat with his back to a stone dyke and looked up at me. 'What did they say to you?' he said.

'I told you,' I said. 'They chased me. You were there, remember?' I looked down the hill, trying to judge which of the dykes seemed familiar and which crooked tree line marked the road.

'You must have done something to annoy them,' Charlie said. 'You usually do.'

'What are you saying?'

He smiled slightly. 'Maybe we should go back the way we came,' he said after a pause, his voice jumping with the cold.

'That'll take hours.' I hauled him to his feet and we continued on our way, Charlie too tired to argue. I didn't want to tell him I was no longer sure if we could even find our way back to the village. I still felt confident enough that we'd come all right at the bottom of the hill. My trigonometry couldn't be that bad.

He kept one pace behind me as we slithered and trudged through the fields, and I could hear his heavy breaths filtering through his scarf. Charlie wasn't the type to openly reproach me, but I could feel the tension growing between us – as if, perhaps, he knew the real reason for my desire to visit Dungowan that day. Every step further I kept expecting his hand on my shoulder and an accusation – you're obsessed, he might repeat again, always following Mervyn, dragging me out in the cold and the wet, losing our way because you believe in fucking triangles, turning the village against us and all for what? For a snatched glance through a pub window? Had it all been just for that? So Mervyn went to the pub every Saturday, or at least that Saturday, but I could hardly tell Charlie that, could hardly cite this cast-iron evidence as reason enough to miss lunch.

'James!' Charlie called. 'Wait.' I turned to see him some yards behind me, sitting again.

The wind whipped snowflakes around him and his face looked smaller than ever. 'I'm sorry,' he said. 'For holding us up. I'm such a wimp.' He glanced up at me again, trying to smile through his cold-shakes. His whole body juddered in small, fast movements and he hunched in on himself.

Squatting next to him, I cast around for some visual clues as to where we might be. I noticed a lone tree standing on top of a small rise to our right, stark against the darkening afternoon sky. 'Give me a minute,' I said pointing. 'I'll climb up there, see where we are. Stay here.'

'You're a good friend,' he said, closing his eyes.

'Don't say that.'

Gnarled and dead-cold to the touch, the tree nevertheless felt reassuring. Its roots were buried beneath and between the intersection of two dykes. It had obviously been there much longer than the walls. Its trunk felt thick and heavy, barely wavering at all in the quickening wind. I scaled it easily enough and scanned around. The dark grey angles of the Big House, squat beneath its snow-covered roof, were faintly visible beyond the other side of the vast meadow, amid the denuded winter trees. 'I can see it!' I shouted back to Charlie. 'We overshot big time.' I hurried back to where Charlie sat, his eyes still closed. 'Come on, we'll get there before dark.'

We made our way over the small rise, past the tree, and began our slow descent to the school. Heavy clouds pressed down on us and I felt a tight knot in my stomach, hunger and something else I couldn't place. Charlie's breathing sounded shorter than ever but every time I glanced around at him he would usher me on with his hand. The ground flattened out as we approached a tangled string of bushes and trees. It was only then I realised our next problem, though Charlie voiced it first.

'The river,' he said. We'd forgotten about the river. It ran straight across our path, with the meadow and then the school beyond. 'We'll have to follow it back to the bridge,' Charlie went on through chattering teeth.

'That'll take ages,' I replied. Charlie looked spent, his cheeks hollow and his eyes only half-open. I could have walked back to the road alone, got help, someone to carry him. I didn't understand, then, why he was so tired but a part of me knew it was my fault, knew I had to do something about it. I thought of the stones skittling across the frozen river by the bridge, of how that felt like a different day, and how I needed to make things better. 'We can walk across the ice,' I said.

We pushed through the bushes and came upon the river itself, about forty feet across. Dusted with snow, the ice held but it didn't look quite as thick as I'd remembered from the bridge. 'Shouldn't it have more snow on it?' Charlie said.

I grasped a stick and began poking the surface close to the bank. 'It'll be fine,' I said.

'But you can see the water moving underneath.' Through the ice the dark grey of the river churned past, noticeable whenever a stray reed went by. 'I don't know about this,' Charlie said.

Beyond the river lay the flat meadow, and less than a mile from that the school.

'I'll go first.' I ignored the fear I'd heard in Charlie's voice. 'We'll go one at a time.' I placed my right foot on the ice and pushed down. It felt solid enough and so I went for it, with swift short strides, feet flat to the surface. As I approached the far bank I heard a rumbling crack beneath my feet. I leapt the last yard and cried out to Charlie. 'Quick!'

The ice between us was still intact but it seemed much thinner now, as if my coming across had weakened it irreparably.

'Are you sure?'

'Just come the way I did,' I shouted trying to keep the panic out of my voice 'Walk quickly.' Suddenly, Charlie began running toward me across the river. 'Don't run!' I called but it was too late.

He slipped and fell forward, his right hand punching a fist through the ice. A rolling, racing, ripping sound rose from the river and all around Charlie the ice broke up, like a bursting star. 'Come on,' I shouted. He pushed himself up but then his foot went through. I didn't dare go back out to help him, the ice too thin for us both. 'Keep coming,' I called. 'There's a solid bit there, off to your left.' I pointed. Charlie scrambled up again, his legs soaked, shambling, not saying a word, his eyes wide and fixed on me. I gestured again, trying to identify clean, solid ice but Charlie kept losing his footing. His trousers were dark to the knee with water.

'One more jump,' I said, urging him towards me.

The ice collapsed. The noise first, a rumble, a gun crack, and then shards of ice jagging out of the water all at once. One moment Charlie's face was looking into mine, set with

53

concentration and the next he was gone, totally submerged into the icy water out of my grasp.

He went under for what seemed like minutes but then his head bobbed up – tugged downstream by the current. His short arms scrabbled desperately at the remaining shelf of ice by the bank but he couldn't get any purchase.

'Hold on,' I shouted as I tore along the bank by his side. Off to my left, I noticed that the ice had given way to the fast flowing river where it widened. Charlie coughed and spluttered, his head ducking below the water again and again. The river bent towards my side of the bank and so I got ahead of him and ventured out to the channel he was moving down. His arm slid from my grasp but I managed to get hold of his scarf. 'Your scarf,' I shouted to him as it unwound from his neck. 'Hold your scarf.' He caught it in his hands just in time and I hauled him in.

It took all my strength to pull him out of the water and drag him to the safety of the bank. We lay together in silence while I got my breath back. Charlie's skin had gone a horrible grey-blue and his breath no longer wisped.

'Charlie,' I said to him. 'We've got to move.' I shook him until his eyes popped open yet he still didn't say anything. In the end, I had to drape him over my shoulder before we could get going.

I don't know how we got back. The meadow looked beautifully soft and flat under the snow, like a freshly made bed, but underneath it was ridged by a succession of small drainage trenches. Each one felt like a mountain in itself as I dragged Charlie towards the school. The darkness came quick and horrible, with only the lights of the Big House windows to guide us. Charlie, sodden and heavy, made no sound the whole way while I kept talking, saying anything and everything, a dreadful reversal of our usual roles. I can't remember what I said. Somehow I got him up the slope from the meadow to the football pitch. We reached the edge of the gravel when I heard shouts and Fran came striding across towards us with a couple of kids in tow and a knot of knitting in her hand.

'James, where the hell have you been?' she said. 'What's going on? Oh my god, what have you done to him?' She grabbed hold of Charlie and said again. 'What have you done?'

'The river,' I said but Fran was already taking Charlie in her arms and ordering the others about.

'Let's get him to the staff room,' she barked. 'It's warm there, and go get his duvet or something. Jenny, run a bath, hot. And bring clothes.' The others ran off to their tasks with Fran virtually carrying Charlie to the front steps, a whirl of activity so at odds with the slow painful march from the river that we'd just endured. I stayed on the edge of the gravel and cast my eyes down to Fran's discarded knitting, the crossed needles an angry clue to the origin of Mervyn's new jumper.

Fran shouted to someone in the kitchen and I looked up as she reached the steps, poor Charlie held completely in her arms. She pushed through the doors with her back and I saw the two of them under the front lamp for a moment, she mouthing something into his ear, he a motionless, drowned rag-doll.

3

'This is Dungowan, then.' Janice swept her hand in a wide arc as we reached the road. 'But I guess you already know that, mystery man.' She couldn't keep a note of bitterness out of her voice.

'I'm sorry,' I said. I wanted to please her. 'It's been a long time.'

'You must have been at the hippy school.' She fingered her fringe again, mollified. 'Bollock House, is what we called it.'

'Bannock House,' I laughed. 'Yeah.'

Someone squawked behind us. 'Janice! Hey, Janice.'

She swivelled around, as a birdlike creature came scuttling along the road – she wore black jeans, a shapeless white t-shirt and cruelly tied back hair. Her eyes darted between Janice and me. 'Who's this?' she said.

Janice began to turn her chin into her shoulder, and took a ghost step away from me. 'Just a guy from the bus.'

'Does your dad ken?'

'This is Lynn,' Janice gestured towards the girl and then turned. 'James. And no, to answer your question. Da's got nothing to do with it.'

'Aye right.' Lynn ripped a cigarette packet from her too-tight jeans. 'Want one?' she offered, after she had lit her own.

'I'm fine, thank you.'

She looked at Janice and tipped her head towards me. 'Ooh, posh.'

Janice tutted and Lynn smoked in silence, her eyes on me. 'Do I know you?' she snapped suddenly.

'I don't think so.' I adjusted the strap of my rucksack.

'You mean you wouldn't ken a scrote like me?' Her chin jutted. 'Is that what you mean?'

I glanced at Janice. 'No. Not at all. I just don't think we've met. I didn't mean to upset you.'

'You didn't upset me.' She sucked at the fag, fast and deep. 'Any road,' she went on, turning to Janice. 'We're having a bevy later, up past the kirk. Big Tam's about. You coming?'

'Mebbe,' Janice said.

'Bring you friend,' Lynn cackled without humour. 'Tam'll love him. Cheerio,'

She turned back the way she'd come.

'She's alright when you get to know her,' Janice said after a moment. 'Bit chippy is all.'

'It's fine, really. Look, I'd better get on. I need to find somewhere to camp. I've got some things to work out, you know.'

She bent her head away from me, stretching her birthmark again.

'It sounds like you've got a lot on anyway,' I went on.

'What do you mean?'

I hesitated. 'With your dad and everything – drinks this evening. Big Tam? I don't want to get in the way.'

'Och, Lynn's talking shite.' She pointed to my shirt and took a deep breath. 'Look, you're a mess. Camp up in that field over there, past the estate. There's some cover. No one'll see you for a night at least. I'll check home and get you in a bit, at least so's you can wash. You cannae sleep in that state.'

'Are you sure?'

Her mouth hinted at a smile and she pointed me to the far side of the village's main crossroads. 'Give me twenty minutes.' She set off with a choppy stride, her arms by her side. I moved through the small village, past the kirk, trying not to picture the last time I stood there. The half-forgotten snowflakes of the past appeared in the sky above me, though, unbidden and, for a moment, I saw again that white-out day when Charlie and I followed Mervyn. And I saw again the aftermath.

The snow melted. The guttering above my window groaned. Fat droplets broke upon the sill, like the tocking of a too fast clock. The football pitch reappeared, a mud-green canvas dotted with a dozen dying snowmen. A crystal sun shone four days straight. Stone-studded footpaths scarred the grounds and black trees shed their snowy decorations, lining the drive like a skeletal guard of honour. Stripped bare by unblinking daylight, Bannock House became its true self once more – neglected, dirty and unkempt. The white illusion dissolved.

The whole last day of that term, autumn 1986, was given over to readying the school for the Christmas party: decorations daubed, special food prepared, the Octagon cleared for a dance. The staff pretended it was a great event. They said the party strengthened the bond between adults and children, a gathering to celebrate the love and mutual understanding on which the school was founded. Which may have been why the preparations usually led to the fiercest arguments – the stress of actually organising something concrete got to everyone. I trudged back from the South Gate that morning, with my head down, determined to hide in my room for as much of the day as possible. As I reached the gravel, I heard a babble of voices echoing from the central hall.

I pushed into the long wide hallway. A splayed circular stairway at the far end twirled to staff quarters above and down to the lower ground floor where the kitchen and the phone cupboard lay. A large corkboard ran along one wall, pasted with the everyday nonsense of school life: washing-up rotas; an *AIDS Kills* leaflet; Fran's yoga timetable; a peeling SNP election poster from 1983; and news of the latest gig from the Bannock Players, an early Celtic music group run by the English teacher. That morning, though, there were about fifteen kids huddled around the notice board with more arriving from the dining room. Something of interest had been posted at last.

'Fuck sake, man,' Keith said adjusting his long hair in his careful, girlish way. 'This is a joke.'

'I got fifty-five,' someone shouted. 'Luke, Luke, fifty-five.' He ran off.

Lone put her hand on Keith's shoulder. 'It doesn't matter,' she said.

'I don't give a shit about the mark.' He smashed the side of his fist against the board suddenly and the AIDS leaflet fluttered to the floor. 'I thought I did better than that, is all.' He trudged into the dining-room. I squeezed through the jostling crowd to get a better look.

Six separate sheets of A4 were neatly tacked to the board in two rows of three. Each page had an underlined typed heading, starting with Mathematics, Class M1 through to M6 and below that it had in capitals *Test Scores* with a list of names accompanied by a percentage figure.

I scanned for my name as those around me sighed, or whooped or mostly feigned a lack of interest while struggling to get a better view – of their own marks and, no doubt, of others.

'I can't believe he's put them up there,' someone said. 'We should totally boycott it.'

'I know. Did you see what Daisy got?' her friend replied.

'She'll be gutted.' Both girls laughed.

I didn't recognise my own name immediately – it was the first time I'd ever seen a list at Bannock House that included our surnames. *James Trefoil 67%,* it said in tightly bunched black capitals. Top of the class. Next came Jennifer Turly. It took me a second to realise this was Jenny.

'Not bad for a girl,' she said at my shoulder. 'Sixty-two.' I spun around, ready for a jibe. Her moley cheeks rose in a smile. 'Almost as good the teacher's pet.'

'Luck.'

She poked her tongue out. 'You don't have to suck up to him to do well.'

I looked back at the lists. Mervyn was a terrible typist. Corrections in red biro tattooed each sheet. At the bottom he had signed them with a single M, the first vertical of which was strangely long like stretched elastic. I scanned down the names, everybody's performance laid out as fact. At the bottom of our class list, next to Charles Bevan, it simply had N/A.

'He did what!' Moira's bellow rose from the stairwell. She appeared, a moment later, red-faced. 'What the hell is going on here?' she said, through quickened, fat-woman breaths. The children spilled apart. 'He really did? I don't believe it.' I saw Lex, coming up the stairs behind her, his eyes pinked by tears.

Moira grasped at the nearest sheet. 'This is outrageous,' she said as she tore it down. She scrunched up the paper in tight fists then pawed at the board for the next one.

I grabbed her wrist. 'Don't!' I cried. 'Mervyn typed them.'

She fixed me with her squinty blue-green eyes, her heavy breaths still audible, and then looked at my hand. Thin black hair wisped around her temples beneath a chequered headscarf. I suddenly pictured her bald, like a sick woman I'd seen on television. 'Get your hands off me,' she said into the now silent hall. 'Never touch a woman in violence.'

I drew my hand back. 'But, I, it's just…'

'We don't do things like this here,' she went on, pulling the pieces of paper down one by one and stowing them in her pockets. 'This is a non-competitive community,' she recited. 'It's the community that matters.'

'But what does that mean? You're talking nonsense,' I said. Tears sprang to my eyes, I didn't know why, but something about Moira's destruction of the test scores prickled. 'They're our scores. Our *individual* scores.'

'Meaningless.' She ripped down another sheet. 'Worse than that, divisive.'

'But how are we meant to know how good we are? If he doesn't test us, we won't know.'

'A test tells us nothing of importance.' She took down the last piece of paper and tore it carefully in two. 'All it does is worry and disturb the children.'

'You bitch,' I cried.

Everyone gasped. As a word 'bitch' had been officially 'disapproved' by the school meeting, along with 'slag', 'slapper' and 'motherfucker'. I saw a sly smile flash across Lex's face. Someone pulled my arm but I held my ground. Moira's head shook in anger. She opened her mouth but nothing came out.

The front doors crashed behind me. 'What's going on here?' I heard Fran's firm Canadian voice and tried to blink back the tears.

'He's gone too far now, Fran,' Moira said over my head.

'James?'

'Yes, no, I mean.' Moira took a much-needed breath. 'James is bad enough but I'm talking about this.' She pulled one of the pieces of paper from her pocket. 'Mervyn.'

The rest of the kids began to leave; now that Fran had arrived and the marks had been taken down there was nothing to see. 'Come on guys.' Fran chivvied the kids away. 'We've got a party to organise.' Moira handed her the scrunched up test results and she examined them quickly. Dark lines cracked the skin around Fran's eyes as she squeezed them shut.

Moira's skin glistened, her face flushed. 'Fran, we've got to take this to the senior committee. Look at them, posted for everyone to see. It's bad enough he had them doing tests at all but to publicise the results. Lex was in floods.'

'That's because he only got thirty-three percent,' I explained to Fran.

She looked down at Jenny and me and at the papers in her hand. 'Today's not the day.' She gestured Moira to the stairway. 'Jenny,' she called back. 'You and James should go to the Octagon, help with the decorations.'

The two women made their way up the stairs, talking in lowered voices. I kicked at a flap of peeling lino.

'That's that,' Jenny said, moving towards the door. She walked on the balls of her feet, with self-satisfied hair bouncing in time.

I rubbed my arm across my eyes. 'What do you mean?

'He's bound to get the sack now.' She twirled back towards me. 'I knew he would.'

'Shut up.' I pushed past her. 'You don't know fuck.'

The party started at six – a free-for-all buffet of saggy baps, tepid sausage rolls and dusty meringues topped with whipped cream from a can. A special treat. I squeezed myself beneath arms of older kids, determined to stuff my face before all the food went. I didn't particularly like any of it but you got into the habit of eating when you could at school. My plate full, I sloshed a couple of tinned peaches on the top and found a seat in a corner of the dining room.

Steam gathered on the window panes, and red tissue paper covered the lights, casting a sinister sheen on the faces of the guests. A spray of joss sticks sent willowing smoke over the heads of the frenzied eaters, mixing with the smell of over-perfumed girls. Their chatter rose and fell with occasional screaming peaks when something particularly hilarious was said. Moira angled her way to the buffet, elbows teapotting aggressively, asking no one in particular whether or not the apples were South African. Beyond her Fran stood at the end of the table nodding as people passed like she was the head of a welcoming line. I ate everything on my plate as quickly as possible, even though I felt sick, and retreated back to my room.

After the meal, everybody would troop across to the Octagon for the dance so I turned the light off in my dorm. I didn't want anyone to notice me as they came past. I sat by the window in the gloom and looked across at the dense shape of the armchair Charlie and I had salvaged a year earlier. Opposite, his stripped bed loomed white as my eyes became accustomed to the darkness. Charlie's mum had picked him up, two days after we returned from Dungowan. Charlie told Fran I wasn't to blame, that we'd gone together, been stupid as a duo. I was only four months older, after all, no-one could accuse me of bullying him into it. (Not that anyone would – Bannock House was too weird a school to have bullies.) Charlie had slept most of the Sunday and only came round in the evening, swaddled in blankets and duvets on the sofa of the staff room, next to its open fire. Fran found me when he'd woken up, told me he was okay.

'I can't believe I'm going to miss the Christmas party,' he said when he settled back into his bed. 'My mum's coming to get me later.' He pushed these words out with difficulty and looked hardly different from the ghostly form I'd pulled from the river.

'It'll be shit,' I said.

His mother arrived as it got dark. I offered to help her pack Charlie's stuff but she shook her head and smiled at me, the lines around her mouth springing up as she did so. She looked like the kind of person that smiled a lot and didn't mind the wrinkles that came with it. But her smile faded quickly after and Charlie was loaded into the back of their Volvo, jammed in with three duvets and the heating turned up full.

'Merry Christmas,' he said as I stood by the car door. 'See you next year.' He closed his eyes and the car rolled away up the drive, spitting gravel from its wheels.

I stepped over our lightless dorm and sat on the naked mattress. Faint music crackled over from the Octagon, the improvised PA barely up to the task. I strained to hear which dance they'd started with, either the Gay Gordons or Strip the Willow, I wasn't sure. When you were there dancing you could tell, or rather your feet could tell, but from afar all the Scottish country dancing tunes sounded the same. They each kept a jigging, skipping time, all done in twos. Everything in twos.

Someone doubled-rapped the door. 'Come in,' I said after a second. There was no lock and I guessed that whoever it was would look in the room, whether I answered or not.

The door levered open slowly, sending a shadow swinging along the near wall and a triangle of light above. Mervyn stood, his crinkled profile black against the hall lights.

He stayed motionless for a moment and I thought I could hear his breathing. 'Why are you sitting in the dark?' he said at last.

I kept my palms by my side and my legs together on Charlie's mattress. 'So no-one knows I'm here.'

'Very wise.' He let the door drift shut behind him and I saw his dark form move to the arm of the chair. He sat with a hand on each knee, leaning slightly forwards, elbows jutting outwards. I couldn't make out his eyes clearly but I felt them on me. 'Not a fan of parties?' he said after a pause.

'Are you?' I said. 'You didn't even come to Halloween.'

He coughed. 'This bloody Christmas Draw thing – it wouldn't look good if I didn't turn up. Especially after the test nonsense.' I stood up and stepped across the room. 'Nevertheless, my tastes are beside the point,' he went on. 'You should come over to the dance.'

I snapped on my bedside lamp and looked at him. He blinked, startled. 'Are you going to stop doing tests?'

'Tests are important,' he said after a moment. 'It helps me stream each of you, work out who needs what kind of help.'

'Sixty-seven's good isn't it?'

'You should be doing much better,' he said, his eyebrows joining. 'Your presentational skills are appalling – positively egregious one might say, if this were any other school. And your reasoning is haphazard with a propensity to leap too quickly to what you think is the answer. You must work out things step by step, not skip to the solution just because you think you know it.' He paused at the same time as the music stopped. The sound of clapping reached us from the dance. 'Overall it's very sloppy.'

I sat down on my bed. 'Sloppy?'

The music started up again, different but the same, and Mervyn and I listened in silence. 'But promising,' he said in the same measured tone. 'You show promise.' His last word swelled in my mind, filling the space between us. It felt final but also like an opening, a stamp, and a contract between us, a foretelling. A promise. The crazy patterned lino between my feet, smeared with sticky stains, a tangled map of this future.

He examined me for a moment longer. 'You need to learn how to take instruction. There's a bond between teacher and pupil. You need to respect that. We need to work together.' He stroked his thighs with his hand, a gentle swishing sound.

'Of course,' I said, though I didn't really know what he meant. 'I love maths. It's the truth.'

'The truth?'

'No one cares about the truth, here. It's all about respecting other people's opinions and different points of view. About working for consensus, about everyone having a say. They call it democracy but I call it a load of bollocks. I just want to know the truth.' I stopped, embarrassed.

Mervyn coughed and furrowed his brow. I'd expected him to agree with me but he suddenly looked vaguely unhappy and confused, as if I'd answered a basic sum incorrectly.

I rubbed the rim of my shoe. 'Do you want me to come to the dance?' I said.

'Yes. I mean no. I mean, not exactly.' He paused. 'Fran,' he said, then fell silent again.

'Are you going?'

He nodded quickly and brought his hand up to his beard. 'I'll put in an appearance,' he said. 'Form sake.' He stood up. 'Coming?' He'd lost interest in me by this time and was half-way through the door.

'Why aren't you wearing your new jumper?' I said as we padded across the landing, he two steps ahead.

He answered over his shoulder as we took the stairs. 'It's very itchy. And stifling.' We broke out onto the path and headed towards the Octagon and the crackling PA system.

'What does streaming mean? Will we get extra classes?'

'Possibly. Split into smaller units for extra work.'

'Will I be with Charlie?' I said, eagerly. 'I know he didn't take the test but he's almost as good as me. I'm pretty sure.'

He sighed. 'I imagine Charles will have to do his extra study period with Lex,' Mervyn glanced back at me. 'At least in the short term.'

'But he's good, really.'

'What did you do to him by the way?' We neared the Octagon but he stopped short of the steps and looked down at me. 'Half dead or so I hear.'

'Don't say that,' I said. 'Don't speak about him.'

'As you wish. But why did you go to the village?' I stayed silent. 'Christ, it's not as if there's anything there.' He scratched his beard as he waited for me to respond. 'Well, I suppose we all must have our secrets. But I advise not going swimming in December again. It's dangerous. Now,' he tapped up the steps to the Octagon and held open the door, 'ready to trip the light fantastic?'

The Octagon had been designed and built by the staff and kids some time in the seventies. For people like Fran it represented all that was good and sacred about the school, a community coming together to create a meeting space. It looked like a badly lit shack to me, with no heating. One long bench ran all the way around the hut, attached to the wall, so you could see everyone. The walls themselves were made from thin planks painted white, forming a succession of sides joined together at rough posts. Its eight rough sides made it an imperfect octagon, hence the name. From these walls the ceiling vaulted, dome-shaped, towards a small skylight at the apex. None of the windows opened. The whole structure rested on stubby stilts and if you looked closely enough you could see the bare ground through cracks in the floor.

That night the large hut was garlanded with Christmas decorations, hippy style. There was no Christian iconography, nothing to suggest the birth of Christ. Instead, ugly crayon drawings of Father Christmas and reindeer and ringing bells sagged from the walls, and bunches of holly and ivy hung from the roof like unlit chandeliers. One-eyed Murdo had rigged extra party lights at intervals around the hut. Power came from fat extension cords taped to the floor, with the glare of the bulbs dulled and cheapened by coloured plastic pinned askew.

A racing twirling song played on the tinny PA and, despite the cold outside, the room hummed with the smell of sweating teenagers. Lines of dancers stood opposite each other, feet beating in time. The music went up a notch and the first couple of each set swung in a circle before exchanging flung twirls with successive partners down the line. Raymond whooped as he swung Lone in the air. Clumps of people stood or sat around the outside, clapping. I looked up to see Fran sat with Moira and a couple of others. She mouthed 'thank you' above my head. Mervyn edged around the benches away from me. I found a darkened spot by the music system and settled down to watch.

In parties past, Charlie and I had run through the dancers and laughed at the older kids pretending to be grown up. We'd stolen food and even danced at times, with each other or as part of three in the Dashing White Sergeant. Sitting alone gave a whole different angle to the night. As it went on, I could see the sweat forming under people's arms and in the smalls of their backs, even the girls. The teachers danced too, with kids and with each other, and they smiled indulgently when every now and then someone kicked a leg too high or swung a partner around an extra time. This was letting go, this was freedom, this was the flowing of youth, all circumscribed by the boundaries of an eight-sided hut.

The music quickened, the dances grew more urgent and Raymond turned some of the lights off, in a dismal attempt at dimming. Moira, who never danced but liked calling out the moves, announced a Gay Gordons. I was shocked to see Fran lead Mervyn onto the floor. He'd been popping in and out all evening, hanging around by the doorways, and hadn't talked to anyone as far as I could tell. But now, he edged behind her, looking warily at his own feet, and they positioned themselves for the start. In front of them, Keith stood with Lone. I watched as his hand moved down her lower back and settle on the upsurge of her bum. She didn't complain.

Jenny stepped in front of me. 'Do you want to dance?' I looked up at her fat cheeks and the coffee moles that spattered them. Her hair fanned over her shoulders, her eyes darkened by too much mascara. 'I know you can,' she went on. 'We learned at the same time, remember?'

The floor was almost full of couples but I eyed a space behind Fran and Mervyn. 'Not dancing with Lex?' I said, even as I stood up and walked over to the spot.

She took my left hand in hers and I placed my right hand on her shoulder, ready to begin. 'Lex's nowhere to be seen,' she said and tilted her chin. 'So you'll have to do.' She wore an open shouldered dress and a smell of vanilla and fresh fruit reached my nose. 'Dewberry,' she said though I hadn't said anything.

The Gay Gordons is a skipping, bouncing sort of dance where the couple move side by side with the boy's arm draped over the girl's shoulder. At the end of each wheeling run, you flip around and go back the other way with only a slight pause in between where you 'address' you partner with a little jig. This meant that though we were right next to Fran and Mervyn, we could only see their faces in the action of flipping around. Mervyn had his head down as he stumbled through the steps and Fran kept talking him through the changes. Once, when we switched direction, I caught sight of his face, his eyes glassy with concentration. A dark purple tongue tipped his moustache, his hands rigid paws as they held Fran. We flipped round and I lost sight, though I heard Fran. 'Good, that's good. And again, one-two, one-two.'

'Gooseberry,' Jenny said out of the corner of her mouth as we skipped away.

'What do you mean?' I said. 'What does that mean?' But she kept her eyes on the dance and didn't answer, though I could see the faint bend of a smile.

Once it was over, everybody clapped even though it was only recorded music. I wanted to ask Jenny what she was talking about but one of her friends ran up with some urgent information about an older boy and she sped off without glancing back my way.

'Not bad for a beginner,' I heard Fran say to Mervyn. 'Can you give me a hand in the kitchen later? It's best to clean up before bedtime.' Mervyn stood apart from Fran, an arm's length away.

'Of course,' he said, hoarse. 'I'll just. I should, well. I've got to…' He pointed at the doorway. 'I'll be there. Shortly.' He drifted to the exit.

Fran stood for a second and swept the hair from her eyes. She placed it carefully behind her ears and then turned on her heel, looking about her. 'Hey James,' she said. 'Does this mean you're finally going to make a girl happy?'

'What girl?' I said, confused.

'Me, of course, Mr Charming,' she said, taking my hand. 'I believe next up is the Haymaker's Jig. And it would be my pleasure to be your partner, kind Sir.' I let her lead me into position, through lines of jostling chattering dancers, kids and adults together, hanging off each other like jungle plants.

I left after that jig. Once you were standing up, it was so much easier for people to persuade you to dance and I never liked the final half hour. They'd play a couple of soppy, more modern songs for the older kids to slow grope. At the end of the night everyone would have to join hands (with arms crossed) and sing *Auld Lang Syne* swaying in and out with each emphasis and all full of friendship and tiredness, community spirit and happiness that it was time to go home, but sadness that another term had ended and the smiling, glistening, fat-cheeked, back-rubbingly sickening good will of it all always made me sleep badly.

A prickling wind shook the trees above and the ground felt slick with frost. Soft light spilled onto the gravel from the kitchen's open windows and I went there, rather than back to my empty dorm.

Someone had left the larder door unlocked and, spurred as much by the novelty of opportunity as hunger, I sneaked in. It was the one day of year when it wasn't worth it, as I'd be going home the next day, but I started to look for food to steal all the same. I stuffed packets of jelly into my pockets and looked up at the huge tins of peaches and baked beans and soup that stood round and silent on the top shelves, like gasholders.

The light bulbs were cased in heavy plastic and they buzzed in my ears as I stood on a chair and reached up for a tin. The room was built in the shape of a large T with the door at one end of the cross-stroke. It had no windows. The way the staff, and Fran in particular, guarded it you would have thought it was Fort Knox. I got back down and eased open the fridge, taking out an industrial slab of cheddar.

A banging of doors from the scullery stilled my hand. 'Well, not educational exactly.' I made out Fran's voice, the lighter version. She laughed. 'But it's good to get loose once in a while. Jesus, who left the larder open?'

I crouched down beside the fridge, the immediate need to hide overriding the much larger fear that I might be trapped overnight in the larder, in the dark, an ice cold midnight feast all of my own.

A man coughed. 'Shall I?' I recognised Mervyn's voice.

'Oh right,' Fran said and paused. She clapped her hands. 'Absolutely, yes. I'll give you a hand.' Their voices faded back into the scullery, drowned out by the rushing water and clatter of pans that signalled the washing-up.

I placed the cheese back in the fridge and put back all the food that wasn't easily portable, leaving only the jelly. On my hands and knees, I crawled out of the larder. I had one chance to avoid detection. If I could make it through the kitchen, using the table as cover, then I could slip out of the door into the hallway and up the stairs without Fran noticing. I wasn't scared of any kind of punishment – it was the last day of term and even if she brought me up in the meeting after Christmas I wouldn't get detention or anything like that. The school didn't do punishment, except that I'd have to pay for replacement jelly out of my pocket money. What I was really trying to avoid was the inevitable lecture about community ethics, about how everyone in society is responsible for everyone else, how harming the whole harms you and on and on and on. Fran would have a go at me for hours. She believed in it too, as if the world wasn't made up of individuals out for themselves.

As I inched under the table, I heard Fran's voice once more. 'It's the definition of neglect if you ask me.' Through the crosshairs of table and stool legs I could make out Mervyn stooped over the sinks, his back to me. Fran was out of view, at the other sink. Mervyn mumbled something that I couldn't catch as he crashed a baking tray on the draining board.

'Huh?' Fran said, her voice higher, more piercing, clearer. 'We all find him difficult. But with a Mom like his, I guess we can forgive.' I stayed still, waiting to hear more, for I assumed from the reference to my mother that they were talking about me. It was thrilling to hear Mervyn's interest in my life. I didn't mind Fran describing me as difficult. The staff always described me as difficult, but only because none of them – apart from Mervyn – could answer a straight question. As I watched, caught between dashing for the hallway door and wanting to hear more, I saw Fran step into view, the two of them framed by the doorway.

'It's good of you to ask,' she said drying her hands on a tea towel. Her hair seemed blonder in the glare of the naked scullery bulbs, not tied back as usual but splayed across her shoulders. She moved towards Mervyn as he turned, his back to the sink, to face her. 'You know, so many teachers here don't really care about the kids. I'm touched that you do. It's kinda sweet.' She closed on Mervyn, obscuring him from my view, and placed her hand on his chest. Then she leant up without speaking and kissed him on the lips.

I crouched, unable to pull my eyes away. Normally, the sight of anyone kissing was enough to make me puke but this looked different somehow. I could see Mervyn's arms poking out either side of Fran, his palms open but unmoving, like he'd been asked to dance against his will. A second later Fran pushed herself away and stepped out of my view once more. 'Don't worry about Moira and the whole test thing,' she said in

71

a voice floating over the gentle sound of stowed crockery. 'I'll speak to her.'

Mervyn hadn't moved but for his hands, which now gripped the sink rim behind him. I stood up and he looked directly at me. His ale-dark eyes were wide in panic and his body rigid. We stared at each other. His purple tongue slowly dabbed his lips. 'That was fun,' Fran said from out of view. 'I think I need a rerun.' Mervyn's head jerked like a trapped animal. Still watching Mervyn, I deliberately pushed a stool to the ground and ran off.

'What the?' Fran cried. 'Who the hell was that?' I rushed up the stairs and away, hoping that Mervyn would stay silent and spare me the lecture. I hoped he knew I understood how hard it is to resist girls when you're standing up, knew that I wouldn't be sloppy any more, that I'd help Charlie become a better mathematician, knew I understood he wasn't to blame for Fran's attentions. Knew that the reason I wanted to come back next year was him and Charlie alone. I hoped he knew all this.

Mervyn's voice drifted up the stairwell as I ran. 'I saw no one,' he said.

4

I flung the tent to the ground and tried to shake the midges from my sweaty neck and ears. The glory of a Scottish summer's evening was so often tarnished by clouds of the black insects, dirty blemishes fretting against the pale evening sky. I stood on the spot of wasteland Janice had suggested, shielded from the village by a high and tangled hedgerow. There was something about her that made me do what she said. The odd mixture of belligerence, vulnerability and authority in her manner perversely made me feel at ease and I even liked her frank curiosity.

The tent confused me. Its poles, designed to interlock in neat, squeak-free ways, refused to bind. I couldn't work out which was the inner and which the outer part of the tent. And there appeared to be only one peg. Even when I laid each piece out, like a giant diagram, I still didn't know where to start. Bannock House, too, lay jumbled in my mind – disjointed, unputogetherable, unclear but so suddenly unforgettable and close and no longer barricaded in an attic of my memory.

I'd filled my head with facts and figures and exam technique, and thought of little else, certainly not about my weird hippy school in the countryside or even what it was all for except to get me to the next stage – the better school, the top university, the highest grade. Even now, I looked on my past as the raw material for a top CV. Bannock House hadn't seemed to fit in to my life, my history, in any way, other than as a quirk of biography. But as I neared, I felt its pull, its gravity, the memories blotting out all else like a fast approaching planet.

'You kidding?' Janice laughed from behind me. 'You're sleeping in that?'

I looked down at my temporary home. The top sagged in a sad arc and I held a disturbingly unused poll in my hand. 'It's only for one night.'

She sniffed. 'Any road, you can use the bathroom at mine now if you like. Clean up.'

'Are you sure?'

'Why wouldn't I be?'

We walked towards the low-rise, boxy estate. 'I can't believe you went to that hippy school,' she said after a moment. 'We used to talk about it as kids. It sounded fucking mental.'

'It wasn't too bad.'

'But didn't yous all have to run around naked and that?' I shook my head. 'No sleeping with the teachers? That's what they used to say. And that the kids ran the place.'

'We used to have meetings, it's true.' I said, thinking of Mervyn's first day, eleven years previously. Had it all started then, before even our lessons?

*

Once a week the whole school would meet in the Octagon, ostensibly to govern the place. One of the older kids chaired the meeting. Even the teachers had to wait their turn to speak. It was an exercise in democracy, or so Fran said. My father described it as a revolutionary way to engage children. At least, that's what he wrote in the articles he published in *The Guardian* and *The TES*. In reality the meeting dealt with tedious admin: who left the cowshed door open; can people remember to put their dishes away after tea; will Jenny undertake to stop calling Lex a chipmunk?

On the first day of term following Mervyn's arrival, Charlie nudged me as soon as we sat down. I had already noted Mervyn's tie, barely visible between the straggles of his beard. Children of all ages trooped in around us, dressed any old how, with the staff scruffier still, as if the school held a jumble sale and everybody bought everybody else's old clothes, none of which fitted properly. Mervyn seemed oblivious to the 60 kids staring at him. He kept his head down the whole time, fingering the tight crease that ran down the front of his trouser leg. He wore purple socks, and kept his legs crossed at a sharp angle. Someone had wheeled out the Calor Gas heater into the middle of the Octagon. It spluttered and hissed but its warmth disappeared upwards while the smell hung about our heads, making me feel sick.

'Next item is Undertakings.' Lone chaired the meeting. We had to call her the chairgirl, not the chairman. 'Only one outstanding Undertaking from last term. James undertook not to taunt Lex. Does anyone have anything to say?' she said, swishing her hair this way and that.

'I haven't taunted Lex for ages,' I said in my defence. 'And even then, I was never that horrible to him.'

'You haven't seen him for ages – we've just got back,' a voice said. People laughed.

I ignored them. 'He kept disrupting the class, that's all.' I noticed Mervyn's head prick up, as if he heard a twig snap behind him on a dark night. Classes were normally a total free-for-all, so one extra kid disrupting things didn't make that much difference, but Lex got under my skin. I wondered if Mervyn knew what he'd let himself in for. Fran sat directly across from us, a hand on each knee, peering at me with her head on one side.

'Can I just say?' someone broke in. 'I overheard James at the summer end of term party. He said Lex was an idiot. It was really aggressive.'

'Am I not allowed my own thoughts?' I replied. 'What about my rights? What about my civil liberties?' I looked to my left at Mervyn and saw his beard twitch with suppressed amusement. Charlie tugged at my arm.

'It's like Stalin's Russia,' I finished, crossing my arms.

Fran frowned.

'We've been through it already,' Lone said. 'Lex, are you happy?'

Lex glanced at me for a second with his insect-big eyes. 'James hit me this morning,' he said, his chin turned into his shoulder. 'At breakfast.'

'That's not true!' Charlie called out, not even bothering to lift his hand. 'I was at breakfast with James the whole time.'

'I wish I had,' I said. 'Lex is a big fat liar.'

Fran raised her hand. 'James has to learn to think of the community as a whole,' she said.

'More like co-mutiny,' I muttered.

'But,' Fran continued, glaring at me. 'I think we've dealt with it for now. I should also say that I was at breakfast too and James certainly did not hit Lex.'

'Aren't we going to tell him off for lying?' I said, but no one acknowledged me. The meeting carried on to the next item. I tried to catch Lex's eye but he hid behind the knotted fringe of his lank black hair. All I could see was his first two fingers set rigid, scratching his cheek in an obvious V-sign.

Bannock House collected misfits – it was almost impossible to get expelled, for one thing. How do you rebel against rebellion? The school ran on a shoestring, so even though it was private a lot of the kids didn't come from rich families. If they weren't on the Tories assisted-places scheme, some of them had been sent to the school by local councils – Bannock House so often the last resort. They literally took anyone. When all other schools failed, they promised to fail too. I was one of the exceptions: my parents had the money to send me elsewhere but they were ideologically committed to the school's ethos. They thought children learned best in a free environment, without rules, tests or timetables. That's why everyone could build tree huts or throw pots or silk-screen flowers on to t-shirts. But we couldn't really spell or add up or point to Venezuela on the map. If you wanted to learn anything at the school, you had to find it out for yourself, which was hard enough without having to share a classroom with the likes of Lex.

He had arrived mid-way through the previous year, I thought for the sole purpose of tormenting me. I remember one of the teachers calling him cute but I didn't think so. He had too many teeth and could never look you in the eye. I assumed Lex was another of those kids who'd been thrown out of all the other schools until his local council despaired. But I never asked him. I never asked him anything.

The meeting rolled on for an age until Lone tapped her pen on the table and swept her hair from her eyes. 'Any other business?' she asked. 'Okay, we've one final point.'

'At last,' someone gasped under their breath, sending a ripple of giggles round the benches.

Leonard, the balding and be-flared woodwork teacher, stood up. 'I speak on behalf of the senior committee. As many of you may be aware, we have a new maths teacher. Not only a teacher, but a Cambridge man.' He smiled. 'Cambridge is a great chair of academic learning, by the way, or so the powers that be are wonted to tell us.' He spread his arms out wide, a hippy on the cross, and boomed. 'Mervyn, welcome to Bannock House.'

Mervyn gave a quick nod and saluted with his biro. It was only when we filed out that I realised he'd been doing *The Times* crossword all along. I watched him stride away from the Octagon, the paper thrust under his arm like a baton.

'Do you think he'd teach us how?' I spoke aloud, though I didn't mean to.

'What?' Charlie said, tumbling on top of me down the Octagon steps.

'The crossword,' I turned to him. 'Do you think Mervyn would teach us how?'

'You're nuts.' He shook his head and ran off after a knot of girls. I stayed on my own, watching Mervyn's back as he marched towards the farm, thinking of that crossword and of all the words I didn't know.

*

'That's mine at the end,' Janice said. 'We'll just go through the back. Mum doesn't let anyone use the front door. Unless they're special.'

Janice's house stood at the end of a grey, seventies style terrace that already looked old and tattered. A red sheet covered the top window and a dark stain ran down from below the bathroom. The small, square garden graced only by a broken bicycle and a half-open fridge. Janice hesitated at the gate, unsure. 'But you had proper lessons and that?' She looked at the ground between us, her head turned awkwardly. 'I mean, like, you've been to uni right?'

'I have, yes.' The birthmark puckered as she twisted her neck. 'But lessons at Bannock House weren't compulsory.'

'You mean you didnae have to go?' Her eyes widened, clear watery blue unruined by the heavy black eyeliner she'd misguidedly applied. 'Christ, didn't everyone just bunk?'

'Not really. There was nothing else to do.'

'But how did you learn anything? If you didnae have to?' she insisted.

'How did you learn to speak English?' I said, a stock response. I scratched the corner of my chin and glanced towards the house. For a moment, a shadow flitted behind the downstairs curtain but Janice didn't seem to notice. 'What was your school like?' I said.

'Shit boring.' She relaxed her shoulders. 'I hated it. I got a higher,' she said quickly. 'But that was about it. Perfect for a dump like John Menzies. Really living the high life.' She looked out across the open slope that lay opposite her house. 'That's where I work, by the way. In Dumfries, thanks for asking,' she went on in response to my raised eyebrow.

'All this, despite being forced to go to classes.'

'Yeah, yeah. I get it. But you should've seen some of the kids at my school. It was chaos even in the classes. If they could have done what they want, it would have been carnage. What's that book? The one about the mad kids.'

'Lord of the Flies?'

'Aye, with Piggy and Ralph?'

I shook my head. 'I've never read it. It was banned in my house for promoting an unrealistic view of anarchism.'

'We did it for Standard Grade. Any road, that's what my school would have been, without lessons. Wall to wall fighting.'

The sky had lost its pink tinge and a cold breeze prickled the back of my legs. We stood for a moment, silent. Her school days took place in a world I would never know except through books and policy reports and the mercury words of hand-wringing politicians. I hardly knew anyone at university who'd been to a state school. And yet Janice spoke of it in such an off-hand way, as if it weren't the most important thing in her life, which I found odd for someone in their early twenties. For everybody I knew my age, school defined who they were. You could hear it in their voices, see it in the way they walked and dressed. And you could tell they still looked at the world through those schoolboy eyes. How could anything more important happen to you than what happened at school?

'God, I'm sorry,' Janice broke the silence. 'I'm such a spaz. I get like that sometimes. Drift off into my own world. You want to use the bathroom?'

I followed her through the unlocked back door and into a bare kitchen, furnished with a small drop leaf table, an empty bottle of milk and a full ashtray. 'Top of the stairs,' Janice hissed under her breath. 'But be quiet.'

I twisted and turned in the rickety bathroom. Dried blood caked my upper lip. A mysterious dirty smear on the left hand side of my face. Mervyn's hands must have been muddy.

Cheap toiletries garlanded the side of the pea-green plastic bath and I breathed in a smell of soap and rising damp.

Wall to wall fighting, Janice had said. We had fights at Bannock House too.

*

I heard the words before I saw them. 'Mervyn loves Fran,' Jenny pronounced each syllable deliberately. Laughter rang in my ears as I rose through the hatch into the maths cabin.

'What are you doing?' I said. 'He'll be here in a minute.'

Jenny turned from the blackboard and held up a chalk-dusted hand. 'Ooops. Here comes the pet.' Behind her, the two names were scored in rounded capitals and separated by a crudely drawn, arrow-pierced heart.

I snatched the board cleaner from its peg and scrubbed at the lettering, an act the class found even funnier than Jenny's original joke.

'Touchy,' she said as she went back to her desk. Lex and the rest grinned at me. I felt like a teacher asked a simple question, the answer to which I did not know.

'Where is he?' I said.

Jenny puffed out her cheeks. 'You should know.'

Lex began chanting. 'Mervyn loves Fran, Fran loves Mervyn.' My cheeks reddened and a wash of warmth rose up my head, despite the cold. Laughter filled the cabin, though I didn't know what was funny and couldn't ask. I stepped towards Lex and grabbed his jacket.

'Shut up.' I shook him. 'Shut up, shut up, shut up.'

'What's going on here?' Mervyn's voice cut the noise dead. 'James, let go of that boy!' I waited for a moment as I heard him clambering up the stairs but his hand didn't grab my shoulder. I straightened and twisted around. 'This is totally unacceptable. Explain yourself.' His eyes were large and alive and his beard quivered.

I looked at the tight wine-red weave of his tie and noticed a dark stain where it disappeared beneath his jumper. No words came. I didn't understand why I'd become so angry, which made it hard to explain the truth without making myself look stupid. Even worse, I suddenly realised how embarrassing it would be for Mervyn if I repeated what had been written on the board, what Lex had been chanting. I reddened anew at the thought that Mervyn had heard.

His eyes shifted, as if he too had realised the truth or at least that saying it would be uncomfortable for us both. 'Sit down,' he said breaking the spell. 'I expect better of you James, I really do.'

'Were you busy in the staff room?' Jenny asked. She twirled her unbound hair with a pencil. 'Is that why you're late?'

Mervyn glanced at her but replied only with a curt: 'Silence.'

I couldn't participate in the class as normal, even though I wanted to fulfil Mervyn's best expectations of me. But that day my hand stayed by my side, not thrusting up at every question. I may have cleaned Jenny's chalked slogan from the board, but its message hung in the air like dust.

The space next to me, where Charlie used to sit, lay empty. Two weeks after the Christmas holidays and he hadn't returned. I assumed he was still recovering from our accident but didn't know for sure, no one had told me or given me a direct answer since I got back. Over the holidays my family received a bland Christmas card from 'The Bevans.' Charlie's mum had signed it for them all and it looked like it was one of many. There was no special message, no *'See you next term,'* scribbled in Charlie's jagged hand. I put the card on the mantelpiece at home, and came down each day to see it crowded out by others my parents received, their atheism on hold.

My father loved Christmas because, he said, it was a time of few distractions. Most of the people we knew went to the countryside which meant he could concentrate on his writing. Before everyone disappeared, we always held a grand party and I was allowed to stay up late. My father liked to trot me out to answer the questions of tall men in open shirts and glamorous women with heavy earrings and bright red lipstick spread across amused expressions. 'No compulsory lessons? How divine.' They'd smile at my mother, yet their eyes would quickly slide away. I knew they sent their sons to Westminster or St Paul's; they might chatter loudly about 'the Left' but they wouldn't leave their kids behind.

Mervyn tapped at the board, but I still couldn't focus. I wondered how long hypothermia lasted, how ill Charlie must be. The library didn't have a medical dictionary and of course the school didn't have a nurse, at least not one trained in anything other than homeopathy. I doubted arnica would do the trick this time. Could it be more than a month? 'James. James. James!' Mervyn's voice brought me back to the cabin. 'How many?'

'Six weeks?' I said.

He stepped back, astonished. 'Six weeks?'

Lex sniggered.

I looked up at the blackboard. 'I mean, twelve over sixty. Or one fifth.'

'Correct.' Mervyn raised an eyebrow. 'Easy to confuse with six weeks, I know, but you got there in the end.' He chalked up the final line of working on the board.

'Is that because twelve times five is sixty?' Lex said.

Mervyn swivelled, surprised. 'Yes Lex, in a way. Well done. Very well done.' He smiled down at him and they looked at each other for a moment. One right answer in fourteen weeks. I snapped my pencil.

The bell went. 'Now listen, this is very important.' Mervyn began scratching at the board again, his body twitching like an eel. 'I've scheduled extra classes for all of you. Three different streams, matching ability.'

'You can't do that,' Jenny squealed, along with her friend, a new girl called Roya or Romy or something equally stupid. For the first two weeks of term she'd worn her raincoat everyday, like Paddington Bear.

Mervyn had been writing down a timetable on the board. 'I've checked with your parents and guardians and they are keen for the extra sessions. They must love you all dearly.'

'My mum never told me,' Jenny muttered.

'Adults don't need to tell you everything,' Mervyn said. 'That's just a Bannock House fiction.'

I'd been put in the top set along with Jenny but I couldn't see Charlie's name. 'What about Charlie?'

'When,' Mervyn glanced at me as he paused, 'Or if he returns, he'll be in the bottom set with Lex.'

People packed their bags around us. 'So Lex gets one on one?' I said.

Mervyn drifted towards the sideboard. 'Until Charlie's return, yes.' His hands flicked through sheaved paper.

Jenny, Lex and the others grumbled their way out of the cabin. It occurred to me that Mervyn only fiddled through his things to stop his hands shaking, his movements were quick. 'Is there anything else?' he said.

'I'm sorry about the six weeks thing.'

He nodded but didn't look up. 'You must focus.'

'Have you done the crossword today? Can you give me a clue?'

'Don't you have a class to go to?'

'What, you mean palmistry with Raymond?' I forced a laugh. 'Perhaps I can pick up History from the lines in my hand.'

Mervyn didn't laugh. 'What was that?' he said absently, looking up at me. 'Get along now.'

I paused at the steps. 'Did you really speak to my parents?' I said. 'About the extra classes.'

'Your father,' he replied. 'Gifted speaker. Orotund.'

Without Charlie I had no one to talk to. I didn't even know what was wrong with him, apart from the fag ends of muttered conversations, words like lymphoma and meningitis but I guessed no one really knew. I didn't want to ask anyone, though, for I feared they all blamed me. In the end, I wrote to my father asking if he could send me a medical dictionary. I'd already given up expecting any kind of emotional information from him but books were a different matter. He could understand bibliographical requests.

Mervyn had become even less talkative since the holidays, and he wouldn't look at me. Something had definitely happened between him and Fran over Christmas, though I couldn't work out exactly what and certainly didn't want to ask. Jenny made it clear enough what she thought but I couldn't quite credit it, not when I remembered the fear on Mervyn's face that night in the scullery. His fingers clamped tight to the sink. Fran whistled and smiled and chatted to me whenever she could, though, and my scowling criticisms of the school left no mark. Was it Mervyn who made her happy? Was happiness so simple, I wondered as I haunted the empty evening classrooms looking for nobody's company but my own.

One day at lunch, the week after we'd been given our new lessons, I walked towards the Big House and smacked my hands together against the cold. I hoped my father would send me the requested medical dictionary and thought again about Charlie's mystery ailment. A sharp stone skidded across the path.

'Loser,' Lex yelled at me from on top of the climbing frame known as the tripod. It was made from three old-fashioned telegraph poles bound together like a wigwam shell with a platform a ladder's length up. A cargo net sagged between one of the poles and a nearby tree. Lex stood at the head of the ladder though you could also climb up it using the metal handholds on each of the three poles.

'Fuck off,' I shouted.

He laughed. Behind him, the sky was almost black with clouds, massive but moving. Some of the other Sparrows draped themselves around the frame or swung entangled in the cargo net. I noticed Jenny's eyes on me and turned away. As I did so, Lex tugged another stone from his pocket and flung it. The pebble grazed my arm as I moved. 'Yes,' he screamed. 'Got you.'

My head grew hot, despite the cold, cold air. 'No you didn't.' I strode towards the tripod and jumped onto one of the legs. The wood was burnished metal-grey, with tiny unseen slivers ready to pierce the unwary. I grasped the hand-holds and began climbing.

Lex looked uncertain. 'No long words?' He peered over the edge at me. 'What would Mervyn say? I guess you're not his pet any more.'

As I reached the platform, Lex disappeared down another of the tripod legs, his voice bubbling with laughter or fear; I couldn't tell which and didn't care. What right did he have to be healthy and active and able to run while Charlie lay in bed? What right did he have to be happy? He jumped the last two feet and turned to look up at me. 'Loser,' he said and swivelled towards the Big House.

I leapt the full fifteen feet or so down from the platform, and tumbled him to the ground. He grunted and squealed and squirmed out of my grasp, screaming for help as he did so. I pushed myself up from the muddy grass and sped after him, easily pinning his sparrow-thin frame to the ground with my arms.

'Don't hit me,' he whimpered, all his bravado gone. 'I'm so small.'

He'd brought his hands to his face and his bug eyes opened even wider, his mouth a horrible gash-come-smile. I unclenched my fists and let him go, annoyed with myself. 'Be careful,' I said. 'You're not as untouchable as you think, even here.'

We both got up. 'Sorry, James,' he said. I watched as he jaunted towards the front steps, his shoulders jutting from side-to-side, confidence restored. He knew I wouldn't hit him, knew he had Moira and Fran and the meeting for protection. As he reached the gravel, he turned slightly and called out in a sing-song tone. 'There's no time to fight, anyway. I've got extra maths this afternoon. Just me and Mervyn. Mervyn and me. Don't be jealous.'

I didn't care about the meeting at that moment, didn't care what Fran might say. It should have been Charlie in that class with Lex. Wind rushed in my ears and I charged, driving my head into Lex's back. We sprawled in front of the Big House and he struggled and cried beneath me but I was heavier and stronger. I took hold of his lank black hair, twisted it in my grip, pulled his head up then jammed his face into the gravel. The shock of the blow broke my hand clear and he scrambled away, yelping. People appeared in my peripheral vision but I had eyes only for Lex. I caught hold of his trousers by the belt and ducked as he wind-milled his arms uselessly. I drove my still clenched fist into his chest. He oomphed to the ground.

For an instant I saw myself: bigger, bullying, wet-eyed with anger, standing over an injured, bloodied weakling. I dived on Lex, ready to hit again, but the flash of self-knowledge slowed my fists and the rushing in my ears subsided.

'This really isn't appropriate,' a voice said.

Someone else cooed. 'Peace, guys, peace.' Yet another said: 'What shall we do?'

Two arms gripped my shoulders, pulling me up. 'Cool it, wee man,' Keith said as he ushered me backwards. I looked around at the gathered circle of staff and kids: nervous smiles and knitted brows couldn't hide their excitement. Theory is never as exciting as action. 'I think he's had enough pal.' Keith gestured to Lex, who sobbed expertly with his head between his knees. He looked like a child half his age who couldn't find his mother, but knew that he if put on a good show he might get a free ice cream out of the tragedy.

Fran's face appeared through the circle of onlookers. 'Dear God, James,' she said, stooping towards Lex. 'What have you done this time?' Her face was flushed, despite the cold, and her blond hair fell about her face unbound. She went down on her knees to cradle him.

Mervyn appeared behind the two of them, a dark form looking down at woman and child, then over to me. His eyes sharpened and the small patches of cheek above his beard grew red. He pursed his lips and, though I knew he was angry, I couldn't quite disentangle the other emotions writ across his face – confusion, interest and, most piercing of all, most evident, a sombre disappointment. Something else troubled me but my head was hot and I couldn't think clearly. He looked away and then down at the pieta on the ground between us.

'Let's take him to the cabin,' Mervyn said. 'He has an extra session with me in ten minutes.'

Fran helped Lex to his feet. He rose between her and Mervyn, who'd stepped beside them to make up the trio. 'I'll have to bring you up in the meeting,' Fran said.

'I don't give a flying fuck about the meeting,' I shouted. 'You can all go and fuck yourselves and the meeting too.' I pushed my way past Keith and walked away. Without Charlie, I was on my own.

'James,' Fran called after me faintly. 'It's almost two. You've got Art with Moira.' At that, my temper cracked anew and I sprinted off, my feet splashing through the puddles of the path, the soot-black clouds rising in great plumes like some malignant gas sent to choke me.

The clouds broke. I plunged into the Tangle and heard the rain as much as felt it: A continuous beat that trammelled the bushes and brambles around me and forced its way into my thoughts. I pushed through a thicket, determined not to go back despite the mud, and the cold and the water seeping through my shoes. Then I remembered the abandoned hut with its smooth, lathe-turned doorknob and headed there, slithering though the damp undergrowth.

This time I didn't hesitate. I stepped onto the rotten wooden decking, cold water running down my back. The small door ground against the jamb but I squeezed myself in and left it ajar to light the darkened room. Inside, it was low ceilinged and I had to crouch to get in.

The single room was about six feet by four and the whole thing was made of soft wood planks long-since filched from the school's timber pile. I traced the bark-crinkled edge of one of the boards with my hand. The roof had been lined with heavy-duty plastic bags and it sloped down from front to back. The ground was visible beneath and the place had a smell of wood and countryside rather than anything man made. It was as if it had sprung up, like the twisted bushes and roots which surrounded it, from nature. There were no signs of previous life, no gutted candles, smudged fag ends or twisted cans of cola.

I slumped down against the nearest wall, thrust my legs out straight and listened to the rattling of the roof beneath the rain. I wouldn't go to Art and learn bugger all about next to nothing. I didn't need a silk screen to express my feelings, or a charcoal daub to explore my inner self. The knuckles of my right hand tingled, blood-flecked.

As I teased the grit from my palms, the shame of my own childishness began to overcome me. An adult wouldn't strike at the provocation of a child, the simple taunts of a cretin such as Lex. I'd hit out like an animal. A grown up wouldn't run away in a huff. My face burnt at the thought of Mervyn's disappointment. He expected better of me. I'd never hit anyone at Bannock House. Charlie had always been so squeamish about the thought of hitting people, and now I'd wasted blows on Lex. He now had sympathy and I had nothing.

It rained still but I had to get out of the Tangle before it became dark. I drew myself up and clambered back through the thick undergrowth. The return journey didn't seem nearly as fraught. My soaked jumper stuck to my skin but my step remained steady and my head felt clearer. I didn't need anyone's sympathy, didn't want Fran's consoling arm upon my shoulder. Lex could keep it. But I knew from now on, I would come back to the Tangle, the hut. I had discovered a place of my own. No one but Charlie knew it existed. It would be ours to share on his return.

As I approached the Big House, the lights of its windows were already illuminating the afternoon gloom. I couldn't face teatime and the dining room – news of the fight would be all over the school. Despite all the nutjobs, real fights were a rarity at Bannock House: everyone had been neutered by the pathetic hippy ethos. I didn't want to be the centre of attention, so I changed in my room and hid in the library until suppertime. Even on a rainy day, you'd be hard pushed to find anyone in the library.

Supper had almost finished when I tapped down the stairs, relieved to see Fran on her own with the washing-up. 'Where have you been?' she said, her back to me as I entered the kitchen.

'I only want a piece of toast.'

She stood in the scullery door and watched me as I sawed two slices from a loaf. 'Moira missed you in Art,' she said. 'And I missed you at tea.'

I closed the Aga door and looked at the torn oven gloves in my hand. Grey from over-washing, the gloves must have been at least as old as me. Fran took her glasses off and polished them on the hem of her painter's frock, a livid pink with purple trim. 'You did a bad thing today,' she said quietly as the light caught the gentle moving lenses of her specs.

A picture of the scene on the gravel came to my mind once more, the gaping excited faces of the crowd, Mervyn among them, and I realised what it was about him that struck me as odd. 'Did Mervyn have a tie on earlier?' I said. 'That must be the first time I've ever seen him without one.'

She exhaled in exasperation. 'You should apologise, James. Go up and say you're sorry.'

The smell of toasting bread wafted up from the Aga, and I scanned the table.

'Can I have the butter please?'

'Apologise.'

'He started it,' I blurted out, hating myself for sounding so like a child. 'Why should I?'

She put her glasses back on and opened her hands. 'What would Charlie do?'

'Charlie wouldn't have hit him at all,' I snapped.

Smoke curled up from the Aga. Fran stepped past me and took the toast out of the oven and strolled around to the larder. She came back out with a tub of St Ivel Gold and a pot of honey and placed them on the table in front of me. I sat down and began spreading. You're probably right,' she said as she sat opposite me. 'But what would Charlie advise you to do now?'

I stepped onto the landing and looked at the five closed doors, my fellow Sparrows preparing for bed in three of them. The chessboard lino was slicked wet from the rainwater of shoes and there was a metal mop bucket right in the middle collecting a drip from the skylight. Fat droplets pinged every second or so. Instead of going to my own door in the far corner I moved towards Lex's. For the whole of the year so far he'd had a tiny room on his own because, I reasoned, no one could stand sharing with him. I knocked but didn't wait for a reply.

The dorm was painted in the same oily orange as mine but the colour felt darker and more oppressive. This was partly because the room was shaped like a cell, a small oblong with a window at one end and a set of bunk beds by the door as you came in. Lex had no posters. Everyone else in the school had something on the walls: ripped pictures of Bananarama for the girls or footballers or Iron Maiden for the boys or Madonna for everyone. Lex had nothing but the blank swathe of orange, illuminated by a sole naked bulb suspended from the ceiling on a long wire. He had no bedside lamp, no family photograph Blutacked by the bed. The tiny chest of drawers under the window also had nothing on it other than his discarded clothes of the day just gone.

Lex lay on the bottom bunk, facing the wall and with his back to me. He was clamped beneath the blankets but I could see from the shape he made that his legs were drawn up into his body, like he was trying to hibernate.

I licked toast crumbs from my lips. 'How was maths?' I could tell he wasn't asleep by his breathing but he made no move and said nothing. I listened to the sound of the dripping from the hallway and caught myself counting each drop.

'What did you learn? It must have been great to have all the time to yourself.' I tailed off, casting around the room for something else to talk about. The polyester sheets rustled as Lex shifted but he refused to turn around. 'You should make the most of it before Charlie comes back.'

'I don't think Charlie's coming back,' Lex said into his sheets. 'I wouldn't.'

'Why?' I said quickly. 'What have you heard?'

He pulled the sheets tighter around him. 'Go away.'

I'd expected him to tell me to fuck off immediately, or gloat about the trouble I'd be in at the meeting or even some bullshit about Mervyn but he didn't say anything more. He lay motionless, like a dead animal. The black window rattled in the wind and I picked at my nails for something to do.

'I'm sorry,' I said at last. 'I won't touch you again.' I didn't know what else to say. His stillness frightened me. I looked up at the solitary, naked bulb and left the room.

The school meeting that week contained the same old nonsense. Murdo the caretaker scoped the room with his single good eye, looking for volunteers to form a maintenance party. No one joined, not even any of the adults. In the end, after a twenty-minute discussion among the staff, it was decided to set up a working group to explore how to increase pupil participation in infrastructure issues. Four members of staff volunteered for that detail.

Mervyn had stopped doing the crossword in the meetings because now he sat next to Fran. He looked small beside her, shrunken back into his jumper, eyes down, while she leaned forward hands on knees, imposing herself as best she could on the meeting and those around her. It was only a matter of time before the agenda came around to her big 'point' – my fight with Lex. She outlined what had happened and I was asked to explain.

I didn't try to defend myself, this time. Without Charlie next to me to laugh at my smart asides, it seemed pointless – worse than pointless, for arguing only made the meeting drag on. As if sitting around in meetings and speaking in front of people were any kind of training or preparation for the real world. The staff would normally encourage the kids to speak up but this time they didn't need any help. Three different teachers in succession made long speeches about the abhorrent nature of violence, and bullying and dictatorship. Moira glared at me the entire time before putting her oar in with a long lecture that ended with: 'Fighting leads to fascism.'

'It's not as if I marched on Poland.' I felt moved to talk at last. I heard a couple of chuckles, although someone muttered. 'What's Poland got to do with it?'

'James.' Lone in the chair pointed her pen at me. 'You must raise your hand to speak. Have you finished, Moira?'

They banged on a bit but no one asked me anything else and Lex kept quiet. As soon as I'd admitted I hit him, there was nothing to discuss. Disputes between kids in the meeting normally revolved around matters of fact, about who said what to whom, who stole whose mix tape and so on. Kids were only interested in the truth. It was the staff that liked to spin things out and talk about the why, the *what does it mean?'* I undertook not to attack Lex for the following week, indeed, not to talk to him at all unless strictly necessary. (That final 'unless strictly necessary' had to be inserted when I asked whether I should refrain from speaking to Lex in the event that a piano was about to fall on his head, or in case he hadn't heard a lorry bearing down on him.) I also agreed to join Murdo's maintenance team.

Feet shuffled, mouths yawned and watches were checked. Leonard the woodwork teacher put his hand up. He wore a jumper of hooped two-tone grey and his spindly hair fell away from his balding head in too-long strands. His features twisted around a small, hairy, button nose making him look like a knot of the burr oak he so highly prized.

'Some of you may know,' he said in a wheezing tone. 'That Charlie Bevan has been unwell. I, as acting chairman of the Senior Committee, received a letter earlier this week from Charlie's dad. Charlie will not be coming back to the school, this term at least. He's suffering from a strain of something or other – the writing, I'm afraid, is rather unclear. Mr Bevan must have been upset, even disturbed, when he wrote it.' Leonard paused, folded the letter carefully and then lifted his head to look around the room. 'I can make out this, though. He writes the prognosis is not good.'

The room fell quiet. Leonard gently closed the leaves of the notebook and twanged the elastic band that held it shut.

'What does prognosis mean?' I said, when I realised the meeting had ended. Leonard looked across at me with vacant, unanswering eyes.

'We can talk about this later, James,' Fran said softly. 'After the meeting.'

I stood up. 'Tell me now! What the fuck does it mean?' I looked around at the others but the staff turned their eyes away.

Suddenly, Mervyn's voice echoed around the Octagon, the first time he'd ever spoken in a meeting. He stared straight at me unblinking and said: 'It means he may well die.'

5

'You've got someone up there, I know you have you wee whore,' a woman's voice rang out from the front room. I stopped on my way down the stairs, unsure, and listened.

'Shut up, Mum,' Janice said.

I folded the dark purple towel she'd given me and looked back at the bathroom door. 'It's not like that,' Janice went on.

'Is it no?'

The door hung open and I moved towards it as Janice continued. 'I said he could use the bathroom. Maybe you should try that some time? It stinks in here. Of you.'

I stepped into the room. Janice had her back to the door. Beyond her stood the owner of the unknown voice, Janice's mum I assumed, facing both of us. She wore a soiled blue housecoat and an expression of angry disgust. 'And here he is, the big man,' her voice hack-sawed through the words. She gestured towards me with a half-smoked cigarette. 'Get your hole did you son?'

'Mum!' Janice shouted and turned to me, lowering her voice but avoiding my eye. 'I'm sorry.'

'No, it's my fault, really.' I placed the towel over my arm. I felt like an apologetic waiter. 'I shouldn't have. I think you've got the wrong impression. Janice was simply being kind, helping me clean up and so forth. Please forgive the imposition, Mrs…'

The older woman exploded in a caterwauling laugh that quickly transformed into a deep, rumbling cough. '*Mrs I shouldn't have. Im-pos-ition,*' she said after she'd recovered. 'Christ, Janice, where did you get him, the 1940s? Fuck knows what Archie'll say.'

'Dad's got nothing to do with it.'

'He's not going see it like that, is he? Think!'

I drifted backwards out of the room as the two of them continued to argue. 'I'm fed up thinking about him,' Janice's voice grew higher, marked against the harsh depth of her mother's tone. I walked through the bare kitchen and creaked open the back door. The crash of breaking glass followed me out the house. 'Jesus,' Janice shrieked. I carried on walking.

There's only so far politeness can take you and getting involved with people is never really a good idea. If all my education had taught me anything, it was to keep my distance, not to intervene. It never leads to happiness. If you don't get involved, you can't be responsible – no matter what Edmund Burke said. No one blames the hermit when things go wrong, do they? How can they? As a policy, it leads to a fairly friendless existence but it's simpler that way. I could handle it. I could be happy alone.

I climbed a small grass ridge opposite the row of houses and sat down. Janice's face had flushed when I'd interrupted her argument. *Get your hole* – hardly the words of mother-in-law material. Janice had gone the same shade when I first noticed her on the bus. Mottled peach. I kept my eyes on the house and made sure she could see me if she came out. Daisies dotted the slope and I looked down to see my hands had already begun making a daisy chain, as if they remembered things my brain did not. I concentrated on threading the stems and tried not to think too much about Janice's father, and what went on in the house below me. I should have left completely but something held me back. Did I really want to know about this shadowy Archie? Or was I simply interested in Janice's pink-white skin and what might happen later under the cover of my poorly assembled tent?

The back door slammed shut, and Janice stormed out of the house. She glanced around and made her way towards me, up the slight hill at an oblique angle, like a sailing boat tacking in the wind.

'Sorry about that,' she said shielding her eyes against the embarrassment, as if the shame were a big bright light shining directly behind me. 'She's been in the house all day, bored. She wants the attention.' Despite her angled head, I could see her reddened eyes and hear a hint of a sniffle in her voice. She'd changed out of the uniform into a tight t-shirt and jeans. I took in the curve of her thin waist and the lithe way she stood, almost bouncing on the balls of her feet, ready.

'Parents,' I said, shifting my weight to the side. She sat down next to me but chose the other side on my right. To hide her birthmark, I thought. Her perfume hung in the air, chocolate sweet and chemically. 'What does your dad do?'

'Drink,' she said without humour. She pulled her arm across her eyes and began pulling up small tufts of grass. She had a couple of dark bruises, grip marks, on the inside of her wrist. I waited but she didn't say any more. Instead, she held her head down until she caught sight of my half-made daisy chain. 'Is that yours? I wouldnae show that round here. People might get the wrong idea.'

'I'm not gay,' I said quickly and tossed the daisies in front of me. 'I don't know why I made it. It's odd.'

She smiled quickly and tossed the white-blonde hair from her eyes. 'So tell me about the weirdo on the bus,' she said finally. 'You said you knew he was a paedo. Why did you lie about knowing him?'

'Did I?'

'Aye, you did.' She looked at me hard for a moment, her thin pale face almost glowing as the night darkened. 'Oh my god, I'm sorry.' She brought her hand up to her mouth. 'I'm such an idiot. You're one of the kids, aren't you? No wonder you blanked him.'

I shook my head slightly. 'He used to be my friend.'

*

Mervyn referred to his living quarters as his 'rooms' but that was far too grand a title. The room – really not much more than a hut – was made of chipboard and perched on a breezeblock base at the end of a row of converted brick farm buildings, like the last outpost of a shabby hilltop station. Beyond it lay the school's small farm, with its three horses, two cows and a fat sow that squealed once a year when it littered. Chickens pecked at my feet as I banged on the door for the first time, one day deep into the spring term.

'What do you want?' Mervyn said, standing in the doorway.

I held up my exercise book like the excuse it was. 'I want to ask you about these simultaneous equations.'

'Can't it wait until the next lesson?' He looked left and right and over my shoulder. 'You really shouldn't be here.'

'But you didn't set them in class,' I said. 'These were extra.'

He twizzled his moustache. 'Very well,' he said, turning back into the room. I smiled. He'd fallen for my ruse.

It had taken me months to get to this point. I'd tried to ingratiate myself by mentioning the crossword, or cracking jokes about the other staff – anything to mark me out as different from the rest of Bannock House. Despite all this, it turned out to be my failings in class that provided the first real suggestion he might be interested in me.

A month or so previously, Jenny and I walked to our extra maths lesson. 'Can you believe Keith?' she said. 'Smashing up the art room like that?'

'It's normal,' I grunted. 'A reaction to this place.'

'It's not normal.' She tutted. 'You're always so negative.'

I pulled up my collar. 'Keith destroys stuff, that's what he does. I don't know why you care.'

We walked on, my face turned into my chest.

'I miss Charlie,' Jenny said suddenly. 'Do you think he's coming back?'

'Don't speak about him,' I hissed back. 'He's my friend. You're just a stupid girl.'

We approached the maths cabin in huffy silence. 'You think you're so special, James,' she said as we ducked underneath. 'As if you're the only one with feelings and thoughts and emotions. Here's a newsflash, a-hole: you're not.'

'Not what?' Mervyn said as we emerged onto the cabin floor. He stood with his feet squeezed together and one hand resting on the board. He reminded me of a dancer at the barre, ready to plié or twirl or at least describe the arcs of geometry with balletic grace: A bearded Nureyev. We ignored his question and sat down.

I couldn't concentrate. Mervyn drew bending curves on the board, plotted points on the x-axis and the y, and then connected them in great chalk sweeps. But each time he asked me a question I got it wrong. At one point, after a third successive mistake, Mervyn broke the chalk against the board. 'Focus!'

Jenny, by contrast, sing-songed correct answers at every turn making my failures all the more stark. When we finished, she packed up her books with prim and proud reproach. I took my time, my movements as sluggish as my mind.

'Hold on a moment would you, James?' Mervyn said. Jenny stuck her tongue out at me as she descended through the trapdoor. Mervyn busied himself around the classroom, making light of his words. 'Is there any reason why your work has been so poor?'

'What's it to you?'

'I'm your teacher,' he said sharply and then began again in a softer tone. 'You need to concentrate. It's all very well being gifted.' He stopped fussing and looked at me, scratching his beard. 'But you must put in the hard work. Apply yourself. *Atque inter silvas Academi quaerere verum.*'

'What does that mean?'

'And seek for truth in the groves of Academe. Horace.'

'Who? What groves?' I said angrily. I relied on Mervyn, of all the adults at the school, to give me a straight answer.

'It's Latin,' he said as if that were answer enough which in a way it was. I knew real schools taught Latin and Greek but I'd never heard it spoken before. Each word sounded complete and sufficient of itself, more powerful and resonant than mere English. I still didn't know what it meant, but at least I knew it meant something and had done for hundreds of years. I tried to think of an intelligent thing to say but then Mervyn spoke again, throwing the words out in a casual way. 'How are things with the new sleeping arrangements?'

Lex had moved into my dorm. A couple of younger girls started in the middle of term, and Fran and Moira decided to reorganise the Sparrows' accommodation. My room was way too big for one and so they put Lex into Charlie's old bed while the girls took his bunk bed cell. I could tell Fran hoped Lex and I would settle our differences, would come to 'understand each other.' This could never happen. What had happened, though, is that we stopped fighting. Lex had been strangely subdued for most of the term, pretty much since the day of our fight on the gravel, and so we spent the nights in silence. I think he knew how outrageous it was for him to be sleeping in Charlie's bed, how impossibly absurd for him to be in his shoes. The only remark he'd ever made in the dorm was to compare my pressed, striped boxer shorts unfavourably with his rank y-fronts: You look like a girl, he said. I hadn't replied.

For all the airy manner of Mervyn's question, I could see him waiting for an answer. 'We don't really speak,' I said.

'Lex is no Charlie, eh?' He paused but made no movement to dismiss me. He pulled at his tie and straightened it. 'How are you getting on with the crossword?'

'The crossword?' I said, surprised. 'What's that got to do with maths?'

'There was a clue in yesterday's paper,' he said, ruffling through a pile of old newspapers by his desk. 'It made me think of you.'

'I haven't really bothered with it,' I answered. 'I don't know how to start.'

'You shouldn't simply give up, just because something is hard.' He closed the stove and gestured towards the trapdoor. 'Let's go.' He stepped back from the fire, hesitated and then said: 'I'll make a deal with you. If your marks improve – if you concentrate, that is, on your mathematics – I will undertake to induct you in the mysteries of the cryptic crossword. Fair?'

I nodded quickly. He followed me down the steps and we broke into the open ground between the cabin and the Big House. He'd set his sights on his rooms and didn't seem to want to speak any more but, emboldened by his offer, I spoke again. 'What's the clue?'

'I beg your pardon.'

'That made you think of me.'

'Oh.' He wetted his lips as he walked and held his head at an elevated angle, as if conjuring up the clue from some space above us. 'You promise to concentrate on your school work?'

'Yes.'

'Jacobite leader pursued by audible ends. Five letters.' He left me after that, his jerky movements taking him into the fading light on the far side of the gravel. I went to my room to write down the strange sentence before I forgot.

The following week, I proudly presented Mervyn with my answer, which happened to be my name.

'Well done,' he said, looking me up and down. He stood in the middle of the rain-lashed football pitch as he waited for training to begin. Despite the weather, he wore no jacket but his jumper and tie were still in place. Dark patches formed on his shoulders, his hair matted flat. As a concession to the mud bath in which we stood, he'd pushed the ends of his trousers into his socks. 'But do you know why?' I followed him as he placed out the cones for shuttle runs.

'You said you thought of me.'

He twisted his head toward me, a half-smile showing through his beard. 'That doesn't count.'

'Well,' I said. 'I looked up what Jacobite meant. They were supporters of King James, right?' He nodded, so I went on. 'In other words, Jacobite leader equals James. I didn't understand the rest.'

'Good start, though,' he replied. 'We'll make a solver of you yet. Hey, you boys!' he suddenly shouted across the pitch. 'Line up in the far goal mouth.' A rag-tag column, in different coloured strips, jogged into position. Mervyn's football training, like his lessons, were the only part of the school day when the kids didn't question what was going on. Though no one would admit it, I think many of them enjoyed being told what to do. I could tell they didn't like Mervyn as a person, I was the only one who seemed to talk to him outside lessons, but they listened to what he had to say. 'You too,' he said, gesturing to the goal with his head.

I hesitated, happier by his side than with the other children. 'But what about the rest of the clue, what does it mean?'

'Jacobite leader equals James, you got that precisely,' he nodded quickly. 'Yet Jacobite leader can also mean the letter J. The leader of "Jacobite", you see. Next, or "pursued by", is "audible" which means sounds like, then a word for "ends", which in this case is aims. Spelt A M E S, because it's only sounds, gives us Jacobite leader, i.e. James.' He'd rattled through the solution in seconds but I'd followed every word.

'That's amazing,' I said. 'Give me another.'

He looked at me sharply, alert, as if unsure whether or not I was laughing at him. 'Get down there in the goalmouth with the others,' he said. Then, as I walked away, almost as an afterthought he said in a soft voice. 'I'll think of one for later.'

So started my obsession with crosswords. I gave up completely on Moira's art classes. Every Thursday afternoon, I would head to my hut in the Tangle and grapple with clues, or try extra maths problems or simply flick through the fluttery pages of my dictionary, reading out words, learning for myself: words, numbers, things. Moira had nothing to teach me. On these days, I would sometimes see Lex trudge to the maths cabin for his extra lesson, a lonely figure disappearing under its shadow. The sight of his shambling, stuttering gait made me sad. Not for him, alone, but for the Charlie-shaped absence by his side. I would turn away, hide in my Tangle, and try not to think of what was gone.

At the end of a maths lesson, I asked Mervyn to give me some extra hard questions. I tried to be as causal and quiet as possible but Jenny heard.

'Extra!' she squealed, outraged. 'James has asked for extra questions,' she called down to the rest of the class underneath the cabin on their way out. 'He's gone totally loop the loop now.' She turned back for a second and whirled her finger around her ear. 'You should take some time off to, you know, be a kid.'

'Piss off, Jenny.'

Mervyn had remained silent during this exchange but when I looked back to the board, he was scratching away excitedly.

'These are simultaneous equations,' he said. 'They're quite tough but should keep you occupied. I'd give you a text book, but we only have the one.' Bannock House had the best wood workshop and pottery in the county, I knew because the staff always boasted about it, but finances couldn't stretch to a textbook.

'What book are they from,' I said pointing to the questions on the board. 'I'll get my dad to send it to me. He doesn't mind sending me books.'

He turned to face me, brushing his hands free of chalk dust as he did so. 'I devised these myself,' he said, his tobacco brown teeth showing amidst his beard. 'You're the first pupil who's ever asked for more.'

Jenny was still taking the piss out of me at tea the next day. 'James is absolutely mental,' she said to anyone around the table who'd listen. 'Extra!'

'Mervyn seemed to like it,' I said eventually.

Keith sat opposite. He looked up at me and adjusted his long hair. 'Mervyn likes everything just now.' He smirked.

'What do you mean?'

He leant forward conspiratorially and hitched his head to the side, gesturing at Fran on a far table. 'He's all happy, now he's getting his hole.'

'Keith!' Lone swatted him on the arm. 'Don't be so disgusting.'

I glanced over at Fran. She polished her glasses and said something to Lex next to her, then looked up. She smiled a question at me and I looked away, my face hot.

Lone badgered Keith. 'You're very immature, talking about women in this way,' she said. He hung his head low, hair like earflaps.

'Cool it guys.' Raymond clattered his plate on the table in front of us. 'Peace and love.' He grinned widely at Keith and Lone. 'What's your beef?'

'Beef?' Keith spat the word out.

Lone flicked her hair. 'Hi, Raymond.' She blinked at him. 'Keith's being childish.'

Keith pushed his stool back, scraping it loudly on the hard floor. 'Fuck this,' he banged out of the dining room. I couldn't understand why he was so angry. I looked between Raymond and Lone but they just grinned at each other, ignoring the rest of the table. 'He'll grow out of it,' Raymond said.

I got up. 'Off to do your homework?' Jenny trilled.

'I don't want to end up an ignoramus, like the rest of you.'

And so it was that the following evening I'd made my way to Mervyn's rooms and stood at his door, exercise book in hand, waiting for him to let me in. He ushered me through a small anteroom that had little else in it but a large and dirty off-white sink, serviced by a cold tap. Above it hung a blotchy mirror with a single crack scoring it from corner to corner. I followed him into the main room, which was more basic even than my dorm. The low-slung bed was a tangle of grey and brown, like a pile of winter coats. An armchair, a stool and a wooden box doubling as a coffee table completed the furniture. A notebook lay open on the box. As the last of the March sun mottled one wall, Mervyn drew a ragged curtain. He rested on the edge of the stool and pointed me to the armchair.

I picked up a completed crossword from the chair and sat. 'Why is this *mood*?' I read out, gesturing at the paper.

He poked fiercely at the smouldering fire, trying to cajole the damp logs into life. 'What's the clue?' he said.

'Condemnation about atmosphere.' Smoke drifted as much into the room as up the chimney, making the place feel strangely windy rather than cosy.

'Easy,' he said. He poured a glass of Gaymers Original Cider from a green plastic bottle as he rattled off how to solve the clue. 'But what about these simultaneous equations?'

He thrust out his hand for my exercise book.

'What are you doing here?' I asked, ignoring his outstretched claw.

He gestured to the hearth. 'Well, I was trying to get the bloody fire started, what does it look like?' The room smelt of rotten apples and onions and something bitter I couldn't quite place. The fire hissed.

'I mean here, at this kind of school. Why here?'

'That's a big question,' he said. He ran his fingers through his beard but didn't answer. A tangle of horsehair came away in my hand and I realised I was tugging at the arm of the chair. 'I could ask the same question of you.' He pulled again at his glass.

'Me? I'm a kid, I have to come here.' I looked at the glass in his hand. 'Why aren't you in the pub?'

He stopped the glass at his lips, surprised. 'I suppose it's hard to keep a secret here,' he said almost to himself, then looked at the cider swilling in the scale-stained glass. 'When one finds oneself approaching Queer Street, economies must be made.'

I wanted to ask him where Queer Street was but something about the mood had changed. It was as if we were having a grown up conversation and I didn't want to ruin it by continuing to ask questions, like a child. 'My dad sent me here,' I said. 'Because he believes in progressive education.' Mervyn raised one of his thatched and unruly eyebrows so I continued. 'Bannock House had one of the best reputations. The guy who set it up was some kind of conscientious objector in the war. I read an old *Freedom* pamphlet about it once. My dad showed it to me before I came here. Anyway, this guy created the whole thing from scratch, when the outside world hated him. He was some kind of visionary. That's what my dad said. An "educationalist." But he got the sack or something a few years ago. Moira said he got power hungry so the senior staff took over.'

'Put out to pasture, eh?' Mervyn said, tossing another log on the fire.

'Well, that's what Moira says. I think he's dead now, or too old to do anything useful.' Mervyn laughed but I wasn't sure why. I went on. 'Ever since then, the school's been run as a collective. You must know all this?'

'I neither know nor care.'

'But didn't they quiz you when you got the job?' I said. I couldn't help myself asking questions. 'Didn't they make sure you agreed with the ethos of the school?'

He pursed his lips and considered. 'They didn't seem that interested in me at all once they found out I was qualified to teach mathematics. I sensed a certain fear of Her Majesty's Inspectorate of Schools.' He paused for a drink. 'And a paucity of suitable candidates.'

'Eh?'

He drew his forearm across his lips. 'They were desperate.'

'I'm surprised they didn't convene a summit to confirm your appointment. It normally takes at least six meetings to decide on whether to serve butter or margarine at supper, let alone a new teacher.' He smiled so I carried on. 'Do you know it took us almost a year to decide whether or not to serve tea *and* coffee at the morning coffee break? The staff think it's useful for all of us to express our opinions, for our voices to be heard – as if *that's* going to be of any help when we're grownups. I don't even like coffee. In the end, Leonard won the argument because he said they'd have to change the name of the whole break if they didn't serve coffee, despite Moira's propaganda about the evils of caffeine.'

Mervyn laughed in a high-pitched, reedy way. 'What are you babbling on about?'

'Moira's latest claim is that Leonard's a Trot. I'm not quite sure what a Trot is, but Leonard's not a great advert.'

'I thought all you kids enjoyed woodwork,' Mervyn said. 'It seems to be what everybody spends their time on. That or art, judging by what they deem to be acceptable usage of a mathematics exercise book.'

'Not me,' I said quickly, nettled that he'd lumped me in with the rest of the school. 'Never.'

He didn't reply immediately and we both stared at the fire. I regretted the sharpness of my tone and wondered how I might take the conversation down a different path. I wanted to show that I was more than a typical Bannock House hippy.

'What's this?' I picked up the notebook from the table. It showed a list of names down one side, with numerous dots against each name and a corresponding number on the other side of the page.

'It's a cricket game I invented,' he answered. 'It's played with dice.'

I looked at the two headings, Gloucestershire and Somerset. 'Have you been playing with yourself?'

He spluttered into his glass. 'I wouldn't put it quite like that. Against myself, is what I would say.' He finished his cloudy pint, ahhing in satisfaction.

'Do you play with Fran?' As soon as I said it, I wished I hadn't. His whole body tensed.

He glared. 'Certainly not.' He pulled the notebook towards him and closed it with a bump. His hands clung to the edges of the book and he looked down at it, as if it might tell him what to say. After a moment he glanced up at me. 'You should go. It's late.' Then he reached backwards and took another bottle of cider from the foot of the bed. A charred log fell from the fire, leaving a fizzling pile of ash in its wake. I stood up, struggling to find something else to say as Mervyn clumsily manoeuvred the log back into place. He gripped it between the poker and a jumper-covered hand. 'You still here?' he said as he sat back down, his tone softer.

'I just thought...' I hesitated and then picked up my exercise book from the table. 'Maybe you could teach me how to play sometime? If you ever needed an opponent, I mean.'

He put his hand out, palm to the floor, and gestured to the door. 'Run along,' he said. When he caught the look on my face, he added. 'Come at the weekend. We can play then.'

Although Mervyn was a member of the staff, he was so different from everyone else that visiting him didn't seem out of place to me. I turned up the following Saturday as planned and from that moment on, my social life fell into place. I had no need for anybody else.

Mervyn lurched to his feet. We'd finished another game of dice cricket and he had decided to re-enact the winning stroke. 'It's all about balance,' he said, pulling the poker from the wood pile like the sword from the stone.

He assumed a batting stance, the poker as his bat. The dice game didn't actually detail the kind of shot batsmen scored with, but Mervyn liked embellishing things when he spoke. 'The key to the sweep,' he carried on, referring to a stroke played against spin bowlers, where you take a long stride forward and bend down, swinging the bat around your front leg, 'is to keep your head still. The sweep is all about poise and balance.'

Mervyn stood by the fire, facing towards me. He flexed his legs at the knee and concentrated his eyes on the imaginary bowler twenty yards behind me. 'Even pressure on each foot and then a controlled leap forward.'

He stepped out with his left leg, ready to meet the non-existent ball. As he did so, he swayed slightly out of line and his foot caught the low tabletop. Such a challenge to his fabled balance proved too much to overcome and the table flipped, sending dice, cider glass and paper flying. Mervyn pitched sideways, crashing into his log pile.

'Bowled,' I said, laughing.

He pulled himself up on one knee, fighting a smile. 'Yes, well. This is a confined space. Give me a pitch. Different story.'

He collected up the spilled debris while I righted the table. 'We can play cricket next term, can't we?' I said. 'You can teach us instead of football.'

'I believe rounders is planned for the summer term.' He refilled his glass from a grey plastic bottle. 'Not taught by me, thank God,' he added, frowning at the cloudy brown liquid in his glass, held up close for inspection.

'But you're such a great teacher. Did you teach cricket at your old school?'

He frisbeed the newspaper to me and licked his lips clear of cider. 'Let's do the word pool,' he said.

I read out the question. The game was ruined slightly for me because Mervyn had already marked the answer with a rough biro circle.

Which of these definitions is correct?
Beriberi:
a) *In Buddhism, the state of near-happiness preceding Nirvana*
b) *An ailment of the nervous system caused by malnutrition*
c) *A Sri Lankan siren*
d) *A Malay word for friends*

'B!' he said, triumphant. He must have forgotten his morning's work.

I tossed the paper back on the table. 'You've already done it.'

Mervyn didn't seem to register my annoyance. He threw a log on the fire and gazed at it as the flames caught. 'I had beriberi once,' he said.

'You were starving?'

'No.' He stood up and scrabbled around for something above his bed. As he stretched to the top shelf, I noticed a grey flash at his elbow, flesh showing through a hole in both the bobbled jumper and shirt beneath.

He stepped back across the room. 'You can also get beriberi from excessive alcohol consumption. I collapsed in Montrose High Street,' he continued in a matter-of-fact tone, a teacher explaining a mathematical principle for the nth time. 'At eleven in the morning. My mates in the pub opposite thought I was pissed.' He sat down and drank from his glass. 'I spent six weeks in intensive care. Six weeks.' He laughed, as if remembering an exciting scrape from his childhood: caught scrumping apples.

I pried apart a piece of kindling with a billhook on the hearth, as I often did. He had difficulty with small things. 'Is that why you left your last school?' I said.

'No.' He looked at me in an odd way, then picked up a length of rubber tubing and craned behind him. His arms shook with the tension of leaning over and I heard a click.

I stood up to get a better look. There were a series of tubes and plastic bottles all leading to a large, dirty barrel on the floor. 'What's that?'

'Homebrew kit. It'll have to do until pay day.' He put his lips to the tube and sucked, spluttered then plunged it into one of the barrels.

I threw the billhook onto the small woodstack, so recently disturbed by Mervyn's tumble. 'You know most of the kids think you're odd?' He raised his eyebrows but didn't say anything. 'They think you're some kind of warlock, sent from medieval times to torment them with insoluble problems.'

He coughed. 'Compared to most of the staff, perhaps I am.'

'They don't understand you at all,' I said, still thinking of ways to get him to take cricket the following term. 'I understand though. You're a teacher. That's what you do. Teach.'

'Quite so,' he said, straightening on the stool, shoulders rising.

I waited a moment. 'Will you teach me how to play cricket then?' I made my eyes as big as possible and squeezed my bottom lip with my teeth. 'I'll do anything.'

He looked at me with an odd, questioning expression. His brow knitted and he scrunched his eyes closed, as if trying to keep something in. Then he broke into loud and forceful laugh, making me jump. 'You crafty sod,' he said. He shook his head sharply and then glanced up at the tiny clock on the otherwise bare bedside shelf. 'It's supper time,' he said. 'You should make haste, else Fran will be most displeased.'

While Mervyn and I played games, did crosswords and cracked mathematical problems, the rest of the school carried on in its normal, pointless, boring way: breakfast served at 7:45; hungry, dirty children scooping cups of warm milk from the frothing pail dragged up from the farm an hour earlier; crusts of bitter burnt toast strewn among streaks of sticky tea; the washing-up clattered and sang; the wood team sawed their way through damp timber and fed the fires until they hissed; children ran through the wet to their classes; Leonard laughed loudly at his own jokes as he showed us how to strike a chisel with a wooden mallet; Jenny skipped to the art room, her pigtails bouncing; ravenous mouths troughed at lunchtime; Mervyn scratched his symbols on the board, and wrote QED at the end of each solution. The meetings went on, the staff shouting above the drumming of the rain, banging on about policy and ideology and who should be in charge of what. And the pupils simply carried on living their lives: they cracked grins at stupid jokes, they sang songs to pass the time, or screamed over silly board games; boys decoded heavy metal lyrics in their rooms and tried to play their records backwards just to check; and the girls trilled and tattled and plaited each other's hair. Mervyn still took football twice a week and we ran around the pitch to warm up, we passed in triangles to practice, we dribbled through cones and we chased the ball and tackled and shot and passed and panted in exhaustion. Murdo the caretaker strode around the grounds in turned down wellies, muttering to himself in incomprehensible Scots; Paloma the red-headed potter sat at her wheel like an earth mother, giving birth to pots as she lectured on the magic of clay; and Moira eating, always eating from the great grey dollops of porridge in the morning to slabs of buttered toast last thing, crumbs spilling from her flabby lips. And then, shortly before the end of term, the Octagon collapsed.

During the night the roof concertinaed in on itself, rendering the hut completely useless. No one died. No one got hurt. It would have been impossible, however, to tell these two facts from the reaction of the staff alone. At breakfast on the morning after it happened, Moira stumbled into the dining room with tear-glistened eyes. 'There's been a terrible accident in the night,' she wailed. 'The roof's caved in. The Octagon.'

She called an emergency meeting immediately. Everybody piled into the dining room but then we had to wait while people went out to find all those who had skipped breakfast. There were lots of yawns and scratching and a great gaggle of Kestrels clung to the storage heater, like a colony of coastal birds. I perched by the front window, next to the other Sparrows. Jenny sat two over with her back to me, Roya in between. As the last of the stragglers came in, Roya took careful strands of Jenny's hair and began to weave them together. I watched as the thin brown-red streaks twisted into a dark cord.

Moira coughed, stamped her foot and then clapped the room into silence. 'We've called this meeting to discuss what should be done about the terrible accident.' She sat in the middle of one of the benches. Lex cosied up to her.

The meeting broke out into various voices, either disputing Moira's version or crying shame. Raymond spoke over the hubbub. 'But was it at an accident?'

I continued to look at Lex, ignoring the chatter. His arms wrapped around Moira's bulk, it was a pose typical of the new him. He'd developed a habit of draping himself over either Moira or Fran at every opportunity, a cloying facsimile of affection. He'd been quieter, too, and we hadn't clashed since our fight on the gravel. I wasn't sure whether I preferred the taunting, irksome problem child to this mute and mooning poodle.

'Who's the chair?' someone shouted above the din. 'You should put your hand up.'

'Quite right,' Leonard said. 'We need to elect a chair.' They spent the next five minutes working out who should preside over the chaos. Leonard kept his hand raised throughout this discussion, which meant he was the first to speak. 'I think the pre-prandial question, the nub as it were, is how are we going to react? I suggest that, together with Murdo, I lead the process. We'll give over woodwork classes to the reconstruction effort.' Mervyn snorted halfway through this speech, but I didn't know why.

'Why should you lead?' Moira said. 'Isn't this a committee issue?'

'Well.' Leonard drew in his stomach and flattened a wisp of hair with his hand. 'As the head of woodwork and chair of the aforementioned committee, I thought –' He left what he thought hanging. Moira's eyes narrowed. I saw a couple of the other staff bristle too and glance from one to the other – all Moira's gang.

'Wasn't it your design in the first place?' one of them snapped.

Leonard raised himself up. 'I'm not responsible for maintenance – it was surely rotten.'

Another argument started up among the adults until Raymond, squeezed next to Lone, stumbled into the fray once more. 'But, I mean, shouldn't we look in to what happened? Could it have been sabotage?'

'Check out Woodward and Bernstein,' one of the Eagles cracked.

Leonard and Moira looked blank but some of the other kids were nodding their heads. Keith put his hand up to second.

'What exactly are you suggesting?' Moira said.

Raymond tugged at his black (mourning) bandana in a nervous gesture. 'You know, I don't mean to accuse anyone or anything. No way.' Moira's eyes remained small, blackcurrants in her Bath bun face.

I put my hand up. 'If you want to know what happened, why don't you call the police? Or even get a proper builder in.'

'Hear, hear,' Mervyn muttered, surprisingly. His accent made it sound as if the word had two distinct syllables.

'No,' Leonard said sharply before regaining himself. He unscrunched his face, trying to smooth away the deep, burr-oak creases round his nose and forehead. 'I don't think that's a good idea. Moira, I'm sure, would agree with me on that.' He glanced at her quickly, before casting his eyes around the room. They rested first on Raymond then Mervyn. He was going for the reproving father look but ended up more like petulant pensioner. 'Raymond and Mervyn are both relatively new here, and don't quite understand what's what. Bannock House is a unique school. Much more unique than most others.' Again, I heard Mervyn snort but Leonard carried on. 'But its very uniqueness makes it prey to the forces of, er...bad people. Yes, bad people from outside. The press, etcetera.' He waited but Moira nodded him on, harmony momentarily restored. He tried again to tame his few, flapping hairs and continued. 'We will rebuild the Octagon, don't worry about that. I can see how many of you are discombobulated by this sad news but the Octagon will rise again. It is a symbol of the school's self-sufficiency, of our democratic spirit.'

'Which lies in ruins,' I called out.

'Yes, thank you, James. As I was saying, the senior committee will discuss the reconstruction details – I expect most of you will want to volunteer.'

Fran, who had been silent throughout the meeting, interjected. 'Shouldn't we mention the inspection?' This question provoked a stir on the benches. Most school business didn't really bother any of the pupils. They sat bored and hangdog as the teachers played out their theories around us. But every so often the school inspectors came to visit, which always caused excitement, at least for the pupils. As far as I could tell, the very word 'inspection' struck most of the staff –

especially the academic teachers – as even more heinous than 'motherfucker'.

The thing was, despite being bored by such things as the school meeting and the endless ideological discussions, most of the pupils were perversely proud of the place as a whole. Bannock House was different, special, unique. The children shared in this sense of chosenness, as if it were a privilege to leave school semi-literate, scientifically ignorant and academically unqualified. I could never understand it but almost every one of the kids loved the school. They seemed happy, or at least as happy as their problems allowed. It was nuts. The inspection was a chance to show off, a rare opportunity to illustrate how brilliant we were at personal interaction and self-expression. In my first year, I'd tried to point out how poor the Geography teacher was by showing up her embarrassing lack of basic knowledge. But the whole plan backfired on me, for the inspectors ended up thinking how terribly advanced I was for a young boy. I heard them chatting as they left the class – they attributed *my* book-learned knowledge to the teacher.

Leonard, who'd furrowed his long sloping brow at Fran, finally answered her question. 'The school inspectors? Yes, thank you for that Fran.' He sucked air through his gappy teeth and continued. 'Due to certain issues with the last report.'

'What issues?' someone heckled before they were shushed.

'Irrelevant issues,' Moira replied over the noise. 'Those idiots know nothing. What's the point of an O Grade eh? How dare they come in here and tell us what to do.'

Fran held up a warning hand but Moira continued. 'How many kids at normal schools are as well-adjusted as ours? Can they speak confidently? Can they think for themselves?'

'At least they can count!'

'You can count, James. I believe that you can count very well indeed. But you can also speak up for yourself and I doubt very much, though you hate us now, whether you'll grow into the kind of man who'll do as he's told. You'll be a responsible, caring individual – hard to believe now, I know, but I believe it. Because of what we've made here – not because you can count, or pass exams or make the inspectors happy.' She breathed out heavily, deflated.

'Never mind that just now,' Leonard said. 'The point is the inspectors are not coming until the autumn term, which means we've got time to prepare.' He glared at Moira and some of her cronies. 'Time to girder our loins.' I heard Mervyn snigger at that, as Leonard went on. 'Which means we need to rebuild the Octagon and forget this dribble about calling the police or outside builders or anything else.'

The meeting broke up with a couple of staff cheerily telling us not to worry and that we'd have the Octagon back in no time just as soon as the senior committee has come up with a schedule of works. They didn't mention the leaking roof on the Sparrows' landing, the split door of the sports cupboard, the blocked chimney in the library or the maths cabin's broken windows. The Octagon was everything. I sat still and watched as Roya's chapped-red hands entangled the last of Jenny's plaits into place. I leaned over her shoulder and noticed the smell of lavender and something else I couldn't place beyond its sweetish tang.

She straightened, nearly knocking me, and clapped her hands. 'All done,' she said. The two of them popped away from the bench like a pair of dunked corks and drifted out on the tide of people leaving. They didn't look back.

On those evenings when I didn't go round to Mervyn's I'd work on my maths or on the crossword or simply think about what we would do the next time I saw him. It became routine. When I knocked, he'd simply open the door and turn back into his bedroom without saying a word. He might lower the volume on the radio or sometimes we'd listen together, laughing at *I'm Sorry I Haven't a Clue* or *Just a Minute*.

He still spent time with Fran, or went to the pub, so I didn't see him every day. But it felt like it was every day, for even if I didn't go to his rooms I'd be thinking of what we talked about or looking up things in my dictionary or studying crossword clues. I even made my father send me a copy of *Wisden's Cricketer's Almanac*, so I could study the cricket results from the summer before. I would lever open the heavy yellow book and try to decode the lists of numbers that it held, the statistical proofs of various truths: West Indian domination; Australian incompetence. It could even give you the unarguable record of individual achievement: a player's performance rendered right down to the last run, wicket and catch. The numbers didn't lie.

One night when Mervyn was at the pub I headed down to supper early to warm up on the Aga. I pulled a stool close to the stove and looked over the *Scotsman*'s (inferior) crossword. The clues lacked subtlety, were barely cryptic at all in fact, but Mervyn said all puzzles, regardless of the quality, were gymnasiums for the mind.

The door to the scullery swung open, and Fran appeared, her clogs clattering. 'Hey James, what's going on?'

'I'm working out.'

She smile-frowned. 'Working out what?'

I lifted my eyes. 'I'm doing the crossword,' I said, raising the limp paper in my hand.

'Right.' She opened the larder and crashed about for a while, putting the things out for supper and boiling the kettle. 'Mervyn got you on to that?' she said, once she'd settled down at the table opposite. I grunted in response.

'So tell me about his place.' She sliced bread. 'Is everything okay?'

'What do you mean? He's a friend.'

'But what do you do?' She put down the knife and looked at me, her head to one side. The kitchen lights flashed off her thick glasses.

'What do you do?' I snapped back.

Her face pinked. 'James.'

'I mean,' I hurried on, wanting to avoid the subject as much as she did. 'Why don't you ask him?' She frowned and walked into the scullery to scrape cups from the shelves. I waited until she came back before I answered. 'We play games and talk,' I said. 'He knows stuff.'

She laughed. 'I know stuff too.'

I threw the paper onto the table and warmed my hands on the stove. 'Why do you work here?' I said.

'Oh god, I don't know. I like kids, I guess. It's rewarding, watching them learn, seeing them work things out for themselves.'

'Mervyn's like that too.'

She looked at me for a moment as if deciding whether or not she agreed. 'You know I'm always here, if you ever want to talk. I know you've been lonely without Charlie.' I shook my head, stung. I hadn't thought of Charlie for days. It hurt to be reminded of his absence but somewhere deep inside me, what pinched at my heart, was the shame I felt at forgetting him. Fran waited for me to respond but when she saw I wouldn't, she pushed away from the table and turned to the walk-in larder, like a boat putting out to sea.

Jenny, Roya and the others streamed into the kitchen, a sullen Lex drifting up last. 'Good evening, Fido,' Jenny said to me, and gave a fake wave.

Fran came back from the larder. 'Fido?' she asked, holding a gleaming white cube of fresh butter in front of her.

Jenny was surprised to see Fran suddenly appear and fumbled her reply. 'Oh, nothing.' She sat down.

Lex clasped a mug to his chest and said in a monotone. 'It's because he's Mervyn's pet.' He blew on the tea and placed it on the table. 'So she calls him by a dog's name,' he droned, as if utterly uninterested in his own words or their effect. 'But she only does it because she likes him.'

'Shut up, Lex!' Jenny and I said in unison. He shrugged.

'As if,' Jenny pouted, her chin set at the angle of maximum haught.

The girls quickly steered the conversation in a different direction. Romantic entanglements interested them more than anything else and a hot rumour revolved around the supposed love triangle of Keith, Lone and the teacher Raymond. 'It's

Scotland versus America for the heart of the beautiful Danish maiden,' Roya said in a silly accent and laughed.

Fran's face clouded but she didn't say anything. She was probably worried about what Keith might do if it happened to be true. Although he was often nice, the whole school knew that Keith could explode at any moment – he'd smashed up classrooms before, and threw stones and been quite wild, when the mood took him.

Lex and I observed a sullen silence throughout the rest of supper and I noticed Fran looking at us, and me in particular. I didn't fit in with the Sparrows any more, not since spending so much time with Mervyn, and maybe she understood. Every now and then the crinkles around her eyes would deepen, as if she were troubled by questions she couldn't quite formulate, let alone answer.

After lights out later that evening, I called out to Lex across the cold dorm. 'Do you really think Jenny likes me?'

He didn't respond immediately, not with the expected *'Fuck off,'* nor the equally predictable: *'Wanker.'* Instead, after a long pause, he said in a slow and weary tone: 'I don't care.'

The way he spoke made me think for a moment that perhaps he was talking about himself. Then I recovered. 'Piss off,' I said.

In the last week before the Easter holidays, a new posting appeared on the board. Unlike Mervyn's previous notice, this one failed to cause a sensation. It was entitled *Cricket Practice*. Underneath the heading it read: *Please Sign Up Below*. A pencil hung by a string and I scrawled my name, first on the list. When I looked again, while waiting for a lift to the station at the end of term, mine was still the only name. Beneath it, someone had scribbled: 'Sassenach Pish.' I made a mental note to tell Mervyn that this didn't refer to a real person.

It didn't surprise me Mervyn hadn't mentioned his cricket plans in person. In teaching matters he preferred to keep things formal, I understood that much about him. He was a puzzle whose solution I was starting to unpick.

6

'I can't imagine being pally with a teacher,' Janice said. 'Mind you, Mary Aitkin ended up shagging Mr Toseland in the fifth form. But he taught art, so what can you expect?'

Janice and I ambled through the cloud grey cottages of Dungowan. 'The teachers never seemed like a separate species at Bannock House,' I said.

The red rims around Janice's eyes had faded as we walked further away from her house but I couldn't help thinking about what secrets lay there. The bruises on her arm troubled me, even though I told myself not to get involved. I didn't mention it. Instead, she'd kept up a steady stream of queries about Bannock House and eventually she tugged again at the strand that started the whole conversation, the strand I'd ignored. 'Aye, that's great and all about your wee games. But what happened with your friend the teacher? He doesn't seem so pally now.'

A spine-shivering shriek pierced the air, 'Janice! Janice!' We twisted around to see Lynn at the top of the road. 'The chip van's about to leave Jan, you want to order.' Beyond her, a white van stood, a small awning poking from one side. Lynn clutched a dark greasy bouquet in one hand and waved at us with the other.

'Hold on,' Janice shouted back and turned to me. 'Have you got any money? We could get a bag of chips. Or share a fish supper?' Romance, I thought. She jogged up to the van and I followed.

Scottish chip shops aren't like their English counterparts. While the English chippy concerns itself primarily with chips and a small selection of fish and meat delicacies, and perhaps some minor sundries such as a pickled egg or saggy gherkin, the Scottish chip shop is a cornucopia of fatal products. The regulars, the fat white oil-sponge chips, the Day-Glo saveloy, the battered dog-fish, are simply the first wave in the shop's arsenal. Shelves of brightly coloured sweets, bitter cola cubes, radioactive lemon sherbets, chocolate bars, mount an attack on the arteries and teeth; the fizzy drinks, the gut-rot Irn-Bru or locally fashioned cherryade open a second front against the lining of your stomach; and then the heavy artillery go straight for the lungs, packed in clean square boxes at the back, the quickest, faster way to death, the cigarettes. They even sold them in singles. The chip van in Dungowan proved itself to be a top of the range model; the stealth fighter of the heart-disease world, for it also sold alcohol.

The two girls realised I had money, which soon translated into a bottle of gin and a litre of A.G. Barr's American Cream Soda. I brought myself a four pack of McEwan's lager to wash down the chips.

We leant up against a dry stone wall, a little way from the village, fingers slick with chip-fat and mouths ready for warm booze. I ate my supper in gulps, licking my lips for the salt. I hadn't eaten since a shrivelled sandwich on the train, a far away place.

Janice and Lynn drove the conversation, puncturing the air with sharp squeals of laughter that grew louder and more frequent as the light-long summer evening continued. I drank the lager quickly and moved on to sipping the gin, which we passed between us. I put my back to the wall and stretched my legs out flat on the ground. Lynn stood and talked, her hands a whirl. Janice faced her, calmer, shyer but in high spirits. Every now and then she'd sit back down beside me, our legs touching.

As the last of the daylight went – hours after the sun had gone down – two boys arrived. Younger and less sure of themselves than Lynn, but I could tell they adored her. She hailed them in a mocking but not unfriendly way. 'Here come *The Proclaimers*,' she said as she jiggled a pair of imaginary glasses. Bespectacled, the two boys eyed me warily and nodded their heads. One said something to the other but I didn't catch it, and didn't really care.

Lynn held up the empty gin bottle. 'We're dry,' she said and tossed it over the wall. 'I've got a bottle of voddy at home.'

'No you haven't,' Janice laughed.

'Okay, okay. My *mum's* got a bottle of vodka at home.' She looked quickly at Janice and some unspoken message passed between them. Then she turned to the two boys. 'Right Laurel and Hardy, come with me – we're on a booze run.'

'But,' the shorter one started to protest.

'Shut it. Let's go. Cheerio you two,' she cooed back at us as the three of them headed to the village. 'Don't do anything I wouldn't do.'

Janice sat down next to me, her shoulder against mine. 'God I'm pissed,' she said. 'But what else are Fridays for?' She let out a soft, nervous laugh. Her hair fell on my arm as she lolled forward. 'Sorry.' She flicked it back, washing her scent over me again. 'It's good fun to see someone new around here. It makes a change.'

I swallowed a burp and closed my eyes. The chips and beer sat heavy. I brushed my hand on the dew-wet grass. 'Why don't you leave?' I said, eventually. Why don't you escape those bruises, I thought.

'That's easy for you to say. You've got an education, money. Looks. What have I got? A higher in modern studies and a bad attitude. What would the world want with me?'

'You shouldn't think like that,' I slurred. 'Modern studies is a highly respected subject.'

She laughed. 'I've never been good at anything, except talking back to the teachers or my boss. A-plus for lip, that's what they always said. F for everything else.' She hesitated and I opened my eyes again. 'I bet your girlfriend's got a degree though. I bet she's pretty too.'

'I don't have a girlfriend.'

'Aye right,' she smiled.

'Honest, I don't.'

'We have booze!' someone cried through the darkness. 'Let's get bluterred.' The two boys appeared, with Lynn behind them, plastic bags rustling, lit only by the distant street lamps. Janice edged away a touch and one of the boys handed me a beer. The conversation started up but I closed my eyes and barely listened.

After a while, I felt Janice's body relax against me again. I took another drink and wondered how far it was to my tent. 'Alright bawbags!' a powerful voice rang out. I craned my neck. A dark figure loomed above us like a cloud, perched on the wall, arms outstretched. He balanced for a moment and then vaulted over our heads with a great cry.

'Tam,' one of the boys shouted in delight. 'You want a drink?'

The big man turned, laughing. 'What's the crack?' he said, taking a beer. He was taller than me and I could see powerful shoulders beneath his shirt and a thin waist. The two boys fluttered around him like by-blown detritus collecting around a tree trunk. His face was in shadow but his head paused when he saw me. Janice's leg stiffened. 'Lynn,' he nodded his head. 'Janice.' He hesitated, then stuffed a hand in his pocket and turned to Lynn. 'Got a light?' The flame illuminated his bristled face, short crop hair. His drink-glistened eyes dipped towards me as the match died.

'How's the rigs?' Lynn said.

'Fucking shite,' he grunted. 'But the pay's great.' The red button on his cigarette glowed again, his eyes still on Janice and me.

'I want to work on a rig,' Lynn went on. 'Do they have women?"

'What could you do?'

'I can cook.'

One of the boys burst out laughing. 'Fuck sake, food poisoning on an oil rig. Piper Alpha all over again.

Tam sat down opposite as Lynn and the boys began arguing. He offered a cigarette across and I took one. He still hadn't said anything to me and I smoked it in silence, the nicotine rushing to my head. By this time Janice had moved and I noticed her standing next to Lynn.

'Back in a minute,' Lynn said. The girls walked towards the lights, picking their way past the two lads, who now lay on the ground, starfished and groaning.

Then Tam was by my side, squeezed close all beer and big man sweat and cigarette smoke in my face. 'Let's get a leak,' he said. 'While the screamers are gone.' He pulled me up and we stumbled to a hedgerow.

His piss roared and steamed and stank beside my sad dribble. 'Me and Jan,' he said. 'On, off.'

'I don't want to get involved.'

'Good job.'

'I don't like triangles,' I muttered.

'You what?' He made everything sound like an accusation.

'Love triangles. Not for me, no way.'

He zipped up loudly. 'Pussy.' He waited until I'd almost finished and then pushed me in the small of the back and walked away.

I stumbled slowly after him and heard the girls talking to one of the collapsed boys. 'Are you alright Davie? Turn him on his side. He's going to vom.'

As I reached them, I could make out Tam with his arm on Janice's back while Lynn knelt beside the stricken Davie. It looked like everyone knew their roles except me.

'How is he?' I said but no one heard.

*

I looked up, surprised. 'Lex?'

'Yes, how is he?' Mervyn repeated. He stepped away from the blackboard and, for the first time ever, sat down in his classroom. He crossed his legs and held my stare. The red splash in his eye had grown bigger over the Easter holidays and now covered the bottom of his left eyeball, like a half-full wineglass.

123

We were alone in the maths cabin. 'His arm?' Mervyn encouraged me to reply but I hesitated further.

In the last week of the previous term Lex had broken his right arm and it still hadn't healed enough for him to hold a pen. At least that's what he said when he got back at the beginning of the summer, toting his spindly limb in a pathetic little sling. He particularly avoided maths and hence I was in the cabin alone with Mervyn, as I'd asked to take Lex's extra afternoon sessions until he recovered. 'Does this mean the class is over?' I said, glancing at Mervyn's awkwardly crossed legs.

He put his head to the side in a sharp, decisive movement. 'Yes, I think so don't you?' He reached behind him and pulled something from beneath the console on which he kept his papers. It was a small, battered flask. 'Just a nip,' he said.

I held my hand out towards him. 'May I?'

'Certainly not!'

'I don't want to drink it. I only want to look at the flask.'

It felt cool and old and only slightly bigger than my palm. The grey-black surface ate the light, like a battered stone on Brighton Beach. I turned it over and fiddled with the tiny, brass-rimmed cap. 'An inheritance,' Mervyn said under his breath. I stretched across and offered it back. He weighed it in his hand for a few moments then drank again. 'You saw Lex's accident, didn't you? Do you think it still hurts? He's missed far too many sessions.' He dipped his head towards me as he spoke, as if asking for the answer to some mathematical question he'd scratched up on the board. I felt he needed an answer.

On the final day of the spring term, traditionally the whole school played a game called Scots and Redcoats. Six or seven of the older kids attempted to guard a small hill top in the nearby countryside and the rest of us tried to sneak in. Half-way through the game, I'd seen Lex standing on top of a dry stone dyke and flick his fat fingers in a V-sign at one of his pursuers. He fell off, of course, and ended up cracking his elbow on a stray stone on the ground. His wails echoed through the valley, until eventually Fran drove him to casualty.

When we came back from the holidays, Lex turned up carrying his arm like a broken wing. Fran and Moira fussed over him and he proclaimed loudly that he couldn't hold a pencil in his hand and that it was 'his right' to be excused from maths. Moira gave him a new homemade sling to replace the snot-stained rag he'd been using and he was allowed to sit in her art lessons and stare out of the window, like that was anything new. From as early as the end of the first week, though, I knew he was faking. I could tell by the way he got into bed in our dorm that his arm didn't hurt that much.

But as I sat there, under Mervyn's unsteady glare, still confused by the fact that he had slumped into a chair during a lesson, I wasn't quite sure what to say. How was Lex? Mervyn brought the flask to his papery lips once more. The pale early summer sun still alive in the sky behind me, I could see my own faint shadow tip his grounded foot. If I told Mervyn the truth, that Lex was almost certainly faking pain, I'd miss out on the extra class for the next couple of weeks. But I didn't want to mislead him either. A certain amount of trust had to exist between friends, otherwise what was the point?

'I don't know,' I said in the end, looking at the floor. 'He squealed loud enough at the time.'

Mervyn coughed. I glanced around the familiar cabin: the cobwebs still undisturbed in its corners; the thin carpet dotted by frayed trip-holes and a pattern all but given up; the silent, cold stove, its small door carelessly ajar. Dust duned along the ridges in the log walls and the heavy tang of Mervyn's liquor hung in the air. 'It's dry in here,' I said.

He pulled again from the flask. 'Probably go up like a Christmas tree. I imagine the roof's made from some hideously flammable substance, obtained cheaply and of dubious legality. Interesting word flammable, inflammable. Same thing, most get it wrong. Should be non-flammable....' he tailed off.

I pointed to the flask. 'Who did you inherit it from?'

He held it up to his face. 'This old thing? My sister gave it to me I think, but ultimately it came from the old man. Must have done.'

'You've got a sister?' It seemed such a strange word to associate with Mervyn, a word that spoke of families and small children and warm sitting rooms.

'Two,' he said before draining the flask. 'Why so surprised?'

'It's not that, it's, I don't know. I thought you were an only child.' I folded my exercise book in front of me and looked down. Even Mervyn had siblings.

Mervyn's hands shook as he tried to fiddle the flask top back on. It dropped to the floor and rolled towards me in a sad arc. 'I never see them,' he said, his eyes fixed on the solitary cap as it rested on the carpet near my feet. I kept quiet and waited for him to continue. 'She must have given me this at my father's funeral. He left me nothing, you know? I didn't expect anything, hadn't seen him for years.' As he spoke, he leaned forward to retrieve the cap but lost his balance and fell on one arm. 'Christ! The drink makes you maudlin.' He lurched back in his chair, fingering the recovered flask cap. 'Spelt M A U D L I N,' he spoke each letter distinctly and then smiled at me. 'You must try not to miss Charlie.'

I flinched. That he would even mention Charlie was one thing but talking in so personal a way was quite unlike Mervyn. I looked up but he had his eyes down, his hand dug deep into the strands of his beard, and I realised he was talking to himself as much as me. Did he miss Charlie too? Or was he thinking about someone else. 'When my father died,' he went on, seemingly unaware I hadn't answered. 'I felt glad. Glad that the old bastard couldn't do anything more to me. It never occurred to me to grieve.' He scratched at his exposed neck beneath his collar and loosened his tie. 'There must be another bottle around here somewhere.' He stumbled over to the cupboard by the stove and pulled out a bottle of cider. 'Splendid. A beaker full of the warm southwest. My faithful nepenthe.'

'Is that a clue?' I said. 'How do you spell nepenthe?'

He slumped back down and adjusted his legs, my question unheard. 'I read an article by your father the other day. On educational theory. He made a few substantive points. Very good on paper, though I got the distinct impression he didn't regularly meet any children. Does he ask you about life here?'

I shifted in my chair. 'I just wish all the teachers were more like you.'

'Do you? Do you really?' He blinked repeatedly. 'Sometimes I wish I was a little bit less like me.' He took a rough heave at the cider bottle. I didn't know what to say but he continued on. 'But the children here have life in them. They've got balls. I like that. You can think for yourselves. That's the thing in your father's article I agreed with.'

'But he talks bollocks,' I blurted out finally.

'It's right to think of the children as people.' He ignored me now, like an old deaf man telling a story. 'They're not a separate species, they're no different from us. Children are simply adults with less experience. We're all people.' Spittle flecked his beard as he spoke. I tried to remember what my father had written, but it didn't seem quite this.

Mervyn took another great swig from his flask. 'So your father doesn't talk to you about life here, then?' he asked again. He seemed keen to know the answer.

'No,' I said. 'Or at least, he doesn't any more.'

He leant forward in his chair and put his hand on my knee. 'So you don't speak about it back home?'

'I write,' I said. I'd lost my bearings in the conversation, Mervyn's hand hot and hard on the tip of my knee. 'Everything I do, I put in in my journal. I don't send it to my dad but it's there.'

Mervyn raised an eyebrow. 'Everything?' He drew back his hand and angled into his chair.

'Everything that I think is important, yes.'

He studied me for a second and opened his mouth, as if to ask another question but nothing came out. Instead, he drew the cider bottle to his lips, the elbow hole in his jumper showing. 'Ahh,' he exhaled. His body relaxed suddenly, and I realised he'd been balled with tension for a few minutes. He seemed

127

relieved, like when a decision's taken out of your hands. 'I wouldn't worry too much about not talking to your father,' he went on. 'I don't think mine ever talked to me before I was five. I can't remember him talking to me much after that either. Except when he caned me, of course. How old are you, twelve? Thirteen? By your age, I still hardly knew him. He liked my sisters, but for some reason he didn't like the sight of my face. Even as a young child I had to eat my meals in the kitchen, on my own, while my father, mother and sisters ate in the dining room. My mother would look in on me every now and then but that only made it worse. I'd hear the sound of the dinner as the door opened and closed, my sisters teasing my father, in some happy conspiracy. As soon as he could, he sent me to boarding school and on the day I left he told me it was for my own good. It had all been for my own good. Eight years old, I was. He didn't want to turn me into a pansy, he said. He didn't care about the girls, he said. They'd be staying at home come what may. I was to go out into the world and so he wanted to toughen me up from the beginning – ready for the army, like him, eating in the mess. Don't want to bring up a pansy. And so he sent me to public school!' Mervyn barked out a sudden laugh but his eyes caught no light.

I picked at the hem of my sweatshirt. Strands like the red cotton in Jenny's hair came loose in my hand and I pulled one the length of my stomach, staring intently as it unpicked from the wider weave. It snapped off and I took another. The wind gathered, rushing through the broken window behind me, a bramble branch rat-tat-tatting against the sill. I looked over my shoulder at the Tangle. It twisted in the blast, early summer-green filaments knitting in the gusts, shimmering, waving. I tried to guess where my hut might be but it was impossible to say. I knew the way from the one spot on the path but as the trees and bushes wove and battered against each other, I realised navigating through the Tangle would never be easy.

Mervyn slurped more of his cider and I turned to face him. His eyes downcast, he didn't seem to notice me any more. It felt like those times when someone cries in front of you and you don't know what to say. If I had been an adult, I might have put my hand on his shoulder or rubbed his back. Instead I changed the subject: 'Did you hear? They finally decided on a new design for the Octagon? Fran suggested they rebuild it as a heptagon to save money.' He didn't laugh. 'She's never been that good with numbers,' I added more quietly.

'Fran? Christ,' he said, standing up unsteadily. 'You really know how to pick them today, James. I'll give you that.'

I packed up my bag. 'What do you mean? Pick what?'

'Not now boy!' He clutched the side of the blackboard to steady himself.

'Sorry.' I went halfway down the steps but twisted around to see Mervyn before I left. He had one hand raised to the side of the board, the other hung loosely by his side and his head sagged. 'Are you coming to tea?' I asked.

He raised his chin and his beard cracked yellow, his version of a smile. 'No, James, I think I'll head back to my rooms. It's been a rather different lesson from the one I anticipated. But thank you for asking. One last thing,' he said, holding his finger up in a parody of the strict schoolmaster. 'Nepenthe is spelt as you say it, with an e on the end. It means: a potion to make you forget.'

'Nothing ever happens here,' Jenny pouted at Fran across the dining room table. 'It's so unfair.'

I'd gone straight from the strange lesson with Mervyn to tea. I sat at a table with some other Sparrows including Jenny, Roya and a glowering one-armed Lex, as well as Fran. Raymond and Lone sat in the far corner of the table while Keith squeezed next to me, his long hair hanging over his ears. The room was awash with shouts and clattering plates.

Fran spooned bright strands of shredded carrot onto her plate. 'We're getting a couple of new Sparrows this term,' she said. 'Eleven-year olds and some more in September. That's something.'

Jenny put her head to one side. 'Is this an infant school now?' She rolled her eyes at Roya.

As I wound thick wholemeal spaghetti against my spoon, I thought of Mervyn. I could understand him eating alone easily enough but the idea of him in any kind of family situation seemed absurd. To me he had become a person who stood outside the normal rules of life and yet suddenly I had to picture him with parents and sisters. I pushed the thought aside and said to no one in particular: 'What kind of school takes pupils half-way through the year?' Keith tapped his fork repeatedly against the edge of the Formica-topped table, a low regular beat.

'We take kids all year round,' Fran snapped. 'We always have.' Then she tried to smile and went on. 'It'll mean you guys will all make Kestrel next term.'

Keith's taps grew faster. 'Nothing happens to Kestrels either,' he grunted and glared over at Lone, who was giggling at a remark of Raymond's. He had lent her one of his hippy-dippy bandanas and she wrapped it tightly around her throat.

'Hey, that's like, Parisian man. Chic,' Raymond said and she laughed again but not like she thought it was funny. I couldn't quite make it out, like a lot of things that day.

Keith muttered under his breath. 'Square Des.' The fork clattered to the floor but Lone ignored him. He picked it up and carried on tapping.

Fran's brow crinkled and she raised her voice. 'Not only that, but I think I'm going to have more good news for you guys. I can't say right now but I think you and Lex will be very happy.'

'What, you think Lex will be made a Kestrel too?' I smart-aleced back.

Lex brandished a Bolognese-spattered fork. 'Fuck off,' he said, his mouth full.

'Look!' Jenny pointed at Lex's raised arm. 'He's been eating with his right-hand. You're totally healed.'

'Busted,' Roya said with glee.

Lex quivered slightly, the fork in front of his face. 'It's not…'

Fran chuckled, shaking her head. 'Caught red-handed,' she said. 'Bolognese-handed.' No one laughed. 'Well, be like that. What it does mean is you'll be back in full classes next week.'

'Keith, will you please stop that noise,' Lone said sharply.

He slammed the fork on the table. 'Am I interrupting something? I wouldnae want to be a gooseberry or nothing.'

'Don't be silly,' she replied.

'Fucking silly, am I?' He got up suddenly and tipped his plate into the middle of the table with a great crash. 'Shower of cunts, the lot of you.' The room went silent. Keith swept his head around in a great arc and we watched as he strode quickly away, the remains of his meal splattered in front of me.

Fran reached forward and turned the two halves of Keith's broken plate the right way up. 'Well, where were we?' she asked brightly, smiling around the table.

'You fucking prick,' I muttered to Lex out of the corner of my mouth. 'Can't even fake a broken arm.'

'Shut up!' Lex dipped his fork into the bowl and ribboned pasta sauce towards me. I bent away and then grabbed him by his shirt, pulling him from the table. It made so much more sense to act, to clasp hold of something concrete, like Lex, than to sit in silence wondering what it all meant: Keith's anger, Lone, Raymond and Mervyn, sitting alone in a classroom, drunk.

'Calm down!' Fran stood up and inserted herself between us. 'What the hell is going on today? You'd think it was a full moon or something.' She sat down between us and we turned back to our food, heads bowed.

Raymond cleared his throat. 'I just want to say it is so totally wrong to throw food around. Not cool. Thousands of kids are dying of starvation in Africa. Didn't you watch *Live Aid*?' Nobody replied. Raymond turned to Lone and said gravely. 'I should know, I was there. In Philly.'

After dinner it was my turn to help with the crockery. All the pots and pans were washed-up separately but each night one staff member and one kid had to do the plates and cutlery. It built community spirit, apparently, though I assumed it was because we couldn't afford to pay anyone. That night I drew Fran. She scrubbed, I rinsed. Lit by the high window above the sink, the milk-white sky visible only when you craned your neck like a prisoner, I stood silent as Fran dunked the blood-red plates in the water and one by one handed them to me soap-sudded. As I clunked them into the wide draining mesh, dripping cold, I thought of Mervyn at the kitchen table of his childhood, alone.

We went on in silence for a few minutes until Fran decided to refill the water in her sink. She cracked her marigolded fingers as the tap ran fresh. 'What is it with you and Lex?'

I shrugged.

She turned off the tap and shifted a pile of plates into the cloudy suds. 'Friends are important, James. Perhaps the most important thing in life. Relationships are the key to happiness. We're all interconnected, and we've got to work that out as best we can. Friends are there for support, you know, but you need to support them too. There are duties involved in friendship.'

'Lex is not my friend.'

'Well maybe he should be. You've got to give people a chance, James. You may feel strong now but you never know when you might need a helping hand yourself. Look at you and Charlie.'

'I said already, Lex is not my friend. I hate him and he hates me, end of story.'

She shook her head and handed me another plate. 'He doesn't hate you. But have it your own way. All I'm saying is give him break, it might help both of you out.'

I said nothing. Fran emptied a huge plastic cutlery container into the sink with a great whoosh. 'Look at Mervyn's classes. I'm sure he treats everybody exactly the same. Everybody deserves a chance. Take it the other way around – when Mervyn first came here none of the kids really liked him, did they? Not many of the staff either.' She sniffed. 'But now math is the mainstay of our curriculum. Who'd have thought, huh?' She glanced over at me when I didn't respond. 'How's it going with Mervyn by the way?'

'Don't you know?' I snapped back, fed up with her lecturing. 'Isn't he your friend?' The image I had of the child Mervyn eating alone, morphed into the version of him I'd left in the maths cabin, clinging to the blackboard with head bowed. The two together troubled me but I didn't want to tell Fran that.

She looked into the murky washing water. 'Sometimes I wonder,' she said almost to herself. 'He doesn't mention...' she began and then faltered. 'No, stupid question, ignore that.' She cleared her throat and spoke once more in her righteous tone. 'It's important that you're good at math. Bannock House needs all sorts. Strong kids like you need to help the rest. The outside world isn't too keen on us James; we need to show that the school works. We've an inspection to pass, remember?'

'Not my job,' I muttered, crashing the last of the knives and forks onto the draining board.

'I know that.' She sighed. 'I want you to understand that we have a lot of struggling kids here, many of whom could do with your help.'

'Like bloody Lex?' I slammed my hand down on the steel drainer. The cutlery jumped. 'Didn't you see him at tea? He threw his food at me, he's the wanker here. Why doesn't anyone give me a break?'

She pursed her lips and reached into the sink to pull the plug and then spoke over the gurgling. 'This is a community built on love, James. Show some love.'

'If you love kids so much, why don't you have some of your own?'

The water drained away in a final flourish and took with it the room's only sounds. Fran's cheeks reddened, her eyes widened and she looked at me as if I wasn't there, not through as much as past me, like she was looking into a future that scared her. I stood still but she didn't say anything more.

Slowly she pulled off first one rubber glove then the other and pinned them to a hook above the sink.

I wanted to get back to the hut in the Tangle. I wanted to be on my own. 'Am I done here?' I said.

She looked back into the empty sink before she answered. 'Yes, I think you are.'

Things returned to normal. Lex went back to maths classes and the two of us rarely spoke, other than to spit insults at each other at supper time. Somehow, once we got into our dorm, we observed an undiscussed but understood truce. Fran's exhortation to friendship remained a distant, unwanted destination as far as I was concerned.

The days grew longer, the weather hotter and many classes became even more 'optional' than usual. Teachers encouraged 'an active engagement in nature' – otherwise known as mucking around – and most kids were happy enough to be outside, planting vegetables destined to die or building tree-huts or feeding cows or whatever pointless nonsense they got up to. Mervyn's classes were the exception. People moaned about going to his lessons but I think they liked having something to do, a point in their week to rely on and a chore to complain about. Mervyn never spoke about his family again and I never asked. Instead, with the sun hardening the ground everyday, we turned our attention to constructing a cricket net. I found an abandoned roller in the bushes and we prepared a plot of grass out by the vegetable patch. I asked Murdo to ram poles into the ground and then Mervyn and I strung up an old fishing net that had been festering in the sports cupboard. As we knotted it to the posts, or pushed the roller up and down, he'd tell me stories about Gloucestershire County Cricket Club and inculcate in me the rules of the game. The dark figure, hanging against the maths blackboard, breathing gin and cider, quickly dissolved amidst the excitement of cricket. Mervyn's mood lifted and with it, so did mine, though I couldn't quite rid my mind of the image of the child eating alone and, sometimes, I would surreptitiously study his face to see if I could spot that little boy, hiding behind the tangled and knotted skein of his beard.

I arrived at supper one evening a few weeks into term. My stomach ached empty, the taste of Raymond's half-cooked American Style Veggie Burgers still clinging to the roof of my mouth. I was the first one there. Pink light from the dipping sun kissed the handrails of the Aga. Fran glanced up from slicing bread as I sat down.

'Where's Moira?' I said as I picked up the crossword.

Fran sawed away at the loaf. She'd barely talked to me since our argument over the washing up and she still didn't look too happy. 'She might be late. She's out canvassing in Dumfries.'

'Who for, the Monster Raving Loony Party?'

'James...'

'It's pointless. Everybody knows the Tories will win. Look.' I held up the front page of the newspaper. 'Even *The Scotsman* says so. And they're leftist loonies too.'

The toilet flushed in the hallway. 'Anyhow,' Fran said. 'She may be late so I've asked Mervyn to pop in and give me a hand.'

'Get off my seat,' Lex said. I turned to see him walk in from the hall, brushing his hands again his trousers.

'It's a free country,' I said and carried on reading.

He pushed me in the back as he went past.

'Fuck off, Lex.'

'No, you fuck off!' he replied with his usual wit.

Fran pointed the bread knife at Lex. 'Did you wash your hands?'

'Didn't you say Mervyn was going to be here?' I said.

She clunked small plates around the table but didn't look at me. 'I expect he'll be here soon.' She glanced up at the clock and then angled her head away. Her hand came up to her fringe and she rearranged it quickly.

'Mervyn this, Mervyn that. You're obsessed.' Lex's voice had a hard edge to it that I hadn't noticed before. I flicked my eyes at him but he seemed intent on tearing a slice of bread into strips.

'Shut up will you, I'm trying to do the crossword. You fucking retard.' It annoyed me that he didn't even look up. 'Just because you can't read, don't hold the rest of us back.'

Jenny came in with Roya and a couple of the new kids. She yawned theatrically and rolled her eyes. 'Oh God, they're at it again.'

Fran brushed past me back into the larder. 'Ignore them, Jenny.' The phone rang, a sound overlaid by a clattering on the stairs.

'I'll get it,' Moira bellowed breathlessly, unseen, returned from her vote-pimping.

'I can so read!' Lex raised his voice, reacting to my last needle. His cheeks coloured, like ripe plums.

'No you can't.'

'I'm dyslexic. It's a condition.'

'You're thick. Which I suppose you could call a condition. A terminal condition.'

He stood up, his pathetic fists balled. I went on, I couldn't help myself. 'You know, if you can't read all you'll be good for is digging holes in the ground, or nothing at all – you'll be on the dole like all the other losers, except you won't even be able to read the giro cheque.'

'I can read,' he shouted again, tears in his eyes. I knew he couldn't read very well – despite hours of one-on-one teaching – and it was the thing that hurt him most.

'You can't.'

'Stop it, James,' Jenny muttered.

'But he can't,' I said and turned back to Lex. 'Can you? Why would Mervyn be interested in you?'

'Mervyn doesn't care about you. He doesn't give a fuck whether you can do the crossword.'

We faced each other, Jenny watching.

'He cares more about me than you. He likes me. We do things together.' The words sounded odd in my mouth. The conversation had taken a strange turn, down a path whose destination I did not know. We were competing but I didn't know the rules of the game.

'He likes me more.' Lex persisted.

'No he doesn't.'

'Does.'

'Fuck off you fucking child.'

'I bet he doesn't touch you.' Lex said.

I heard Fran's clogs step back into the kitchen behind me. 'In my last lesson, he touched me here, here and here.' Lex put his hand to his crotch on the last word. 'And then he asked me to touch him too.'

The back of my neck tingled, despite the warmth of the summer sun purpling the kitchen around me. The kettle rattled on the stove. I could smell a toast crust burning. Fran stepped past me. 'Lex,' she said halfway between a question and a warning. Then she stopped. Behind Lex, framed in the doorway from the scullery, a late arrival to supper. He held each jamb with outstretched arms and his hairy head hung loosely, as if pulled down by the weight of his beard. I didn't know how long he'd been there or what he'd heard.

Lex remained oblivious, his back to Mervyn, and said as if stating the obvious: 'He did it in extra maths this week. If he liked you so much, wouldn't he ask you too?'

'Great news everybody,' Moira tumbled through the other door, jolly and fat from the phone. She clapped her hands, a sweaty smile across her face. We all turned, to stare at her. No one spoke. No one moved.

She put her head on one side and pinched her eyes at Fran. 'I did say good news, didn't I? You look like someone's died.'

Part 2

'The true object of education is the generation of happiness.'

Herbert Read

7

I woke up. Orange blossomed bright. In the morning sun, the cheap tent had turned from flimsy windbreak to tropical hothouse. My head thumped. I scraped a fat tongue along the roof of my mouth and chomped the dryness away. I held my hand up against the garish tone cast by the tent – perfect if lost in a snow-storm, not so great after a gut-full of gin and lager and regret. I couldn't remember getting back to the tent, could barely piece together the later stages of the evening. As I swept the sleep from my eyes, the acid tang of vomit wafted in through the open flaps. I couldn't remember doing that either.

Images flashed through my mind. Big Tam shoving me as I pissed; Davie puking in the long grass; Janice's white-blond hair a blur of light in the darkness; the bruises on her arm. I reached up and traced the line of a bump above my right eyebrow, as if I'd been hit. The dirt on my trousers suggested a tumble and my collar was ripped. Big Tam's fist on my shirt, a scuffle, the upside down head of a drunken fall.

I changed and pulled down the tent. Pictures from the evening came, now, unbidden and in horrible profusion. It had all been a big mistake, talking to Janice, the chips, the booze – partying with the natives. Friendships always created these invisible lines, points of intersection between people, impossible to judge. I couldn't remember what Tam had said exactly, maybe that Janice and he were an item, but I remembered his breath on my face, his fists at my neck and the shambling one-sided, one-punch fight. A hot flush came over me, at the thought of stumbling away from the scene, incoherent and defeated: so much for my faithful nepenthe, so much for forgetting.

Did Janice stare after me? Did she implore me to stay? An image came to me, as I looked over my shoulder, of Tam turning back to her. He had his hand on her wrist as she looked into his face, half-lit by a streetlight, her eyes wide. Fearful? Excited? I couldn't quite tell. Then his large body obscured her from view. Scraps of earlier conversation blew about my booze-emptied mind. Janice had asked again about Mervyn. Why was I friends with a paedo? Was it true? What did I know?

I strapped the rucksack on my back, the tent hanging wildly askew. From the road, Dungowan's few rooftops glistened slightly in the fresh early morning air. Birds sang, loud and irritating. I'd told Janice about Lex's accusation, that was it – *'bad kid,'* I'd said. *'Problem child. Couldn't believe anything.'* I reached the road and looked back at the small and dirty village. Janice and Tam, him closing in on her, swallowing her: her house, her odious mother; and the unseen paternal drunk, Archie. She needed a friend, someone more able, stronger than the feather-light Lynn.

A dog barked from a distant house away to my left. Long, plaintive howls as if the poor beast had just woken up with my hangover and realised it was chained, hungry and alone. Finally, a woman shouted and the howling stopped. The throbbing in my head did not. I waited a moment longer and then turned down the hill away from the village, away from Janice and her problems. 'Lex lied,' I'd told her the previous night. I think I even repeated it. But I couldn't remember her reaction.

*

'He's lying,' I said. 'You're a fucking liar, Lex.'

Moira stepped further into the kitchen. 'What is going on?'

Fran opened her hand out to Lex to usher him into the hallway. 'We shouldn't talk about this now. Lex, come with me.' Her eyes flicked up at Mervyn, then at the confused faces of the other kids. I could see from their expressions that only Jenny really understood.

'But it's not true, Fran,' I said. 'You know it can't be true, of all people.'

'Teacher's pet!' Lex cried but there was something desperate in his voice like he knew he'd overstepped the mark, or made a mistake. Sometimes when you know you're wrong, it's the most upsetting thing of all.

Fran held her hand up to quieten him and then looked carefully at me, her face pale. 'That class he was talking about,' I went on in gasps. 'The extra maths? I was there, see. It couldn't have happened. I was there.' I took a breath. Beyond Fran, Moira loomed, silent, wide eyed. Mervyn still stood in the other doorway, saying nothing. 'Mervyn lets me do my own work in the corner. I've got my exercise book upstairs with the date, if you want to check.'

Fran glanced from Mervyn to me and back again. 'Is this true?' she said.

'It's true,' he replied to her but he looked at me.

Lex's eyes blinked hard, his cheeks flushed red. The kettle rattled on the hob. His head quivered, frustrated that I'd caught him out in his horrible lie. 'I hate you,' he cried at me, flinging a stool to the floor. He pushed past Moira and ran off, through the hall and up the echoing stairs.

Fran ran a hand through her hair. 'Christ, what a kid. I better go after him.' She squeezed past Moira and then out, clacking across the hallway.

Moira fixed me with a glare. 'James, what was that all about?' I shook my head and looked at the hard white table top. She bent down and righted the fallen stool. 'Jenny, you can tell me. What's going on?'

'Oh, nothing.' I could almost hear the shrug in her voice. 'It's just another happy meal at Bannock House.' I tried to smile a mute thank you in her direction.

Mervyn swaddled his hands in a pair of frayed oven gloves and silenced the whistling kettle.

When it came to sex, I was an innocent boy. I used to overhear some of the older kids talk about it, of course, and I picked up fag ends of information here and there through the giggles and trills. But it was hard to connect the bandied code words with anything in the real world. It took me ages to work out what 'coming' meant, for example. My dictionary didn't help. It wasn't until I had my first wet dream that I understood.

If the subject came up at all in classes or at the dinner table, Moira or Leonard or whoever would deliberately act unembarrassed. They refused to call it sex, too, instead speaking of it as 'lovemaking.' Free love, so they said, was part of being a healthy human being, a beautiful thing in itself and not something to feel dirty about. But as with much else at the school, this atmosphere of openness and hatred of taboo didn't extend to hard facts. There were no sex education classes, no cold diagrams explicating how the figure marked x would inseminate via the shaded area marked y. All the details, the science, were either assumed on behalf of the pupils, or simply not known by the teachers. We kids were left to theorise and speculate in a vacuum.

This same vacuum existed in the aftermath of Lex's allegation, except that none of the kids were that bothered about it after five minutes. Sex, as a general topic, could keep people interested for ages. Mervyn and Lex, as a specific gossip item lasted the duration of the next day's coffee break. It didn't occur to any one that Lex was telling the truth, not with his track record. And everyone believed me. I was trusted because people always hated me for telling the truth, from commenting on ready-to-burst spots, to pointing out ill-fitting clothes. I sugared no pills.

As the next day's coffee break ended, only Keith appeared troubled by the whole thing. He came up to me in the dining room as I stirred milk into my scum-filmed tea. 'Wee man, what's the gen?'

My spoon tinkled in the cup. 'What do you mean?'

'Aw, come on Jamesy. Mervyn and Lex and that, don't hold.' He swept his hair from his face.

'Lex is a liar, we all know that,' I said. 'How many times in the last year has he bullshitted you?'

142

'Aye, but fiddling's a bit different.'

'Mervyn couldn't have done it,' I said carefully. 'I was there. That's the point.'

Keith stood close to me, up against the table. But he stepped back as I spoke and cast his eyes around the room. Cups rattled. Children laughed. The acrid tang of burnt coffee hung in the air. 'Och, I know he's probably lying,' he said. 'But why?'

'He'd do anything to avoid extra maths.' Keith shook his head in a way that may have meant he agreed with me, or not. 'Do you think Moira and Leonard will do anything about it?' I asked. I feared Moira might use the allegation to discredit Mervyn's teaching, to run him out of the school – even though she, like everyone else, knew it couldn't be true.

Keith cleared his throat. 'What can they do? He's a lying wee scrote, like always. At least that's what they'll think. That's what they always think.' He tensed his jaw.

'I meant about Mervyn.'

'Nothing, of course,' he said quickly, dismissing the idea. He picked up a sugar cube and began grinding it into the table. 'That kid is fucked up, man. Really fucked up.'

'Charming language, as ever Keith,' Moira heaved herself through the door beside us, followed by the gangling Raymond.

'That'll really impress the ladies.' Raymond winked at us. His arm swung across like a crane and settled on the coffee pot. Keith dashed the remains of his sugar cube across the table and walked out.

Moira tapped a teaspoon against her cup. 'Can I have everyone's attention? Thank you. I've got good news and bad news. Some of you may already have heard on the radio this morning, but I'm very sad to say it looks like the Tories have won yesterday's election.'

'What election?' Paddy asked.

'Is that the good news?' I muttered.

Moira glanced at me. 'Maggie Thatcher is most certainly not good news. Even you'll come to realise that one day,

143

James.' She turned back to the room. 'The good news is that Charlie Bevan has recovered. He'll be coming back to the school in the next couple of weeks.'

I looked up at Moira, who rammed a piece of toast into her mouth. 'Is it true?' I said. 'Is he really coming back? I thought the prognosis was bad.'

Her jowls wobbled as she chewed. 'You mustn't believe everything you're told. Apparently he had glandular fever, according to his mum. His dad got a bit fraught, I believe, which may have led to the misunderstanding. Or it could have been Leonard – he's never been too good with words. But what can you expect from a couple of white, middle-class males?' She dabbed the crumbs away from her mouth and peered at me. 'It'll be great to have Charlie back, all the same. Such a creative boy, so nice. And it will cheer up Lex. They're such good friends.'

Over the next two weeks, the sun shone on Bannock House. Lex's lies and disgrace faded into the background. Charlie was coming back. And Mervyn and I had made great progress on building a cricket net. We began to practice in the evenings. I had become so used to Mervyn's chat about cricket, talking of the laws and techniques and scoring, that when we finally got to play I couldn't believe what a poor player he was. A wiry medium pacer, he could never put any real zip on the ball. His technique with the bat was okay but his eye terrible. He would play a classical straight drive but somehow see his middle stump uprooted all the same.

I was a much better player. As a bowler, I had real pace. One evening, not long after we'd got the net up and running, I hit Mervyn above the hip with the ball. He pulled up his jumper. A blue-green mark appeared on his side, a round bruise the exact size of the cricket ball. It was a shock to see the sallow, strangely creamy skin of Mervyn's stomach. I felt queasy as he hopped around.

'Bastard,' he said. 'Good delivery.' He was pleased I gave everything. I could tell by the way he picked up the bat again, and said: 'Bowl.'

We ambled back from the nets afterwards. 'Good stuff,' Mervyn said. 'You were really getting up a head of steam.' In his right hand swung a thin, weathered bat while in his left he carried a crumpled cricket bag. He bought the whole set from a man in the pub and was immensely proud of his kit. From what I could see, it must have been older than him. 'I think we've got a good chance of selection, at least for one of the sides. Murdo's agreed to drive us to the games.'

At my prompting, Mervyn had arranged for the two of us to trial at a local team. The nearby town had some kind of short form pub league on Wednesday nights and we'd decided to try our luck.

'Do you think Charlie will be interested?' Mervyn said after a moment.

My chest tightened. Charlie's name sounded odd in his mouth, like he relished it too much. I didn't think cricket would work with the three of us, but I didn't know how to say that. 'I'm starving,' I said, spinning the ball from one hand to the other. 'Could you get me something from the larder?

His eyes shrunk behind their tangled brows. 'Can't you wait until supper? It could prove difficult tonight.'

'I don't want to get you into trouble,' I said slowly as we walked on. 'Another time, but I like the strawberry jelly.' I brought the ball up to my nose and breathed in the deep beaten leather and cut grass smell.

Cries, laughter and then a burst of applause reached our ears as we approached the Big House. The air shimmered with gravel dust. A game of badminton had sprung up. Someone had draped a high net over a line strung from the dining room window out to an improvised pole. We watched a raucous game of doubles; the rest of the audience sat on the wide, bent front steps. Raymond, in nothing but long shorts and a yellow bandanna, circled the players with a heavy black camera to his face, click-click-clicking. 'Awesome,' he whooped at a successful smash.

The front doors opened and Fran appeared at the top of the steps. 'Hey guys,' she called and raised her hand. She picked her way through the straggle of kids. 'Good cricket?' She stood before us, hands on hips, as if she were trying to flatten them. I noticed beyond her Lex get up and go inside.

'It was a net,' Mervyn answered. 'We had a net. You should say net.'

'Okay.' She had been looking at Mervyn but then her eyes dropped to me and she shifted her weight from one foot to the other. 'So James, you must be excited about Charlie's return?'

I shrugged.

'What with him being your best friend.' She dropped the words lightly but the fixed smile on her face surprised me. I shrugged and shambled away towards the steps, leaving the two of them together. Radio One's Top 40 wheedled from a ground floor bedroom, the high notes strained by tinny over-amplification. Dust swirled above the badminton game as I sat to watch. The shuttle looped and faded from one side to the next accompanied by grunts and swishes.

Off to one side, Mervyn and Fran talked. They had wandered to the edge of the football pitch. As I watched, he turned his head away from her, out across the meadow, the long grass bending in the wind, a vast snot-green sea of ruffling filaments. She put her hand to his arm and said something. Behind and above them, the horizon pinked. It was one of the few perfect days Bannock House ever had, with a wide, cloudless sky and a hot wet heat. The sweat ran down my spine as I straightened to swat away an insect. In that moment, Mervyn nodded at Fran. She reached up; her hand pressed to his chest, and kissed him. Then she stepped back, turned and shouted out. 'When do I get a game?' Mervyn continued to his rooms, down the dust-swirled path to the farm.

I didn't go inside. The midges stuck to my sweaty neck but the angled sun, the empty sky and the gentle wind shuffling the full trees around us held me there, gazing at the badminton in a vague and distracted way.

Jenny edged along the bottom step towards me. 'There goes Merv the Perv,' she said, her eyes following Mervyn out of sight. 'Your hero.' She tossed her hair over her shoulder.

I shielded my eyes with my hand. 'He's not my hero.' Her freckled shoulder was bare and I could begin to trace how the small brown specks coalesced as they stretched around her covered back.

'Does he touch you where no other teacher can?' she carried on. 'Does he make you feel special?'

'It's not like that,' I said. 'That's just Lex's lies.'

She sighed. 'I'm teasing you, James. Loosen up.'

I picked at the grey seam of the cherry-red cricket ball in my hand. 'You wouldn't understand.'

'Are you gay?'

'No!'

'There's nothing wrong if you are,' she went on unperturbed. 'My mum used to be gay. It's cool.'

A great whoop went up from the game and the players shook hands beneath the net, smiling. Two new partnerships took to the court and warmed up. 'He's a friend, that's all. You probably don't know much about it.' I carried on over her protests. 'There are duties involved in friendship. Things you have to do.'

She looked between her feet and, in reflex, clasped the plait from behind her back and pulled it free. Her head tossed from side to side, the conversation over, but I suddenly breathed in a fresh, clean smell, released with Jenny's hair. I turned back to the game. Moira and Fran had formed an alliance, a parody of a staff versus kids sporting event. Fran leapt and sprang and swished wildly to little effect. Moira by contrast swung her racquet in lazy arcs, sending the shuttle from one corner to the other with no apparent effort but bamboozling disguise. As Fran stumbled around her, fat Moira stood in the centre of the court and controlled the game with a strange unhurried grace, as unexpected as it was beautiful.

'Shambolic.' Mervyn shook his head. 'They spent an hour wittering on about the damn Octagon – an hour! They could have fixed it by now.' He threw his hands up in the air in mock exasperation. 'Then five minutes on whether or not to expel one of the boys. Just five minutes.'

I watched as he pulled his tie loose. We sat in his room, after he'd returned from a staff meeting. 'I don't know why I bother to attend,' he went on, gritting his teeth as he wrenched open a bottle of cider.

'Which boy?' I said. It never occurred to me that Mervyn wouldn't reply, that such a subject as possible expulsion might be thought of as confidential. I expected him to tell me everything. Outside the classroom, we spoke as equals.

'Keith,' he said. 'Apparently he smashed some of the carriage windows, in a fit of frustrated rage. I must say I have some sympathy.' He tossed the bottle top through the door into the ante-room beyond.

'So what? He's always broken things. In my first year he totally destroyed Paddy's hut with his bare hands.' Mervyn raised his eyebrows above his up-tipped glass. 'He's not nearly as bad as he used to be. Why start hassling him now?'

Mervyn smacked his lips together in satisfaction and held onto his beard for a moment. 'Paranoia, I'd say. Leonard and Moira are getting worried about what the local council might think. They're scared of the inspectors too.'

'But Keith? He'd end up in borstal if he had to go to school in the real world.'

'Oh, don't worry about that. He's not going anywhere. Fran wouldn't allow it – nor would I for that matter. Keith tries hard at his mathematics.'

A knock rattled the outside door.

We looked at each other, momentarily non-plussed. No one visited Mervyn's rooms but me. 'Enter!' Mervyn boomed theatrically.

The hinges of the front door screamed. 'Hello? Hello?' Charlie's high, reedy voice tip-toed in front of him through the ante-room. He appeared before us, unsure and absurd in too-short shorts and Dunlop tennis shoes. 'Fran said I'd find you here,' he said, seeking my eye.

His full ginger curls made him look like a clown. 'Oh right,' I said, stifling a smile.

'She wants you to come to the cookery lesson.'

Mervyn snorted.

'Tell her I don't want to,' I said. I looked up at Mervyn, expecting him to share my smile. But his face was serious and intent on the doorway, where Charlie stood. He examined him from beneath his dark brow and the light flashed in his ale-dark eyes for an instant. A draft tickled the back of my neck. I dug my fingers into the tangled horsehair spilling from the chair's arm.

Charlie stood at the door, over my right shoulder, with Mervyn in front of me and slightly to the left. I had to crane to see Charlie but Mervyn had a clear view. We were three points of an imperfect triangle. Charlie turned his foot up on one toe. 'Fran said she was sure Mervyn wouldn't want to keep you.'

The triangle snapped. 'No, of course not. No, by no means.' Mervyn bustled himself about, as if he hadn't been staring stock still and mute a moment before. 'Go along with him.'

Charlie and I shuffled back towards the kitchen, dust eddies worrying our feet. He'd returned to the school ten days earlier yet we still couldn't talk to each other properly. I had expected the same old Charlie bounce, his good nature, his open smile by my side. But when I saw him get out of his mum's car, with Fran and Lex waiting, I was disappointed. He hadn't changed – he looked exactly like he did before he went away. A little paler, if that were possible, but still the same old Charlie. And that's what disappointed me. I had grown in the meantime and he had not, I was changed and he remained the same. My wish had been granted and in that moment, I realised it wasn't what I wanted at all.

When Fran said she wanted to put Charlie and Lex together in the same dorm, given the 'problems' (a Bannock

149

House euphemism for lying, cheating and slander,) I didn't mind moving in on my own to the small room. It would have been childish to object. Charlie and I sat next to each other at supper that evening and he chattered away, but I couldn't hear anything he said – it seemed so alien, like he was from a junior school. I tried to show him the crossword but he looked at me blankly and giggled. I remembered that he was four months younger than me but, whether it was his illness or something else, I felt much older now.

And so, as we headed to the cookery lesson we didn't have much to say to each other. Under the shadow of the Big House, gravestone grey against the wild evening sky, Charlie finally spoke. 'What do you do at Mervyn's?'

I flicked my head. 'Stuff. You know, I'm really into maths now. And the crossword. It's not your kind of thing.'

He pulled at the fringe of his long sleeved, hooped-blue sailor boy t-shirt. 'Everyone really seems to rely on Mervyn now,' he said almost to himself. 'It's like maths is the most important subject.'

'Of course! The staff are paranoid about the inspection.'

'But we passed last time.'

'Yeah but Mervyn's an amazing teacher. He makes the school look like it's improved academically. More efficacious,' I said, rolling the new word around my mouth, still unsure whether or not it was quite right. Charlie said nothing but I knew he didn't understand. I went on. 'The school would be fucked without him, just ask Fran.'

Charlie hung back as we went through the side door, like a little child who didn't know how to operate the handle. 'Aren't they going out?' he said.

We made our way through the hallway. Charlie said something about having to do extra maths by himself, taking Lex's place on Thursday afternoons in order to catch up, but I switched off. I didn't want to know. The kind of equations he talked about I could do in my sleep. As easy as two plus two equals four.

'At last!' Fran called out as we entered the kitchen. A fine white haze hung in the air. Keith and three other kids stood at the table sifting flour into identical metal bowls. 'We're making a roux,' she went on as she walked towards us holding out aprons. 'I told you that's where he'd be,' she said to Charlie.

Keith looked up from his task. 'Alright lads?' His hair was bound back in a tight pony-tail. He wore a purple apron and an expression of contented concentration. 'Get yersels a bowl.'

Leonard and Raymond stood by the larder door and as I knotted the apron around my neck, Fran drifted back to join them. 'It's all about priorities,' she said under her breath.

'Tap it with your hand, gentle like.' Keith smiled at me. 'The finer it is, the smoother the sauce.'

'Sauce?'

'Aye. We're making a roux, the basis of all your classic white sauces: béchamel, parsley, mornay. If you cannae make a roux, you cannae cook shit as far as I'm concerned.' He slapped flour from his hands. 'That's belting, Jenny, you'll need to melt the butter now.'

As we went about making sauces, I glanced over at Fran. She, Leonard and Raymond hissed at each other. 'Utter nonsense!' Leonard blurted out, loudly. 'I will not stand for it and neither will Moira, of that I'm most sure.'

'Last week you called her a splitter,' Raymond said.

Leonard flung his arm out wide. 'At least she's splitting from the right side.'

'None of us want it to go down!' Fran said.

'Hey,' Keith shouted. 'Wheesht! We're trying to concentrate here. If you want to argue, take it outside.'

The three adults turned around, startled. Fran's cheeks reddened slightly. 'Sorry,' she said. Leonard harrumphed and strode from the room, his flared jeans swishing.

'Yes, chef! Sorry, chef!' Raymond tried to make a joke of it, but he sounded like a chastened child. I turned back to the Aga – each of us had a thick yellow paste in our pans, and

151

Keith, smasher of windows and destroyer of huts, held Jenny's wrist as they carefully added milk to her roux.

'A little at a time,' he said as we watched. Charlie's tongue tipped his top lip and he darted a sudden glance at me. The smell of burnt butter prickled my nose, like cracked nuts at Christmas. 'Keep stirring!' Keith snapped. Behind us, Fran noisily collected the empty flour bowls.

She spoke quickly. 'I'm just going to, you know.' I looked at her while the others carried on with the sauce. She cleaned steam from her glasses. 'Keith, you'll be okay here without me?'

Still, intent, Keith murmured back. 'Whatever. Aye.'

'Good, yes.' She stared at me for a second. 'I'm, er, popping over to see Mervyn.' She nodded and left the room.

Raymond leered towards me. 'Don't be jealous,' he said and followed her out.

'It's like a real sauce,' Charlie said in excitement. 'How cool is that?'

Crazes came and went at Bannock House. They lasted for what seemed like months then ended the next day without a word. Conkers, football stickers, playing three-and-in. Kick the Can, British Bulldog, Red Rover, Red Rover send some small scrote over. Ripped jeans, black-eyeliner, brightly coloured friendship bands. Rock bands too, until the kids realised they couldn't play more than just one chord. Everyone took up drums and listened to AC/DC, Iron Maiden, Mötley Crüe. Or else new waved with Duran Duran or Ah-Ha or, secretly, Madonna. Except for Paddy, who blared out Shostakovich on his new Hi-Fi.

When it rained kids sat indoors with Cheat, Hearts, contract bridge, backgammon, knock-out whist and Buccaneer. Charades, Guess Who, and homemade skits – no TV at Bannock House, no modern-day innovations allowed. Jigsaws, yo-yos, paper fortune-tellers, draughts and games invented on the spot. Some even played Monopoly until Moira confiscated the set because it encouraged capitalistic exploitation. The old boot.

Swimming in the river was different, in that it happened every summer come what may. In the term when Charlie returned, there were enough hot days to make even me yearn to get into the river.

The older kids would cycle far down the Bannock Valley road to the more hidden spots but we Sparrows had to be content with swimming in The Hook.

In the week before half-term, Fran arranged a swimming trip. She officially cut afternoon classes – I don't know how she managed to persuade Mervyn, but she did, and we all scrambled into the back of the van, one-eyed Murdo at the wheel. I was the last one in, squeezed in the backseat next to Lex. Charlie's ginger curls bobbed excitedly up front and I could hear him chattering to one of the new Sparrows, something about swimming trunks. I wanted to tell him to call them 'shorts', that trunks made him sound like a kid, or an old man, but I didn't bother. We juddered away from the Big House, gravel groaning. Exhaust fumes drifted up through the hole in the floor by my foot. No one spoke much. Fran tried to get a song going – *Down By The Riverside*, I think – but it was too hot in the van, despite the breeze blowing through the rusting bodywork.

Mervyn sat in the front seat, his rod-straight back contrasting with the wildness of his hair, twisting in the wind. I tried to picture him in shorts, his sallow creamy skin water-slicked.

Fran barked suddenly. 'Hey Murdo, wake up, we're here.'

Murdo pulled the van onto a verge, the breaks squealing as he did so. A sheep-mottled field rose away from the road opposite. We tumbled out of the van, and Jenny and the others rushed to open the rickety gate to the footpath. Charlie turned to me quickly. 'Are you coming?' he said.

'I'll be there in a minute. Oh, don't forget to take your watch off,' I called after him. He was so proud of his calculator wristwatch.

He laughed as he caught up with the rest, straggling through the woods. I waited for Mervyn.

The trees dappled and twisted the light and, every now and then, made a rushing sound, like running water, when the wind picked up. Ahead of us Fran held Lex's hand, half-dragging him down the leaf-strewn path. He trailed a ripped red and white towel behind him, its edge drooping along the ground like a broken cape.

Mervyn carried nothing with him except the newspaper. 'Aren't you going in?' I said.

'I don't swim,' he replied stiffly, the start of a cough sounding in his throat.

'Then why have you come?'

He looked at the two figures ahead of us. 'I've been asking myself the very same question.' He tapped the paper against an open palm. 'His master's voice, I suppose.'

We walked on in silence. I glanced up and noticed the red splash in his eye had spread. The wind had blasted his hair upright and back from his face. He looked liked a dirty lion, except for the shirt, tie and moth-addled jumper. 'Isn't that hot?' I said. The burble of the river merged with the delighted cries of Jenny and the others as they reached the bank.

'It is a warm day. But I don't see why I have to change my attire solely in order to satisfy the bizarre requirements of a curriculum that includes bathing in class time.' His beard shimmered as he spoke.

I picked up a stray branch from the ground and threw it into the woods, as if expecting a dog to chase. 'Sorry,' Mervyn said. 'I don't mean to be so brusque. Difficult issues.' He nodded towards Fran as she aired then flung down a picnic blanket on the river bank. 'And I forgot my flask.'

The Hook was more of a crook in the river than an actual hook. After travelling over a large shelf of shallow rock, the river dropped down and then almost bent back on itself in a horseshoe, before carrying on straight again. This created a twisting whirlpool in the tight bend but also – after the Hook – some deeper clearer spaces for swimming. Because of the shallows upstream, the water caught some of the sun's heat. Which meant it was one degree above arctic.

As we arrived on the high bank, with tall trees on either side, everybody was in various stages of undress. Mervyn drifted over towards Fran and threw his paper down beside the blanket. Charlie ran into the shallows, turned and waved. He looked like a Swan match, his wood-white body topped by the startling red hair. Lex balled himself up some feet away and poked and clawed at his shoelaces. Mervyn propped up on one elbow, his back facing away from Lex. He gazed upstream, towards Charlie and the shallows. I wondered whether Charlie was waving at him or me.

I threw my stuff to the ground. Jenny pulled off her t-shirt in front of me. She'd already changed into her swimming costume and, for the first time, revealed her newly swelled chest. From nowhere her body had begun to look like a woman's. I was so surprised I simply gaped. She saw me, snorted in derision and then took three quick steps to the bank. Her new body, white flashing arms against the black sheer of the costume, bent awkwardly and plunged into the water. Someone else sprinted past me and bombed in after her.

'Don't fancy it James,' Fran said from behind me.

'What do you mean?' I snapped back.

She worked at the side of her long cotton skirt. It took me a second to realise that she too would have a costume on under her clothes. 'The water, of course. Are you going in?' The skirt fluttered to the floor around her.

Even at the height of summer, the cold river water hit your heart like a hammer. I bobbed up gasping. Around me, the heads and flailing arms of children crowded the water. Charlie laughed and joked with a new kid, splashing each other in the shallows. I headed to The Hook itself and hauled myself up on the rocks and dangled my feet in the bubbles. The sun caught the water downstream, filtering through the high trees. Lex doggy paddled across the current and clung on to the other side of The Hook. His black hair stuck to his head with a strangely smart parting, like a mannequin. He ducked into the bubbles every few moments but said nothing.

Down the river, Fran swam breaststroke a couple of widths, puffed theatrically and then pulled her frame onto the bank opposite. In the midst of all those perfectly formed children, lean and lithe, she seemed huge and misshapen, her grey puckered thighs glistening wet. She stooped for her towel and then stood in front of Mervyn, her back to me. Arched to one side, she towelled her hair as it hung down beside her. Mervyn held his hand up to his eyes and said something but I couldn't hear what. He'd moved to face her and the newspaper lay open on his lap, like he'd been eating chips. They were obviously having some kind of conversation but the splashing of the water, Roya and Jenny's giggling and the distance shut me out. Lex popped up out of the bubbles again and gasped. I ignored him.

Fran lay down on the blanket in a sun-bathing pose and turned her head to Mervyn, still talking. She tented a bare leg and stroked it idly. Mervyn shook his head sternly at something and I saw him tense. She lay there open and ready, he sat on the ground, knees bunched into his chest, as tight as a ball of new wool – only the straggles of his beard gave any hint that he might unravel. He said something else and Fran straightened up on one elbow.

'Bomb!' Roya leapt into the river, mushrooming water onto me.

'I'm going to dive,' Jenny called from the high bank. 'Show me where the rock is.'

Lex bobbed up from the water again. His bug eyes, river-slicked black hair and marble smooth, markless skin, pinking at the cheeks in the cold cold water, all of a sudden made him look like an impossibly beautiful girl. I'd never seen him like that before. As I watched, his eyes widened slightly but hardened too and went cold, colder than the mountain cold water bubbling around my ankles. It was as if he no longer saw me, no longer saw anything at all. Slowly, he descended into the bubbles and pushed out into the river proper, still underwater, his white shape like driftwood. Something about the way he slid off into the current, unprotesting and passive, made me nervous. I dropped into the river up to my neck, not quite sure why.

On the bank, I saw Fran sit up and pull the towel across her legs roughly, covering herself, her face set tight. Mervyn got up, his back to her. Jenny plunged into the river beside me but I looked across at Lex's disappearing form – still submerged.

'Lex,' I shouted over the girls' shrieks. 'You fucking idiot.' I struck after his unmoving form, the cold of the water jangling in my chest. 'Lex!' I reached him as the river thinned again downstream. His face down, his arms and legs limp, he only moved when I grabbed him around the waist.

He uttered a muffled, wet cry but I managed to pull him to the bank, lower downstream than at the Hook itself. I flopped him onto the mossy grass as he spluttered.

'What the fuck are you doing?' I said through heavy breaths, the last words I ever spoke to him.

He looked at me with the same dark, still eyes. 'You don't care,' he said. Then he tried to struggle clear of my arms.

Fran came running. 'James,' she cried. 'Get off him. Jesus Christ. I leave you two for one second and you're fighting. Quit it, James!' She looked down at me, ragged half-wet hair on her shoulder, moon glasses glinting. 'I saw you grappling him – if you can't be nice, can't you just leave him alone?'

She'd wrapped a thick multi-coloured towel stiffly around her waist, making her look bulkier than ever. Her loose yellow shirt had dark, damp patches down either arm. I rose and watched as Lex walked past Fran with a slow tread back to the picnic blanket.

'This is the fucking limit,' she scowled. 'Bloody kids, I don't know why I bother. We're going back.' She turned and shouted out to the river as she marched up the bank. 'Everybody out, we're heading home.'

A chorus of protest sang out but Fran bustled about collecting her gear, unheedful. Jenny dried herself next to me as I pulled long shorts on over my swimming costume. 'What did you do?' she hissed.

'Nothing.'

'You must have done something,' she said under her breath. 'Fran's totally livid.'

As we trudged back through the woods, Fran stomping ahead with Lex a stride behind her, I suddenly realised who was missing. 'Where's Mervyn?' I said, as Fran counted us back over the gate to the van.

She turned away. 'He left,' she muttered.

'Just like that?'

'I don't bloody know!' she snapped. 'He went to the pub or something, okay? Enough of the questions already.' She slammed the van door behind me. 'Thank Christ it's nearly half-term.'

Murdo, who'd been asleep in his seat when we'd got there, bent around and scoped us with his eye. 'All aboard?' he said but no one replied. The high-spirits of the swimming jaunt, the giggles, the expectation, had all evaporated on the walk back to the van. Murdo ground the gears, released the clutch and pointed us back to Bannock House. I looked through the windscreen, now clearly visible in the empty space next to Fran. She held her head high and steady the whole way back. She didn't speak a word. No one suggested a singsong this time.

8

My head cleared as I descended the hill towards the school. The sun tipped the trees as it rose. Off to my right, at the bottom of the hill, the road tailed along the Bannock River – I traced a route Charlie and I might have taken that day in the snow but I was only guessing. Two birds sprang from the tangled hedgerow by my side.

When I was a very small child, before I went to school, I dreamt of friends. I invented them like an honest little cliché. We would have tea together, or drive in cars or put out fires. I found comfort in these imaginary companions but yearned for the real thing – I knew they were only faint shadows of the children that awaited me as I grew up. But somewhere along the line it didn't happen like that. I was too eager, or not eager enough. They played games, the rules of which I didn't know. They shared a common but obscure language. I'd look at how children befriended each other. It didn't seem to take much, sitting together in class. Not liking football or liking football. But my edges were always too rough, my home life too different. It was easier to understand friendship in the pages of a book than it was to work out the codes, the shared assumptions that dictated the what-was-what and the who-liked-who. I'd never had a best friend, or even simply a companion, until Bannock House. Until Charlie.

As I neared the bridge, I could make out the flow of the Bannock River, the slow, brown water, reed streaked. What I found harder to see was myself in the first terms at Bannock House, my time with Charlie. It remained opaque and fragmented, unlike the next year, Mervyn's year. My mind snagged in the reeds of those later memories. The day of the swimming trip at the time felt like a release, an opening of a new chapter. The Mervyn-Fran axis snapped. They split up, which for me was an opportunity. Mervyn no longer subject to her whims or demands on his time, free to give more of himself to the pupils, to me.

Better even than this, after half-term Lex failed to appear. He left the school for good, to be replaced by a snot-nosed boy called Billy, a tiny scrap of a kid with city-white skin and a Glasgow accent. Billy even took Lex's bed in Charlie's dorm.

I stood on the bridge and turned my face to the sun. The river ran soft beneath me, murmuring as it squeezed and twisted between the stone arches. I tossed a stick into the current and stepped across the road to watch it drift past and away. At the time, I asked Fran why Lex had left. 'Did his mother not like the school anymore?' I said.

'His Mom? Lex's in the care of the local authority, James. I thought you knew that.'

I hadn't known. I didn't even really know what care meant, except that his mother couldn't look after him or didn't have enough money to pay someone else. Like mine. Instead, this news slipped off my back and I concluded that Lex's departure finally erased the slur against Mervyn. I probably even thought in those words. Is there anyone more pompous than a twelve-year-old using language freshly swallowed from the dictionary? Handing words out here and there like blessings to an ignorant race. Did I treat Janice like that? I thought back to Big Tam and Lynn and Janice's house. Her vulgar mother (did you get your hole son? Not, did you avail yourself of my daughter's charms, my good chap? Maybe I'd have responded better.) The bruises on her arm, Archie. I tried to picture again big Tam turning away from her. Was that relief in her eyes? Entreaty? Fear? An old Land Rover rattled past and the image dissolved in the kicked-up dust. I set my feet to the road again and followed.

Small flies buzzed around me. The smell of dew-wet grass and cowshit hung in the air, mingled with the gravel dust from the side of the road. That summer after half-term, in the wake of Lex's departure, felt like victory. Mervyn's place at the school was secure, his time free to spend with me on crosswords, maths, and on my education. Life freed of irritations. My pursuit of knowledge unencumbered, the staff so fearful of inspection that academic exhibition was almost encouraged at times. I had started to grow, too, that summer and by July I was already three inches taller than Charlie. He had to turn his face up when he spoke.

*

I squeezed beneath a clinging briar and popped out onto the path, freeing myself from the Tangle.

'Hello?' Charlie called from behind me.

Startled, I muttered over my shoulder as I set off to the Big House.

He ran up and walked with me, but behind a little. 'Did you ever find that hut again?'

Over the months it had become easy for me to navigate the Tangle. I'd step through it by heart, noticing the smallest signposts. Since Charlie had been away, I'd torn down branches and brambles and made the path clear. But I didn't want to share it with anyone else. 'I was just taking a walk.' I stopped and looked down at him.

He giggled and put his hand up towards my face.

'I've got cricket in a minute,' I snapped. I swept his hand away and jutted my head towards the Big House.

'With Mervyn?'

I nodded. His voice, so high and small, held me there even though I wanted to walk away. A gust rattled and rustled through the rhododendrons lining the path and two fat leaves fluttered to the floor beside our feet.

Charlie kicked them away. 'What do you and Mervyn do?'

'I told you, we're going to play cricket.'

'At other times? In his rooms.' He bunched the hem of his t-shirt in his right fist and squeezed. 'Is it okay?' He released his fist and then tightened again, a gesture that I didn't recognise but one that made him look much younger.

'What do you mean okay? Are you worried about the extra maths?' He had his own session with Mervyn, now that Lex had gone. 'It's easy. I know he can be a bit grim faced if you get it wrong, but he wants you to do well.' I lifted my chin and turned towards the Big House again. 'It's okay.'

He fell in step. 'I don't want to upset anyone,' he said after a moment.

'Complaining about Mervyn is the last thing you should do. Imagine the school without him? We would never survive an inspection. Academic attainment: nil. Timetabling: lessonless.' I laughed.

We crested a slight rise and the slate grey angles of the Big House came into view. 'You like the school more than you used to.' Charlie said. 'My parents would be upset if it didn't work out here.'

'At least your parents care enough to be upset.' I spat it out as we reached the gravel. I didn't mean it to sound so harsh but I wanted to end the conversation. Mervyn was waiting for me on the front steps.

'Where are your whites?' He stepped from foot to foot and his eyes jumped.

I held up a plastic bag.

'Give them here,' he said. He stowed them in his ancient cricket bag. 'We're not going to a jumble sale, you know.'

Charlie wandered past me and held onto the rusty iron railing, his head down.

'Where's Murdo?' I sat down on the steps. Murdo was our lift.

'He's running late.' Mervyn sat down beside me. 'The carburettor or something equally arcane and mysterious. Nothing works here.' He pulled a chunk of stone from the crumbling step and looked at it. 'Till the dust beneath.' It broke between his fingers and fell into smaller pieces on the gravel. 'All is frangible.'

I watched Jenny and Roya amble across the football pitch. 'That means breakable doesn't it?' I said. Roya shot me a quick glance over her shoulder, though I knew she couldn't hear us.

'Yes, yes it does.' He brushed the dust of his hands and looked at me. Then he licked his lips. 'Anything of interest in that inferior Celtic rag today?' That was his way of referring to *The Scotsman*.

Charlie coughed.

'Where's Billy?' I said, over my shoulder, not looking at him.

'I don't know. Maybe I'll…' he tailed off and then tapped up the steps to the door. 'I'll go and find out. Good luck at the cricket.'

'Nothing in the paper,' I said turning back to Mervyn as Charlie closed the door. 'I thought of one just now though. *Fields available for jumble sale*. Four letters.' Every now and then the evening sun would wink and blanch from behind the high clouds. I squinted against the light and hoped Charlie found Billy inside.

Mervyn's head pricked up and his eyebrows bushed together in the middle. 'Leas,' he said after a pause. 'Excellent, if a little on the simple side.'

In the distance, the minibus choked. I stood up and looked out over the meadow. That morning, for the third time in two weeks, I'd woken up with sticky boxer shorts having dreamt of Jenny in her swimming costume. It made no sense to me. I knew what it was, I'd overhead enough conversations, but I didn't quite know what it meant. And it confused me to think that Jenny might in any way be connected. I couldn't ask Fran. Charlie was way too young. Keith would know, but might tell everyone about it. I looked back at Mervyn as we heard the bus finally kick into life.

'Mervyn,' I said slowly. 'You know about girls?'

'On the whole, good students when they take the subject seriously. But prone, in my experience, to think mathematics unimportant. Or to give up on their own abilities too easily.'

'No, I didn't mean…' I tried again. 'What happened with you and Fran?'

'That's none of your business,' he said angrily. 'Just because this is a boarding school, it doesn't mean I can't have a

163

private life.' From the driveway, the minibus trundled towards us. Newly painted in corn yellow with cack-handed, child-designed flowers in blue and red, it had recently been the subject of an art project. Murdo peered through the windscreen at us, his bare arm hanging from the window.

'There's a wee problem with the starter,' he shouted from the window, not stopping. 'I've opened the side door on the other side, I'll loop round and you jump in.' He began a slow circle on the gravel and we readied ourselves.

'I am sorry I snapped at you. I know you're trying to be friendly,' Mervyn said as we waited. 'Sometimes things simply end.'

'Ready!' Murdo cried as the bus edged along side. Mervyn and I ran. First he threw his cricket bag in and then leapt on the bank of seats. I caught the doorframe and tumbled in on top of him. Murdo chuckled in triumph. 'Nae bother.'

Mervyn lay still beneath me, tensed. Then his arse bone twitched sharp into my stomach and I slithered off him, laughing. 'When are we going to get a new bus?' I asked Murdo as I slid the door shut.

'Aye well, that's a matter for the committee. Other priorities may take precedence.'

'Such as painting it in bright yellow?'

Mervyn snorted and Murdo darted his one eye into the mirror. 'Is it just yous two?' he asked as we swung out of the school gates. 'No one else keen on cricket?'

'Or me,' Mervyn muttered.

'Just us,' I said.

The cricket pitch had open fields on three sides with the modern classroom buildings of the local comprehensive fringing the other edge. Along one side you could make out the tops of cars as they flew by on the nearest A-road and a row of conifers protected an end from the wind.

Mervyn, who'd been quiet on the journey, suddenly came to life at the sight of the other players. Men and a few boys threw catches to each other and unpacked bags. 'Can you smell that?' He held his nose up in the air. 'A freshly cut wicket. Nothing like it – except perhaps cider.' With every word, Mervyn's vowels became more pronounced as if the act of walking out onto the pitch was taking him back to the fields of Gloucestershire.

A large middle-aged man with pork-chop cheeks hailed us. 'Hello, our new recruits.' He offered his hand. 'Nice to see you again, Mervyn. Is this your boy then? James, you say. I'm Angus,' said the man, in an accent not unlike my father's brusque English. 'That's my boy, Rory.' He pointed at a plump carrot-top throwing catches to himself in the outfield.

'Posh Scots,' Mervyn whispered.

'Right then, we're mixing up the teams. Mervyn – I said you'd keep wicket first up. Okay?'

Mervyn clapped his hands and started rooting around for kit.

I pulled my trousers off and looked around for my whites. Mervyn bumped into my back. 'Give us a bit of room, will you?' I said, hopping.

'Sorry.' He stepped away, his hand kissing my side as he steadied himself.

'On you go Mervyn, chop chop,' Angus bellowed as he pointed to the middle. 'They can't start without a keeper, can they?'

Mervyn scuttled off and Angus turned to me. 'James, we're batting. You come in second drop, give it a bit of a bash eh?'

The umpire called play. At first, I felt embarrassed for Mervyn. He wore his same old black trousers, partially obscured by the wicket-keeping pads, and a white shirt so dirty it was impossible to believe it had ever been washed. It had large seventies style lapels and frills down the front. But the rest of his team seemed to enjoy him leaping around and calling out from behind the stumps.

'Impressive beard, your old man,' Angus said as he helped me find some batting pads.

'He's not my dad,' I said.

'Oh, right.' He looked at me as I pulled on my whites. 'Those won't do lad.' He pointed to my loose boxer shorts. 'The box will never stay in place.'

'Box?'

'For your balls, man. Never bat without a box.' He rooted around in one of his huge, coffin-bags. 'Here, take these – Rory's got spare.' He handed me a pair of Y-fronts.

After I'd changed, I sat on a rise at one end with my pads and gloves on. Our openers were quite good but that didn't stop Mervyn shouting: 'Well bowled,' after every ball, even if the batsman smashed it to the boundary. In between overs he'd chatter to the batsmen, trying to put them off. His teammates loved it.

'Don't I know you?' a shrill voice sounded close by.

A slight teenage girl peered at me, her hair violently pulled back, her face bird-like and twitching. 'I doubt it,' I said, turning back to the game.

'I know you. You're frae the hippy school.' She sat down a short distance away, also facing the game. 'You told me to "fuck off".' She said these words as a statement of fact rather than recrimination.

We sat in silence and watched the cricket. I pulled some dead grass and fluff from my hair, snared earlier that evening from the tangle, when Charlie surprised me coming out. It must have been sticking out of the side of my head all along. Maybe it was why Charlie giggled. He would have told me if I hadn't snapped at him. 'Are you a fan?' I said with a gesture at the game.

'You kidding? Nah, I'm waiting for my dad. He's the school janny.'

I shrugged, uncomprehending.

'The janny?' She flicked her head at the school building. 'The jan-it-or,' she said in a mock English accent. 'You know, caretaker. Cleans the bogs and that.'

'I thought caretakers had to be sad and lonely weirdos, as part of the job description,' I said. 'I didn't realise they were allowed kids of their own.'

166

She laughed. 'He is a wee bit of a saddo, actually.'

I ripped off and on the Velcro of my batting gloves. 'What's the school like?' I asked. I could see rows of huge glass fronted classrooms. One on the ground floor looked like a science lab, with all sorts of equipment.

'It's shite,' she said. 'Boring. Does everybody at your school speak like you? Dead posh.'

'But you get to study lots of different subjects, right? You learn a lot at least. There must be good teachers.'

She looked at me with her sharp face set hard and then cackled. 'What are you on? You been sniffing glue?'

'I just thought,' I said. 'It doesn't matter.'

'No one cares about the lessons. Except for some of the rich cunts from Muirdale. You're rich aren't you? I bet you're rich.'

I turned to face her again. 'I don't have any money, if that's what you want.'

'I'm only asking.'

A cheer went up from the middle, Mervyn's voice rising above the rest. I watched as the opening batsmen stomped off, his face a furious scowl, his stumps splayed. 'I'm in,' I said.

'My name's Lynn,' she called after me. 'Thanks for asking.'

I remembered what Mervyn first told me about cricket, the loneliest team game there is, and I felt the truth of it as I walked out. All the fielders moved back to their places, eyeing me with predatory interest. The bowler stood at the end of his run directing people about. Angus was the other batsman and he ambled out to meet me before I got to the wicket. 'Ignore your chap, Mervyn.' He glanced back towards Mervyn who was adjusting his leg pads. 'He's been sledging everyone – childish stuff really – but you just concentrate on hitting the ball. Start slow, there's no hurry.'

When I got to the stumps, Mervyn came alive at the sight of me. ''Ere comes the pretty posh boy,' he shouted out in an exaggerated West-Country accent. ''E don't like it up him.'

167

I took guard and settled in to face my first ball when I heard him whisper. 'Go on ya jazzer, smack it through the offside, this bloke can't bowl.'

'What's a jazzer?' I thought, just as the ball came down. In confusion I slashed at it and missed by a mile. Behind the stumps, Mervyn leapt up in ecstasy.

'Howzzzat?' he screamed, claiming the catch.

'I never touched it!' I stared back at him in disbelief, only to see a weasel grin cracking through his beard. The umpire had given me out.

'You cheating bastard,' I said as I trudged off. 'You know I didn't hit it.'

'That's cricket,' he replied. In that one glimpsed moment of a life forgotten, he looked as happy as I'd ever seen him, sweat-damp hair stuck to his forehead, large lapels flapping and one catch to the good.

I couldn't bring myself to speak to Mervyn the whole way home, cheated out of my first real innings by his lies. Yet his eyes shone with exhilaration, even as we stood facing each other on the gravel. He smelled of stale sweat and unwashed clothes, and didn't seem to notice my chagrin.

'Do you want to come back?' he said. 'We can finish the England-Pakistan game, you only need 200 to win.'

I hesitated. 'I can't believe you cheated,' I said at last.

'What do you mean? It didn't bounce.'

'But I never hit it.'

He pursed his lips. 'You didn't hit it. Not never.'

I shrugged. 'Whatever. Anyway, supper's in half an hour. I'm starving.'

'Don't worry about that.' He turned towards his rooms and swished his bag in a beckoning motion. 'I've visited the larder on your behalf. That gives us a good hour.'

Mervyn pushed open his door and flung the cricket bag to the floor. The room smelt fetid and peaty. 'Can I open a window?' I said.

He looked at me quizzically, but nodded. He grabbed a glass, poured a pint of cloudy cider from a grime smeared plastic bottle and glugged down two-thirds in one go. 'Where were we?' He sat on the stool and refilled his glass.

'You said you had some food?'

I took my favourite place on the armchair, its stuffing now more out than in. Mervyn conjured up a couple of colourless rolls and a thick slab of cheddar. As I ate, I watched him organise the game. He muttered to himself and licked his lips in between quick pulls at his cider glass. 'Play!' he said at last.

After we'd gone a couple of rounds and once I'd finished my roll, I spoke. 'Sorry for asking about Fran. I already knew you'd split.' He looked up and I realised, looking into his half-red eye, dulled by booze and damp hair still clinging to his forehead, that he couldn't tell me anything about girls, that was one subject to which he held no answers. But in that same moment another, different more unsettling thought occurred to me, one that had been brewing ever since I'd seen him on the cricket field and noticed how the solid, organised Angus had regarded him askance. How different Mervyn looked and seemed from the other adults around him, how odd. 'What I really mean is,' I went on. 'Are you going to leave?'

'Why on earth would I leave, dear boy? England is on the verge of a famous victory. My fast bowlers are ravaging your middle order.' He flourished his arm in the air. 'That's two victories in one day, if you count my superb conning of the umpire earlier.'

'Leave Bannock House,' I persisted, annoyed. 'Now that you and Fran are history.' I didn't feel like mentioning any other reasons why he might want to give up on the school.

He set down his pencil and took another drink. 'You think because everybody hates me, I'd want to leave.'

'No! I mean, everyone doesn't hate you. The kids don't.'

'They seem to enjoy the classes,' he said. 'But you're the only one who passes the time of day.'

I rubbed the green stains on the knees of my whites. 'You could teach anywhere,' I said, quietly.

His yellow, crooked teeth showed through his beard. 'But don't you know? The parents love me. No one in the recent memory of the school had ever been given a written report before I came along.' He laughed to himself, shaking his head. 'I'm not going anywhere. Especially with this bloody inspection coming up next term. They daren't fire me. In fact, with a view to the impending visitation of Her Majesty's august inspectorate of schools – and the need to impress – the senior committee have asked me to run a Classics option next term.'

I didn't want to push him away, didn't want him to think about it too much, but I couldn't help myself. 'But don't you want to leave? I mean, why are you here?'

He picked at the bold black dirt beneath his fingernails. 'Have you got better at mathematics since I arrived?' he said, raising his head.

'Of course, you know that.'

'And has everyone else improved too, do you think? I mean, the other pupils.'

'Yes, I'm sure they have. They couldn't have got any worse.'

'Well.' He grasped the pencil again and pointed it at me like a magician about to cast a spell. 'That's why I'm here.'

The gravel shimmered with the pinks, yellows and oranges of t-shirts and summer dresses. White-brown legs and arms and shoulders scissored about, topped by tangled hair and caps and flower garlands. It was the Bannock House scavenger hunt.

On the last day of every summer term, the whole school gathered together in front of the Big House. Divided into four teams, each captained by an Eagle, we had to scour the grounds for various pointless items. Lone, the Dane, led my team which included Keith, Fran and Jenny as well as about ten others. The dining tables had been arranged in a wide horseshoe facing the Big House, with a judge's table at the hub. Lone ambled long-limbed towards us with the list. She read aloud as she stuck it to the Formica-topped table. I forced my head between her and Fran. Lone smelled of rose water and sun cream.

Typed on A-4 and copied using the ancient Gestetner machine in the office, the list was like something from a different age: an army manifest or a telegram. My eye ran down the first few items:

A daisy chain large enough to crown the team's biggest head

Something black and white and red all over

A soft-boiled egg

A piece of broken glass (Found only – DO NOT break anything)

A B flat

A Saltire

A length of half-inch tubing

The milk of human kindness (a thimble full)

Some European currency

An election campaign poster

The list went on, obviously trying to cater for all ages (didn't everyone know the silly riddles by now? They were the same every year.) I stopped reading when Keith spoke. 'I'll get the Saltire. James – give me a hand.' He walked off quickly, his hair trailing after him like a cape.

Lone gazed at his back for a second. 'Go on then.'

People shouted around me in excitement. *'I know where that is.' 'Paddy's got one.' 'What the hell's one of those when it's at home.'* A couple of kids ran past me up the steps and I saw the flash of Charlie's red curls as he argued with Billy. I hadn't spoken to him much recently, I didn't seem to have the time, but for a second my mind went back to the previous summer. We'd insisted on being on the same team, even kicked up a fuss until Moira bent the rules. We stormed around the school, collected items, hid duplicates to beat the rest and laughed at the foolishness of it all while enjoying it just the same: a happy day, full of excitement and glee and pleasure unrestrained. It seemed such a strange and unusual idea now. I tried to pinpoint the time when it wouldn't have been odd, when I was the person I used to be.

'Jamesy, come on,' Keith shouted and I ran after him.

'Where are we going?'

He waited for me to catch up. 'There's a Saltire hanging from the top of the flying fox. You can get on my shoulders. But we better be quick before any of the others have the same idea.'

The flying fox ran from a rickety wooden construction high up in the branches of a large tree up near the North gate. As we approached, I could see the Scottish flag hanging damply from a pole on the take-off platform, like a plastic bag. Keith and I clambered up to the platform and then he bent down. 'On you go, wee man.'

I vaulted onto his shoulders and stretched up to the ancient knot. It felt slippery in my hands and, with Keith swaying beneath me, I struggled for purchase. At last, the string broke apart and I pulled the flag clear. 'Got it,' I cried.

As we walked back, Keith draped the flag over his shoulders like I'd seen athletes do on their laps of honour, or drunken football fans after a defeat. 'What's it like in care?' I said idly.

He stopped. 'Hey, fuck you pal. My maether loves me.'

'I didn't mean. Not you. I was just…'

'Who told you anyways?' he flicked his hair. 'It was only for a few months. Fuck, is nothing secret here?'

'I didn't mean. I'm sorry.'

He took a deep breath. 'Look Jamesy, it's fucking shite alright. Happy now?' He stomped away, the Saltire flapping behind him.

Back at our table, Fran and Moira argued. Jenny stood between them, her head arching from one to the other. Keith brandished the flag and tossed it on the table. 'There you go.'

Lone glanced at him as she crossed it off the list.

I listened to the argument, which was about whether or not it was fair for Jenny, as a girl, to make the daisy chain.

'Moira, you're a judge.' Fran said. 'This is none of your business.'

'Sexual equality is everyone's business.'

Fran sighed, and Jenny lifted up on her toes. 'I don't mind, really,' she said.

'It's not a question of minding. It's a question of what's right.'

'But it's only a daisy chain,' Jenny replied.

'The assumption that making a daisy chain is girl's work is all wrong, that's the problem. It's the kind of institutionalised sexism we're fighting against. It's what Bannock House is all about.'

'It is NOT what Bannock House is all about,' Fran rapped her knuckles on the table, as if she meant to smash down really hard but thought better of it just before she got there.

'Look,' Jenny said before Moira had a chance to respond. She gestured at me. 'James can help.' I nodded, as much in embarrassment as anything else. 'Great.' Jenny smiled. 'Women's Lib in action.'

'I hate it when they argue like that,' Jenny said. We walked along the far edge of the football pitch, on the verge that ran down to the meadow, scouting for daisies. 'It's as if they forget we're there at all.'

I held up a fistful of flowers. 'Surely this is enough?'

'I don't know,' she looked at me thoughtfully. 'You've got a pretty big head.'

'What?'

'Well, you're going to have to wear the daisy crown. You've got the biggest head in the team by far.'

'No I haven't,' I said, scraping the stray hair away from my forehead. 'I'm just a kid.'

'I didn't mean that kind of big head, stupid.' She laughed and sat down on the grass, knees first and feet bent out behind her, impossibly twisted. I slumped down opposite, my legs awkwardly crossed. She showed me how to split the flowers and we began threading them together.

On the far side of the pitch, we could see the hunt continue: people ran to and fro carrying various objects with them, or stood around tables studying the riddles. 'What did you talk to Keith about?' Jenny asked after a while.

'Nothing.'

She brought another stem up to her mouth and wetted it, making a faint sucking sound.

I tried not to look but she noticed my noticing, though she didn't say anything. 'I think Lone might be sleeping with Raymond,' she said.

I ripped one of the stems. 'Ugh! That's gross.' I threw away the ruined flower.

Jenny passed me another daisy and carried on threading. 'She's seventeen.' She looked down at the long chain in her hand. I had only managed to lace two together, compared to her elegant and lengthy curve. 'Give it here,' she said. Our hands touched and I felt heat in my face. I turned away quickly and looked back towards the activity on the gravel.

'Your friend Mervyn not coming today?' Jenny said lightly.

I glanced at her, unsure of the word *friend*. Sometimes the sarcasm of girls was hard to detect. 'Piss off,' I said.

'Why are you so angry? It's a simple question.' She put the last of the daisies to her mouth, the closed circle hanging down beneath her chin.

'Mervyn would probably say it was trivial or childish or something. Piffling pipsqueakism.'

She laughed and pushed herself to her feet.

'What?' I said feeling an unexpected smile come to my lips.

'Trivial, silly and childish. Nothing like crosswords then?'

I craned my head up towards her. 'Or dice cricket?'

She looked quizzical for a moment, then leaned forward and crowned me with the crooked daisy chain. 'Perfect,' she said.

Moira clambered up the front steps and rang the bell. 'Twenty minutes,' she called. 'This is the twenty minute warning.'

'Paint the windows white,' someone shouted out and laughed. 'And crouch under your beds.'

'Very funny, Andrew.' She rolled her eyes. 'I am not talking about the nuclear holocaust but about the end of the hunt – each team has twenty minutes left. This is your last warning.'

Lone stood over our team's table, checking our booty against the list. 'We're still missing the tube.'

Keith spoke from behind his hair, avoiding Lone's eye. 'I tried the workshop, the bike sheds. Even the kitchen. No dice.'

'Don't look at me,' Fran said as we all turned. 'I'm beat. But hey, I think we've done great if we're only missing one thing. It's not all about winning.'

'But I want to win,' Jenny replied. 'Isn't that the point?'

'I've got an idea,' I said.

Mervyn's rooms, his shack, reminded me of a cave, grey and uninviting despite the afternoon sun. The curtains were half-drawn and the whole thing looked somehow lightless. I knocked on the door a few times to no reply. A distant cheer went up from one of the scavenging teams but the sounds faded as I pushed open the paint peeled door and stepped into his small anteroom. To the left, the door to the toilet hung open: the rank, dark stinking hole of a toilet that only faintly flushed. I stepped into Mervyn's room proper.

He was laid out, splayed in a ragged cross, his head at the wrong end of the bed, one foot on the floor the other (still shod) buried into his only pillow, his haystack hair wildly askew. The sounds from outside didn't penetrate, the silence felt heavy and the windows remained shut, trapping the stale air. A picture came to me of my old dead cat, still and small on the road outside my house. But then Mervyn's beard twitched and I knew he was alive.

I bent down to wake him up but hesitated, suddenly repelled by the thought of touching him. The room was a mess, with a few coins, dice and the usual inhabitants of his small table strewn across the thin carpet, the table itself upturned. Beyond it, the cricket bag lay discarded, never properly unpacked from the one and only time we played. Angus never invited us back. Mervyn's only pint glass rested on its side, poking out from under the armchair where it had wheeled. The room smelled of rotten apples and off-cider, mixed with Mervyn's stale sweat and something danker that I couldn't recognise, as if one of the animals from the farm had crawled in there to die and never been discovered.

It seemed wrong to rouse him, or at least uncomfortable. Instead, I tiptoed through the debris to Mervyn's homebrew kit parked in the corner past the end of his bed, complete with its array of half-inch plastic piping. I felt sure he'd let me borrow some tubing, so reached down to pull one of the pipes free.

Mervyn's hand shot out and clamped around my wrist. 'Stop, thief!' he said. His eyes opened slow and distant but his head didn't move. As he focussed, I tugged slightly with my hand. He didn't let go.

'It hurts,' I said.

He stared at me unblinking. Dust motes swirled between us. When he spoke his voice came out deeper and thicker than normal. 'Does it?' He looked from my face to my wrist and back again. 'What do you want?'

I felt the coarseness of his bony fingers and the rough edge of a thumbnail but I couldn't take my eyes off his. 'Can you let go, please?' I said, quietly.

His grip tightened. 'What do you want?' he repeated, more loudly.

'I only wanted some tubing. For the scavenger hunt.'

He closed his eyes again but kept hold of my wrist. Then he angled his head towards the ceiling and pursed his lips as if savouring the fetid air above him. His grip relaxed, his hand slid up my wrist and fluttered the tiny hairs on my arm.

I pulled away, the spell broken. 'It doesn't matter. If you can't spare it, I mean.'

He slapped his lips together and pushed himself upright on the bed, swinging both legs onto the floor as he did so. 'Of course I can spare it,' he rasped. 'The question is, why should I?'

'I don't know. Why should you do anything?' I made to leave.

'James. Don't be so stupid. Take it of course. Take as much as you want. Anything. Pass me that glass will you.' I clambered around the home brew kit, pulled a length of tubing from one of the barrels and then reached down and picked up the fallen glass. As I did so, I noticed behind, tucked further under the seat, a short black curl. The dark plastic of the watch face, complete with the tiny buttons of its calculator, caught my eye as I straightened.

Mervyn gestured to one of the opened bottles. 'Fill it, if you please.'

I hurried back to the door. 'Stay,' he said. 'We'll, er. There's the crossword, or where was it, some of the cricket game? Or, I don't know, something.' His words petered out as he looked at the freshly charged glass.

'Maybe later. I've got to take this back. For the hunt.'

'Tally-ho then,' he said, without looking at me.

When I arrived back at the gravel, the judging process had already started. Andrew, a freckled and gangly Eagle, was arguing with the judges. 'I tell you, that's A B flat. I'll show you again.' He lay down flat on the ground. 'Andrew Banks. A B flat.' Everybody laughed.

'Alright,' Moira said through a smile. 'You can have that. Next.'

I handed the tube to Lone. 'James, you're a hero,' she said.

'Where did you get it?' Jenny whispered. But I shook my head. I didn't quite know how I felt about my encounter with Mervyn but it wasn't something I could tell Jenny. Her mole-spattered cheeks bunched in a smile. 'I think we're going to win,' she said. I looked around for Charlie but couldn't see him anywhere.

Jenny was right. We won, not that there was a special prize or anything. Everybody got a fun-sized Mars bar just for taking part – Bannock House always rated effort over result. As everybody packed up the tables and began to return the various scavenged objects, Leonard appeared carrying a fat ream of paper. 'Listen up, all,' he called out, dumping the paper on the judging table. 'Please each take one of these leaflets to your in locus parentuses. Erm, yes. To your parents or whoever.' He handed them out.

'What's this?' Moira asked sharply peering at a page.

Leonard spoke past her, as people drifted over. 'It's nothing really, a small communique, outlining some ways forward for the school.'

Moira wobbled. 'I wasn't told about this. What the hell are you doing?'

'Something, Moira,' Leonard replied. 'We've got to do something, the inspectors are coming next term.'

'Have you seen Charlie?' I said to Jenny as we wandered back to our dorms.

Roya bundled into her. 'Why don't you try the art room?' Jenny giggled as she pushed Roya away. 'We so beat you.' I left them to it.

Leonard's leaflet was full of the same old stuff. I half-read it as I made my way to the art room. Lots of *Strategic Planning*, a smattering of *Equality*, many *Thoughts on the Future*. The gist of Leonard's message, so far as I could tell from the mangled grammar and abused vocabulary was that the school expected to pass next term's inspection with *colours flying proud*, any additional support parents could offer would be greatly appreciated. By this last request I thought he meant money, though it wasn't specified nor did it say at any point what the extra money might be spent on.

The art room had wide glass windows opening onto the patio that looked out over the school. I stopped just short when

I caught sight of Charlie and Billy. They worked on something that I couldn't see. Charlie's curls hung loose, his face stern with concentration and smeared with a gash of black paint. I didn't call out but kept watching, hidden. I wanted to confirm a suspicion. Suddenly, he brought both his bare arms up in a great sweep and flicked a brush towards the floor. I turned away, my question answered.

Leonard's leaflet had a small NB at the end. *Next term, the school will be offering a Classics option. As always, this will be non-compulsory but we hope to have at least three children taking the class. It will bolster the school's academic portfolio in the eyes of the Inspectorate.* So much for ideology. So much for the nuances of educational theory. When it came down to it, they were relying on someone who knew things, a man who could take complex ideas and explain them in ways that children understood. A person who could point out that NB meant note well, from the Latin *nota bene*. A teacher. They were relying on Mervyn, I realised, as I felt the new scratch on my wrist. Then I thought of Charlie's wrists in the art room behind me, unadorned by his usual black, plastic, calculator watch.

9

I gripped my own watchless wrist and tried not to think of Janice's bruises. The dark purple marks on her forearms bloomed in my mind. Had I deserted her? She'd be somewhere back in Dungowan, her day off she'd said. Perhaps I could help, do something. Then I laughed at the false romance, the image of the white English knight prancing through the village to save the bonny lassie in distress.

Life isn't like that. Maybe if you're one of those diary-keeping girls, with swirly writing and circles above the 'i's, with big fat hearts and exclamation marks. But is it even like that for those girls? That's a make-believe world too. They find that out the first time Clive or Jake or John or whoever waltzes off with someone else and cleaves their big fat heart in twain.

The road curled around and suddenly I could make out the dark green mass of the Tangle, away to the right. I hadn't walked up this road for ten years. My legs quickened unbidden, as if they knew something my brain did not. I reached the South Gate, now just two lonely granite gateposts with nothing to connect them. Prongs of the rusted gate griddled a nettle patch on the other side of the fence, long discarded. The pitted drive dwindled in front of me past the Tangle and up to the unseen Big House. I stepped back into the school.

I expected everything to be smaller, the old cliché of the adult returning to a childhood place. But I'd forgotten another, earlier return. I'd forgotten a lot of things. As I jumped out onto the gravel from the minibus, in the autumn of 1987, Fran called out to me. 'Hey lofty.'

'What do you mean,' I said.

She laughed. 'You must have grown four inches, at least. What are you, five ten, six foot? Anyhow, you're a Kestrel now – your room's downstairs.'

I wasn't much taller now, ten years later, I realised as I picked my way down the drive. My bag hung heavy on my shoulders but I walked on, collecting that final term in my mind like burnished wind-blown leaves.

Round the last corner of the drive, the Big House came into view. The storm-cloud stones of the walls swallowed the pale morning sunlight; the front steps had lost their banisters. All of the ground floor windows were boarded up, with keep out stencilled across chip-board shutters. A sad broken half-moon marked the glass pane of my old dorm window on the upper floor. The only sign of recent activity was a Land Rover, parked askew, the one that had sped past me on the road a few minutes earlier.

I didn't want to go into the house, though. Instead, I shrugged my rucksack to the ground and took off down the path, past the overgrown, daisy-speckled football pitch, to Mervyn's cabin. I took the same walk ten years earlier, on the first day of that term, autumn 1987.

*

Fran pointed me in the direction of my new room, a small one-bedder on the ground floor, with a window opening out onto the vegetable patch. I threw my bags down on the stripped mattress and headed straight to Mervyn's. I hadn't had a meaningful conversation about cricket in the whole of the summer holidays and neither of my parents talked to me about crosswords, or anything much. The memory of the end of the previous term – the day of the scavenger hunt – still troubled me, but I put it to the back of my mind in my eagerness to see Mervyn again. I'd spent the vacation thinking about what else he had to teach me.

From the outside his hut looked smaller and more ramshackle than I remembered. I had grown four inches over the summer break and my limbs felt loose and unattached, an adult body controlled by an unpractised brain. I peeled a thin shard of paint from the doorframe as I waited for him to answer my knock.

The door opened. 'Need a new coat?' I said, holding up the paint before it crumbled.

'Not on my bloody wages,' he said and turned back into the room.

As it appeared from the outside, so the room felt even smaller from within: everything diminished, including Mervyn. I could see how flat the top of his head was, how thin his arms looked. I folded my newly long legs into the armchair and looked across at him.

'I'm half-way through a re-run of the Nat West final.' He pointed to the open scorebook on the table between us. 'Or do you want to start a new one?' He brought his eyes up to mine and I noticed that the burst blood vessel of his left eyeball had spread, the white almost entirely obliterated by a livid red – made all the brighter by the dark hair around it.

Behind him, the homebrew kit had grown – the only thing that hadn't shrunk in my absence. It had an extra barrel along with more higgledy-piggledy tubing poking out of it at random. It had become by far the biggest thing in the room. 'What's been happening here?' I said.

He mumbled something and I held my hand to my mouth. I'd forgotten the rank, rotten smell. By the fire his ancient cricket bag lay open, all the detritus of the summer stuffed in there unwashed and unpacked, abandoned for another year. 'I've been struggling with the crossword,' he said, as if that encompassed the entire vacation. He handed me his paper.

I knew two of the unsolved clues instantly. He took a large gulp from one of the school cups, no sign of his signature pint glass. I opened my mouth to announce the missing answers but the sight of him glugging down cider from a mug made me hesitate. 'It's a toughie,' I said. I placed the paper on the table and waited for him to finish his drink. 'Where did you go to school again?' I asked.

He looked up, surprised. 'I went to what is known as a "minor" public school. About twenty miles from Malvern

College, which is major. Very much the first division, unlike my lower league affair. Mallards, it was called. Known as Maladies to most of the boys.'

'But did you learn a lot?'

'Beyond the clichés of institutional cruelty and British superiority?' He laughed, though I didn't get the impression he thought anything funny. 'I suppose. I had a good mathematics master. One who believed in the subject, understood its power. Logic is liberation, and logic is based on maths.' He paused and examined me with renewed curiosity, as if recognising my increased height for the first time – our eyes level when before he had looked down on me. His face broke into a confused smile, as if I'd cracked a joke he didn't get and never could. Then he tossed his head in three of four, short sharp shakes – some way between a full shake and a shiver – and continued. 'Learnt some Latin too. Keen on Latin at Mallards. In fact, I shall be passing on some of this erudition into your supple and sapling mind this term. You're taking the classics option, I trust?' He gestured to four neatly squared piles of paper on the shelf above his bed, which I hadn't noticed before. The piles looked clean, fresh and totally at odds with the rest of the room. Four pin-sharp red and black striped pencils rested on each top sheet. 'My lesson plans,' he added.

'Can I have a look?'

'No you cannot,' he replied sharply. 'It wouldn't be fair to the others.'

'Like anyone else will care,' I flipped back.

'What an ugly sentence,' he said. 'And an ugly thought.'

I crossed and uncrossed my legs, trying to find space, giving me an excuse to duck my head. 'But never mind about that,' he said. 'Let's crack on.' He pointed to the dice cricket game on the table. 'Not to put too fine a point on it, playing solo doesn't have quite the same frisson.'

After we'd finished the game, I went to tea. I asked Mervyn if he wanted to come, but he said he wasn't hungry. He had preparation to do for the following day, he said, as he had a whole new class of Sparrows. Neither of us mentioned the last time I'd seen him, when he grabbed my wrist on Scavenger Hunt day. As I walked away, I wondered if he even remembered. Or was it simply added to the things we didn't talk about?

The rest of the school changed little. Jenny, Roya and I had been promoted to Kestrels and so we went to bed an hour later than before. Raymond became our houseparent, thus making every supper 'awesome'. The Octagon stood roofless and unusable. I briefly fell back into the old routine of visits to Mervyn and reading in my hut but I began to find other things to do. The two girls shared a room opposite mine and I found myself in their dorm as often as I was in my own. They'd decorated it using cast-offs from Roya's mum's ethnic stall and it felt cared-for, comfortable and cosy. I'd sit on the snug two-seater sofa and listen to their music, the air honeyed by perfumes and sweet soap and a dusty pot-pourri.

Conversation was much easier too. I realised the girls held Raymond in as much contempt as I did, and we'd laugh about him behind his back.

'Peace and love is, like, totally awesome,' Jenny trilled one day as she flicked through a magazine. I stood outside and leaned through the window, my back to the path.

'I know,' I said. 'It conquers all bad things. Just as long as you have a tambourine too.'

'And a joss stick.' Roya laughed.

'Hey James,' Charlie said. He stood down the path from me, out of sight of the girls.

I twisted my head. 'Hi.'

'Me and Billy are going to the flying fox, do you want to come?'

I squinted at him.

'Tina might come too,' he went on, uncertain. His hair was cut short to his head and he stood much shorter than me. I don't know whether it was his illness or if he were a late developer, but he hadn't grown up at all in my eyes both physically and mentally. He could still wear the clothes he wore the year before and still looked like a Sparrow. I felt I

184

was growing into somebody else every day – he looked like he'd stopped.

'Who's Tina?'

'One of the new Sparrows. It'll be fun.'

'No thanks,' I said, turning back to Jenny. 'But I'm sure you'll have fun.' I smiled as I emphasised the last word and Jenny smiled too. Charlie shuffled off down the path. 'What time's the chart show on,' I said loudly to Roya but I didn't look Charlie's way again.

I also went back to art classes. 'Your room's so bare,' Jenny said one day. She stood, framed in the doorway, tutting. 'You need some pictures.'

'Piss off.' I smiled, so she knew it wasn't like the way I used to say it.

'Come back to art. You can paint your own.'

So the next Thursday, I went back to Moira's class rather than going to my hut in the Tangle.

I sat next to Jenny. 'Wow, that looks great,' I said as I leaned over her shoulder and tried to see beyond the dark mole on her left breast. 'Who taught you how to do that?'

'Oh, I tried some stuff out for myself,' she said, pleased I liked her experimental block printing. 'You don't always have to be told how to do things, you know.' She smelled like fresh fruit and vanilla. 'This one's for your wall,' she smiled up at me, her moles like stars dotting the Milky Way.

As half term approached, the school's paths rustled with the brown-gold, apple leaves of autumn. I'd been taking classics once a week, with Keith and another boy, but had stopped going to the extra maths sessions. Instead, I kept to my usual class with Jenny and the rest of the Kestrels. One day she and Roya appeared as I was making my way to the class and we bundled into the maths cabin together.

Mervyn stood waiting at the board. He glowered at us as we sat. The lesson, on matrices, was a recap of something he had introduced the previous term and a pall of boredom fell over the class. Jenny drew a sketch of a huge bear up on its haunches, as if attacking, in her exercise book. As she showed it to me, she completed the picture with a big M on the bear's chest. I laughed.

'Silence!' Mervyn rasped.

'Sorry,' I mumbled, and rolled my eyes at Jenny once his back was turned.

Mervyn rat-tat-tatted chalk against the board. 'Now, James, what's the quotient of this matrix?'

I looked up at the three by three grid of numbers enclosed by two large brackets. 'Pi,' I said with a straight face. He put his head to one side, puzzled. My eyes slid to Jenny. 'A nice juicy steak and kidney pie.' She giggled, along with everyone else.

Mervyn frowned at me and took a deep breath. 'The answer is twelve,' he said. 'A little more than the average mental age of the class.'

As we left, he called me back. 'James, hold on a moment, will you?' He waited until we were alone. I perched myself on one of the desks. 'We're still friends, I hope?' he asked. His voice was stern and precise but brittle too, like a thin sharp stick.

'What do you mean?'

'You can't behave like this in class. It's disrespectful.'

I looked at the carpet's frayed edge. Thick, dry dust lay in small drifts in the corners. 'I was just having a laugh.'

He shuffled over to the sideboard and ruffled through some papers. 'Will I see you in my rooms later?' He turned back to face me, holding a sheaf of notes. 'It's been a while since I've had any help with the crossword.'

'I don't know, maybe?' I said. We both looked at his hands as he held the limp paper before him. Soot-black dirt lined the tips of his yellow finger nails and I struggled to remember when exactly I had last been to his rooms. 'We'll see,' I whispered, unsure what else to say.

As I reached the steps down from the cabin floor, a host of Sparrows appeared, chattering and squeaking around my feet. They greeted Mervyn with enthusiasm and surprising informality. Charlie gave me a quick glance but didn't say anything and didn't smile. Instead, he called out a joke to Mervyn, something about another round of torture.

I didn't manage to get around to Mervyn's rooms later that night. I saw him early the next morning, walking past my window towards the woodshed. He looked a bit wobbly, his eyes shrunken and his hair totally awry. As I gazed after him I noticed for the first time he carried his right leg a little heavier than his left. Not quite a limp, but his movements were no longer as sharp as before. I hesitated then pulled my window up and called out to him but he didn't hear me. For some reason, I was glad.

As the days got shorter and the cold bit, I took to visiting Fran in the kitchen while she cooked the evening meal. I didn't quite know why, but it seemed as comfortable a place to be as any other. A couple of weeks after half term, I sat on a high stool at the table and watched as she moved between larder, table and stove, her clogs click-clacking on the stone floor. A large soup pot steamed and the sky outside darkened.

'What are the committee going to do about the Octagon?' I asked, thinking of its non-existent roof. 'All ready for the inspectors?'

'God James, not now. I don't think I can handle another dose of your piss-taking.'

'No, I didn't mean –' I paused as she took her glasses off and squeezed the bridge of her nose between thumb and forefinger. 'I'm serious,' I said.

She sat opposite me and put her glasses back on. 'You're serious today, huh?' She pulled her hair out from its scrunchy and then retied it even tighter. The bright bulbs above the table caught the grey streaks as she did so. 'Well, serious says there's a hell of lot to do just keeping the show on the road, let alone sorting out the Octagon.'

'I was interested, that's all.'

'Do you realise what I did today? I cleaned up the breakfast things of fifty kids, I taught three classes, I ordered a week's worth of food – after arguing for twenty minutes about our bill with the cash and carry – I'm in the process of cooking a meal for those same kids, most of whom will complain when it's done, then I've got a committee meeting, then I have to put seven Sparrows to their bed, then, maybe, I'll worry about the Octagon.' As she went through the list, she marked each item off on her ringless fingers. 'Or perhaps I'll worry about something else, like when am I ever gonna buy some new clothes, or whether I can afford a flight to visit my folks in Athens – that's in Canada, not Greece,' she broke off when she saw me perk up at the classical reference. 'Or whether I'll ever meet anyone ever again. That's not to mention the inspectors themselves, or Leonard and Moira's endless arguments, or rotten apples, or the Big House's leaky roof or inappropriate staff-pupil liaisons.' Someone clattered into the scullery and she stopped. 'There's a lot to worry about.'

'I'm sorry.' I said. She breathed out heavily. Her purple top, as familiar to me as many of my own, had faded at the elbows and, as she stood, I saw a strand of cotton trailing from its hem. I realised I knew Fran's wardrobe better than I knew my mother's. 'Do you want any help?'

'It's not your fault,' she said. 'I'm not blaming you. I'm not even really complaining.'

'Complaining about what?' Raymond stepped in from the scullery, large and enthusiastic. Charlie hovered a step behind him.

Fran regarded him with a level gaze. 'I was just telling James that though I'm not complaining, I have many worries,' she said. 'Including the appropriateness or otherwise of certain liaisons.'

Raymond paused uncertain, and then broke into a wide grin. 'Oh right. I get you. There's that Canuck subtlety again. Awesome.' He strode around the table into the larder. Fran looked after him, her face dark. 'Charlie and I are working on, you know, something inappropriate I guess. We're liaising.' He spoke over his shoulder while Charlie stood by the doorway. The three of us waited silently as Raymond crashed around, banging crockery and tins in cheerful oblivion. He whistled something like *Yankee Doodle* or *Camptown Races*, then reappeared a moment later. 'Well, folks. I can see you all have a lot to talk about.' He held up a plastic bowl. 'Also, I'm going to take this. I hope it's not inappropriate, or anything?' He flashed his even teeth. 'Peace and love. Come on Charlie, we're off to be inappropriate together.' Charlie smiled weakly at Fran and the two of them left.

Fran shook her head as the whistling echoed up the stairs. She turned back to the Aga, her shoulders slumped. 'Can I help?' I said, again.

I prised open the huge tins of peaches using the industrial opener clamped to the kitchen sideboard. You plunged the lever down and then worked it, car jack style, until the lid came away like jagged orange peel. 'Are you annoyed with Raymond because of Lone?' I asked.

'What was that? What do you know?'

'Nothing,' I said automatically. 'But she's seventeen. Doesn't that make it okay?'

She wiped a large knife on a tea towel. 'It's not always about the numbers. But don't you worry. Nothing's going to happen. That's if anything even has happened. There's no proof.' She drew breath for a moment and looked up at me. 'It's just that, the school has enemies. If the tabloids ever got hold of anything, they'd rip us to shreds.'

'Really?'

'It happened in the seventies, some nonsense about skinny dipping. I don't know if we could stand it now, though. Not with everything else.' She chopped apples on a battered wooden board and threw them into a vat-sized fruit salad.

'Can we have more than apples in it this time?' I said.

'Don't be cheeky.' She frowned at me but I knew she didn't mind.

I joined her at the table and sliced up the tinned peaches, slopping them in with the apples and oranges. Smelling all that fruit made me feel awake and the rhythm of our chops almost sounded like music.

'You and Charlie don't talk so much now,' she murmured.

I threw a tin into the rubbish. 'He's so young,' I said. 'We're in to different things.

She pinched out a smile. 'And how's Mervyn?'

'Fine, I guess. Maths is fun and I like classics. He's a very good teacher.'

Fran sliced up the last of the apples. 'He's given up coming to most of the staff meetings.'

'He always said they were a waste of time.'

'Do you know if he's been eating?' She stilled her hands and looked at me. 'I haven't seen him in the dining room much.'

I put down my own knife, the peaches done. 'I don't know. You should ask him.'

She swivelled away from the table and dried her hands. I didn't quite know how to take her questions. It seemed like normal conversation but she listened to my answers with more care than before. I didn't mind, so often when you say things people barely hear you.

'I wrote a poem,' I said after a moment. 'About the London hurricane.'

She smiled. 'That's good, James. Must be the first time in ages.'

'It was after you said that thing about poetry and emotion. I wrote about a felled tree, lying there lifeless and cold.'

'Is it time?' A high-pitched voice startled me.

A waifish, girl-boy Sparrow with close cropped dark hair stood in the doorway, holding the bell in two hands. Fran spoke past me. 'Yes Tina, thank you. Please ring the bell.'

Fran waited until Tina left and then reached forward towards the table. 'Next time you see Mervyn, give him this. He should eat.' She passed me the last orange, unpeeled. It felt no bigger than a cricket ball in my hand. I glanced back at Fran and then we both looked down at it. We burst out laughing.

At lunch break the next day I spun the orange from hand to hand and looked around at my hut. Jenny had asked where I disappeared to and my mind was full of plans to invite her to the Tangle, to share the hut with somebody at last. The smell of orange peel clung to my hands. I hadn't taken it to Mervyn's rooms the night before, hadn't been there for weeks. I would give it to him in my maths lesson that afternoon, even though it was silly.

The maths cabin appeared to be empty as I clambered up the steps but I suddenly felt two bony hands pushing me through the trapdoor from behind.

'Oi!' I shouted as I fell forward, the hands falling from my arse in the crash.

As I twisted around, Mervyn's head rose through the floor. He hoisted himself up to his waist and leaned over me, his weight resting on his arms: a confused animal, dithering between fight and flight. He licked his lips.

I shifted backwards. 'This is for you,' I said, holding up the orange. 'It's from Fran.' The bell rang.

He blinked hard, and then climbed to his feet. 'You were dawdling in the entrance. I'm sorry if I knocked you over.' He put out his right hand to me and gestured.

His eyes swam, one brown in red, the other dark brown in stained white. Fascinated by the sight, I could only extend a hand towards him. He hauled me to my feet and we stood, facing each other. 'Why don't you come anymore?' he said in a quiet voice, the distant bell still ringing, his heavy stale smell in my nostrils.

'I –' I didn't know what to say, because I didn't really know.

Mervyn looked down. He still held my hand in his.

'Hurry up.' Jenny's voice approached the cabin. 'Merv the perve will kill us if we're late.' They clattered beneath us. Mervyn let my hand drop and turned away to the blackboard.

'Mervyn.' I held my other hand out to him. He looked around quickly. 'You forgot your orange.'

Throughout the lesson, I couldn't help glancing up at the fruit. It stood on the sideboard, like a paperweight, a reproach, an unsatisfactory answer to his perfectly reasonable question.

After a while Mervyn abruptly wrote down four equations on the board. 'I must see to something,' he said. 'Work through these and I'll be back in five minutes.'

We looked at each other but he ignored us as he left. 'Weird,' Roya said.

'He probably needs the toilet,' Jenny replied

Roya groaned. 'Ugh, what a thought. Mervyn on the bog.'

'Shut up,' I snapped. 'Let's get on with the questions.' Surprisingly, everyone fell silent and carried on working. Mervyn had never left mid-class, and he seemed distracted when he returned a few minutes later.

When the lesson ended, Mervyn tossed back our homework from the week before with a succinct verdict for each of us. 'Adequate. Good. Messy. Excellent. Absolute Rubbish.'

I glanced down at my mark. 'Fifty-five percent? That's not bad.'

Mervyn waited for the others to filter past him and climb down the steps. Then he snatched up my exercise book. 'Look, wrong! Wrong! Wrong. Sloppy, stupid, lazy, arrogant. You should be doing much better than this.' He slapped the book with his hand on each word. 'You've found more interesting things to do with yourself, I expect.'

'No, I mean.' I cast around the sparse cabin for something to say and focussed on the orange. 'Is this about? I could come round tonight if you like?' I stood up and stepped towards him, though as I spoke I suddenly thought of his hands on me from the beginning of the lesson. Something not quite right.

'It's your marks I worry about,' he said, ignoring my comment as he put the chalk away. He turned back towards me, his face near mine. 'This level of performance won't make anyone happy.'

I could smell the booze on him, the sweet-bitter tang of strong cider. 'Have you had a drink?' I almost laughed. 'In the middle of the lesson? Is that why you...'

'How dare you say that,' he glowered, as if to put me down like a traditional teacher. But then he pushed his hair-covered cheeks out and in, deflating his whole body. He slumped into a nearby chair. 'Keep it to yourself. You can do that for me, at least.'

'What do you mean?'

He sat below me like an empty sack, his clothes shrivelled and folded about him. His eyes flicked up from beneath his wild brows. 'I just needed a drink, that's all. It's a trifling matter. Something between friends?' His voice rose in pitch, holding the question.

I looked away, embarrassed, unable to speak. Heat rose to my cheeks and anger welled inside me, the smell of cider hanging in the air between us. How was I to know what to say? My eyes flitted from the tinder dry rafters, decorated with ever-growing spider-webs, to the dusty corners of the cabin before they settled on the ripped hem of Mervyn's mud-stained trousers. 'You know,' Mervyn went on in a stronger, harder voice. 'You're the reason I'm here. I wouldn't be here were it not for you, don't forget that.'

'What do you mean?' I gulped.

From outside, Jenny's voice drifted in. 'James, James,' she cried. 'Come on, we'll be late.'

I scrambled to the trapdoor, my question left unanswered. Half-way down the steps, I turned to him – my face at floor level. His head hung heavy between his legs and he didn't look at me. 'I won't tell,' I said and left.

*

The past is a narrative we write to make sense of the present. I went through the rest of my education telling myself I'd outgrown Bannock House. That autumn term proved the school couldn't contain me academically; I moved on. That's what I said when I started acing exams at my hothouse London school: I'd gone through a 'hippy phase' and come out the other end ready for academia, eager for the successes that would make me happy. Bannock House was nothing but a near-forgotten blip, discarded like a childhood friendship. It was a fiction I'd been polishing for the last ten years.

I stood in front of Mervyn's old rooms. That story, the version I'd constructed, now lay in total ruin, as clear to me as the derelict remnants of Mervyn's chipboard hovel. The walls remained upright but the roof had fallen in. The door hung open on one hinge. Around it, the farm buildings lay silent: no clucking, no moos, the stench of dung long gone. I stepped through the doorway but could see no vestigial sign of Mervyn's life there. The cracked toilet bowl gaped dry; a bird's nest bundled in the fireplace like the matted hair of a tramp; weeds seeped through the floorboards.

Back outside, I tried to regain myself. Why had I assumed it would all still be here? Had I come to revel in the decay, to mark time or what? I should be back in Oxford, London, anywhere but this past, this different story. It was splitting apart the nice little narrative I'd constructed for myself. I felt the bruise on my face.

At that moment, a purple mark blinked in the corner of my right eye, a figure glimpsed through a far passageway. The driver of the Land Rover on the gravel, or Fran, I didn't know which but I set off after them, another past, a different version, opening up in front of me.

*

One morning well into the November of that term, a heavy bone-chill wind swept across the school, dark clouds pressed down, collars tipped up. The dining-room thrummed at coffee break, with bunches of kids huddled around the storage heater, their gloved hands cupping mugs like chipmunks with nuts. I poured myself a drink at the top table.

Leonard and Moira bustled past me, their faces snow white with fear. 'Listen everyone, lend me your ears,' Leonard said. No one showed any sign of having heard him, or of wanting to lend him anything.

Moira raised the handbell in her right hand. The sound filled the enclosed space, shocking everyone into silence. 'The time for talking is done,' she said, hinting at more talk to come. 'We've had the call. The inspectors are coming this week.'

The room gave out a collective gasp. Keith stepped forward. 'This week?'

'That's right,' Leonard leapt in before Moira could answer. 'Thursday and Friday. The statuary three day's notice.'

'Statutory,' I mumbled.

He twisted to look at me, spindly hair falling over his wood-knot face. Moira carried on before he could ask me what I meant. 'Classes for the next three days are suspended,' she said. 'Go to where you normally go to after break, and the staff there will have something for you to do.'

'Like what?' someone asked.

'Projects,' Leonard took over. 'Last minute maintenance, painting and etcetera. Also, the Thursday meeting will be held next week – given the Octagon's unfinished.'

'Whose fault is that?' Moira muttered.

Leonard pushed his shoulders back. 'I don't know, whose is it? Perhaps the chair of the Senior Committee?'

The kids in the room gathered around some of the Eagles for direction and ignored the squabbling adults. As so often the case at Bannock House, the pupils worked out what needed to be done and then went about trying to do it. I once thought this trait evidence of a failing school.

'We better pull our fingers out, guys.' Keith glanced around at the nodding, eager faces. 'Everybody do as much as you can.'

'What class have you got now?' Jenny asked me.

'I'm in woodwork,' I replied. 'I'm sure Leonard will have some ideas, if he can fart out the right words.'

She laughed. 'See you later.' People clinked their cups down and clapped their hands, encouraging each other to get to their classes and start work. Everybody wanted to help. Moira and Leonard broke off their argument, surprised, as we streamed passed them.

'Excellent,' Leonard said. 'Well done.'

'Yes, very well done,' Moira added. 'It gives me such a profound feeling of happiness when I can inspire the young.'

I volunteered to strip the ivy from the side of the Big House. The dark green mesh stretched up as far as my old dorm and it had infiltrated the window where I used to sit. I went upstairs to rip the twisted fibres free from the window sill by hand, rather than hauling at it from the ground.

The same tin bucket from the last year stood in the middle of the top landing, placed to collect leaking rainwater from the skylight. I moved it into the bathroom and hoped it wouldn't rain in the next two days. Back in my old dorm, the window pane was still cracked, asterisked by the stone in Lex's long-forgotten snowball. Over time the untrained ivy had insinuated itself between the sash and the sill. I began to tug the spindles clear. They left little sucker marks on the dirty white paint of the frame, dotting it like a rash.

I looked around the room, now home to Charlie and Billy. The oily orange walls were the same but I couldn't see any trace of my past life, or of Lex's, apart from the crack. The two beds hadn't been moved but the strewn clothes and posters seemed too young and too small, as if they belonged to a different race of being altogether. I hardly spoke to Charlie now; I didn't play the silly games that he and the rest of the Sparrows so enjoyed, running through the corridors, screeching. I tried to ignore their antics and had no classes with Charlie or the rest of them. I was too advanced.

The door grumbled open and Roya appeared. 'What are you doing here?' she asked.

I yanked clear the last of the ivy and held it up. 'What do you think?'

She tilted her heavy head. 'Where's Billy?'

'How should I know?'

'You like asking questions don't you?' She held the door open, her long nose pointed like an accusation. 'But you never answer them. You never do anything. Look at you and Jenny.'

'What that's supposed to mean?' I reddened. Did they know about my wet dreams, or about the method I discovered to alleviate them?

'Boys are so dense.' She sighed, tired with the world. 'Anyway, this isn't the advice pages of *Just Seventeen*. I'm looking for the Sparrows. They should be helping me in the pottery.' She fiddled with the zip on her bulky anorak.

'I'll find them.' I knew they must be in Mervyn's class. He was the only teacher who wouldn't have known about the impending inspection.

The cabin sat squat and dark against the Tangle, a thin wisp of smoke coughing from its chimney. Ducking underneath, I heard Mervyn's voice going through Pythagoras' theorem – as clear and lucid as he'd been the year before. I climbed through the trapdoor and halted half way up the steps.

He stopped with his chalk to the board when he saw me. 'What's the meaning of this invasion?' he said.

Six or seven sparrows including Charlie, snot-nosed Billy and the waifish Tina, sat quietly in a tight semi-circle, pencils poised. Charlie smiled at me but I ignored him. 'All classes are suspended,' I replied to Mervyn.

'Why? And on whose authority?'

'The inspectors are coming.' I clambered up into the room and spoke to the class. 'Everyone's helping to get ready.'

The kids shifted in their seats and whispered, waiting for Mervyn's response. 'This week?' He paused and turned to the class. 'Very well, you better go. But remember the theorem. I'll be testing you on it before the end of term.' He rapped the blackboard with his knuckles.

Billy pulled repeatedly at the frayed cuffs of his bright green jumper and stood in front of Mervyn: 'What are you up

197

to later?' he said. 'You can help us get ready.' He turned to me, as if I were the authority figure in the room. 'Where are we meant to go, James?'

Charlie glanced quickly up at me and then back at Mervyn. 'We can come round after tea? To your rooms.'

Mervyn straightened and tried to look stern. He pushed his chest out and pretended to be very busy. 'I may be available for some peregrinations of the mind, provided all set questions have been attempted.' He surveyed the small bobbing forms beneath him, his flock. 'But I will not be taking part in these piddling efforts in cosmetics, administered by pettifogging nincompoops!'

To my surprise, the children laughed.

Tina, the pale bell ringer, touched Mervyn's arm. 'See you later,' she said.

'Can we play crib this time?' A plum faced girl said to one of the others.

Billy sighed. 'Boring. Mervyn can do his impressions.'

'Nincompoop,' she replied.

'Go to the pottery,' I spoke over their heads as they descended through the trap door. 'Paloma and Roya need help.' The way they spoke to Mervyn – and in particular Charlie – disturbed me, somehow, but I didn't quite know why. It was the familiarity, the friendly disdain, that prickled my skin. Was I jealous of them, of him, for myself?

Tina looked up at me before she left. Her black hair cropped, her skin sickly pale, I noticed for the first time her bug-big eyes, too large for her face. She clattered away with the others, leaving me with the sharp-sweet tang of cheap perfume and a stomach sick with unease. I went down the steps after her, pursued by Mervyn's silence.

The School spasmed into action: people shouted at each other; toted mop buckets across the gravel; scrubbed and painted and rushed. The air thrummed with anxiety, transmitted by the short, sharp yelps of the teachers and by the unusual concentration and quiet of the pupils. Time sped. Jenny and I spent most of the day cleaning up downstairs. We soaked graffiti from the walls, scraped green mould from the corners of the bathroom and squashed silverfish under our heels. We even dislodged the ancient cobwebs that garlanded the long dark corridor between our rooms. I had never worked so hard in my life.

Kids crowded into the dining room that night, subdued and hungry. I sat opposite Fran, her eyes dark and hollow behind her glasses. She offered a half-smile. 'Working hard?'

Before I could reply a loud shout echoed from the hallway next door. 'You dirty bastard!' I bolted from the table, eager to catch any confrontation.

Keith stood by the main front door glowering at Raymond, who had both hands up in supplication. 'Cool it, K.' Raymond said, with a hint of amusement in his voice.

Lone muffled in a long woollen jumper, held her head on one side. 'Keith, let's eat some food. Forget about this nonsense.'

'Shut it,' he squeezed the words out of his mouth, his eyes firmly on Raymond. 'You're as bad as he is.'

She sighed then tried to push past me into the dining room. 'Why don't you stop them?' I said.

'If Keith wants to be an idiot, it's up to him, no?' she said.

Fran appeared by my side. 'Keith, what are you doing?' she asked calmly.

He glanced at her and stepped forward. 'This fucking raj is for it, Fran, I'm sorry. He's well out of order.'

Raymond crouched down and turned sideways. 'I warn you, Keith,' he said, adjusting his bandana. 'I know Kung Fu. I will defend myself.'

Keith ran towards him and yelled. 'Kung Fu, my arse.' He launched his head flush into Raymond's face and they both tumbled to the floor.

Fran cried out and she and a couple of others rushed to pull them apart. Keith grunted and shrugged them away. 'Now that's a fucking warning, you hippy cunt. Stay away.' He shook his head and banged out of the front door into the night.

Fran and the pottery teacher, Paloma, helped Raymond to his feet. His nose bled. 'That was totally not Kung Fu,' he said through his hand as Paloma took him to the downstairs bathroom, muttering something about arnica.

I gestured towards the front door and looked at Fran. 'Should I go after him?'

She took off her glasses and squeezed the bridge of her nose. 'Leave him to cool off.' She paced back into the dining room and spoke almost to herself. 'This is not what we need right now. We need to be whiter than white.' Plates clattered and mouths munched but no one said anything more, other than a table full of Sparrows, who giggled like infants.

At the end of the meal, Fran leaned over and put her hand on my arm. 'James, can you help me with something?'

I nodded as she waited for the table to clear.

'Can you make sure Mervyn doesn't get too drunk tomorrow night? He can't turn up smelling of booze in front of the inspectors.'

'Why me?' I said. 'I mean, can't you tell him?' I hadn't visited Mervyn for ages and I knew that turning up with that kind of advice wouldn't make me welcome.

'Just do what you can, okay?'

As we rose the Sparrows bustled past us and out of the door. 'Gobbledegook,' Billy cried amidst the screams. 'Nincompoop,' Charlie's voice echoed down the corridor in reply.

Those same Sparrows screamed and lurched and laughed again, later that night, as they bounced along the corridor. I heard them from the downstairs bathroom as I lay immersed, tracing the cracks in the paintwork with a soapy finger. (Two days cleaning wouldn't change how run down the school was, how much in need of repair.) I gripped the plug in my toes when the outside door banged open. 'He's mental!' Tina screamed.

Three or four sets of feet scuffled past. 'I know, but you're as bad.' I recognised Billy's voice.

Charlie's high, posher pitch came next. 'Do you think he'll do it again?' he said. Their feet pounded out of earshot. I pulled the plug and let the water gurgle away, unable to move. A chill crept into my chest that had nothing to with the cold air around me.

Jenny hadn't witnessed the fight between Keith and Raymond and so I told her as we went to supper.

She scowled. 'That's wrong.' Her dark, fierce eyes shone even in the dismal light of the back stairs.

I shrugged. 'It's just a fight.'

'Don't you see! It's means that Raymond has been sleeping with Lone,' she cried. 'This could ruin everything.' She turned and ran toward the kitchen, leaving me in a swirl of vanilla and fresh fruit.

I arrived a few moments later to find her stood across the table from Raymond, pointing. 'It will be your fault if we fail,' she said, her mole-speckled face flushed.

Raymond held his hands wide and open, his shoulders raised. 'Keep cool, Jen. I'm not sure what you think but you've got the wrong end of the stick.' His voice sounded stuffed up and I saw a wodge of cotton wool poking from his nose.

'I have not.' She stamped her foot. 'We need to be whiter than white.'

'There's nothing going on.' Raymond grinned. 'Look at me, I'm an old man of twenty-nine. You can't imagine a girl like Lone has any interest in me?'

Jenny flicked her head, urging me to speak. I stayed quiet. 'Everybody knows,' she said, glancing back at Raymond.

'Don't listen to them.' Raymond waved his hand airily. 'Most of the women here are wizened old hags. They're jealous of Lone, that's all.'

I felt my chest tighten again but I didn't know why. 'Peace and love,' I said.

Raymond turned to face me, bemused.

'Exactly.' He clapped his hands. 'Peace and love. There's nothing wrong with sex. Hey, we wouldn't be here without it.' He placed himself on a high stool and pulled the teapot towards him. 'I never expected you kids to be such prudes.' He chuckled to himself. 'But, whatever! Lone and I are just friends.'

'Thanks for the support, James.' Jenny said over her shoulder as we went to our rooms. 'You were a real help.'

'What good would it do? If we don't know, then the inspectors can't say either.'

Jenny didn't speak to me at all the next day, the eve of the inspection. She gave me a haughty glance at breakfast, flounced past me at morning break and avoided my eye at lunch. It wasn't until tea that we spoke, when I mustered the courage to apologise for not backing her up against Raymond. I didn't really mean it, but for something so easy to say it had a huge effect. She immediately forgave me and suggested we go for a final clean up session in the art room. Telling the truth isn't always the right thing to do.

The art room was the biggest classroom in the school. Jenny swept and I had the dustpan. Every so often, I would look out over the dark school grounds, the lights of the Big House blinking through the wind-shook trees. Moira worked away in the far corner, her back to us. Across the hallway, through the glass doors, Leonard and some of the Eagles erected safety notices around the equipment. This happened at every inspection, after which the signs were immediately taken down. As far as I knew, no pupil had ever been injured by the power tools – perhaps because they'd been trusted with using them, trusted to know that putting your hand into a circular saw wasn't a good idea.

Jenny put the broom against the far wall. 'That's it. I'm tired.' She pulled her hair free from its band. 'There's nothing more we can do, it's up to the teachers now.'

I emptied the pan. 'And us.'

'Yes, and us.' She smiled at me. 'Are you coming?'

'I'm going for a walk,' I said.

'Here, take my torch.' She handed me her bike light, then skipped to the door, where she turned. 'I like working with you. I'm glad you've helped.' Then she left, as if it were the easiest thing in the world to say such words, and to mean them. I put the dustpan under the sink and noticed Moira mumbling to herself, picking up and putting down paintbrushes at random.

'Are you okay?' I said.

'Yes I'm fine.' I waited, expecting some rant about the iniquity of outside government interference, or the immorality of the Right, or Leonard's megalomania but she simply looked down at the brushes in her hand. 'You all get so tall,' she said, her fat form still and somehow noble, as if she'd stepped out of a painting. 'It's like you become different people.' She walked over to the door. A crooked strip of paper ran from the floor up to near the ceiling, marking the heights of pupils over the last few years. Extra sheets had been stapled on it, with big bunches of names between five and six feet.

I stepped beside her and found my own name: The first entry, an inch above Charlie's, with Lex's name squeezed in between. Now I'd out distanced Charlie by many inches on the chart. Adjacent to these, on a bright, white new piece of paper, I saw the names of the latest Sparrows, including Billy and Tina.

Moira put her hand to the paper and gently smoothed out a crease. 'All we want is for you to be happy, to grow up happy.'

The buzzing of the overhead lights grew louder and I didn't know what to say. I'd always been ready to argue with her but I couldn't then. How could you argue with that? 'I better go,' I said.

As I strode out into the night, a tight chill gripped my chest once more. Fran's words came back to me. Make sure Mervyn's not too drunk. But the thought of going to his rooms awoke a sense of dread, for me, for him, for the school. I walked through the vegetable garden in the near dark, trampling on Fran's spinach. The younger five-foot me would have laughed at my unease. Why did I care about the school now? It shocked me, but I did. I loped past the cricket net, ruffling my hand through the twisted netting. I carried on, down the drive, trying to gather up the courage to go to Mervyn's.

The wind rose and fell, catching the ankles of my wide trousers. I paused at the Tangle. I could find my way to the hut with my eyes closed, so often had I been there, so well did I know each knot and gnarl of the path. I planned to take Jenny on the day of the Christmas party, to show her where I spent so much of my time. No one else had been there. I turned back along the drive, past the dark, brooding shape of the maths cabin. Unlit, it merged into the Tangle more like an overgrown bank of nature than a man-made structure. I picked up pace and carried on, past the cabin, across the gravel. My legs propelled me forwards unbidden and, though part of me didn't want to, I found myself hurrying towards Mervyn's rooms. The thing in my mind that had been snagging like a jersey on a nail suddenly sprang free. It was nothing to do with Raymond and Lone at all.

Sat on the end of the row of farm buildings, Mervyn's chipboard hut looked more alone than ever, a temporary afterthought appended to a solid stone edifice. A single outdoor bulb burned from the corner opposite, outside the byre, casting a weak glow over the muddy, dung-stained flagstones. A thin yellow band escaped the side of the hut, the light breaking through the gap in the curtains. The small window to the left of the front door was dark, though, and as I peered through I could see the sliding door that connected Mervyn's room to the hallway was shut, only a thin wedge of light at the bottom hinting at what lay beyond.

I put my hand to the door but then hesitated. A faint fast beat filtered from inside, the first time I'd heard Mervyn ever listen to music. As far as I knew, his knowledge of the subject didn't go beyond crossword terminology. *Soft* equals Piano equals P; *Opera* equals N O R M A. The paint on the wooden door had almost totally peeled off, leaving only flaking streaks down the side and a sad island in the centre. A back draft of wind brought the smoke cascading down from the chimney, drifting around me like mist. I smoothed my hand across the door, feeling for creases, and then rapped three times.

No one answered. A great crash shuddered the hut, followed by some high-pitch squealing. I wanted to turn away, to go back to Jenny, Roya and Fran and the warm kitchen, or their brightly coloured dorm or the Tangle or anywhere but here. I wanted to, yet I raised my hand to the door again and pushed it open with my palm, the Yale lock either snibbed or broken. My throat constricted and my chest tightened as I pulled open the slide door.

The bedroom thronged with snotty young Sparrows. Frantic stringed folk music strained out of a small tape recorder and the room was hot with smoke and cider. Charlie sat coiled in the armchair that I still, with a lurch, regarded as mine. Billy crouched by the wood stack, grinning. Tina and another girl tickled each other on the bed, giggling, on the edge of hysteria. And in the midst of it all sat Mervyn on his favourite stool, side lit by the high flames of the fire. He barely acknowledged my entrance. He was too busy tapping his feet to the beat. His eyes flickered wildly and I could tell he'd been drinking heavily.

I stood in the doorway. None of the children took notice of me other than a brief glance, just another guest at the party. Mervyn banged his head in time with the music, and Billy leant forward to sneak a sip of his glass. 'Oi! That's mine you cheeky bugger.' Mervyn shot out a hand and snatched the glass back, slopping some of its contents on his trousers. 'Where are your manners?' He grinned and took another gulp. His voice sounded coarser, more common than normal, unlike the precise terms he used in classes.

No words came to me. The stifling heat, so unlike the pinching cold outside, the music, the smoke, the noise of the screaming children overwhelmed me. Mervyn shook his head from side to side and mooed his lips for a moment, still ignoring my presence. 'What's Lothario doing here?' he suddenly snapped at Charlie in the chair. He didn't look up at me.

Charlie turned his head to me, eager to help. His familiar bright red curls framed his face, but he didn't smile. 'What are you doing here?' he challenged. His cheeks didn't bunch, his eyes didn't shine.

I looked from him to Mervyn but couldn't say anything. The girls stood up on Mervyn's bed. 'Can we plait your hair?' Tina called to Mervyn. 'Or your beard?'

'Come here,' Mervyn said to Charlie. 'I suppose he wants his chair.' Charlie stood up and Mervyn put his arm out. 'Sit on my lap,' he said.

A kicking dancing beat started up and Charlie grasped his hand and clambered onto him. The two girls on the bed and Billy all stood up and jumped in time to the new base line. Charlie, sitting on Mervyn's lap like any child, bounced up and down to the music. Mervyn grinned as the boy gripped his thighs, a gurgle in his throat, the kids cackled in delight.

I watched, motionless, unable to step forward or to turn away. Mervyn gurned theatrically, increasing the hysteria.

'It's hard, it's hard,' Charlie squealed in excitement as he wriggled. 'I can feel it through his trousers.'

I put my hand forward in a half-movement which caught Mervyn's wild eyes. He glared at me. 'Too much is it? Jealous?' He raised his voice over the music, Charlie lurching on his lap. 'Boys and girls go round and round. Round boys, boys round.' He ended up shouting, as Charlie slipped off him.

'It's not –' I faltered. 'The inspection. Tomorrow. We've got to be whiter than white.'

'You've changed your tune,' he rasped. 'You lied for me once, remember? It's your fault.'

'You shouldn't drink,' I muttered weakly. 'We were friends.'

'I never asked you to be my friend. I never asked.'

The music ended abruptly. 'Watch this!' Billy yelled. He tossed a plastic bottle into the fire. It flamed up, all blue white and green together. They all stared but I turned and ran, the smell of burnt plastic caught in my nose.

10

I couldn't find anyone. The dark figure I'd seen had disappeared, lost amidst the deserted school. I pushed at locked doors, rattled dirty windows but could find nothing except my own memories. Eventually I ran up the small hill that overlooked the grounds. The arts and crafts building had been demolished. Only the concrete foundations remained, any trace of former function gone. The wood must have been sold, the asphalt on the roof recycled. I sat down on the brow of the hill and gazed out over the school, an empty silent shell. It held only visions of my past, that final night now vivid in my mind. Moira's gentle words, uttered a few feet from where I sat, and then my own discovery of Mervyn in his rooms; the picture blazing in my mind, a night I'd done my best to forget, to deny, even to myself.

Do we learn to lie to ourselves at the same time we learn to lie at all? Parents laugh at their young children when they catch them out in a transparent falsehood; they chide them gently 'to always tell the truth'; yet we all know that one of the symptoms and necessities of growing up is a facility to be elastic with the facts. How could we protect ourselves if we were forever honest? Had I taken this too far, and deceived even myself, deliberately forgetting my own sins, obliterated them in an act of misremembering? But surely, if we can't maintain a lie we would be lost, useless, condemned to an endless tangle of guilt and blame?

Mervyn was right. It was my fault he stayed at the school. He was right ten years ago and he was right yesterday on the bus. I lied. I never attended an extra maths session with Lex, was never in a position to disprove his allegations against Mervyn. I lied to Fran, to everyone, that suppertime because to me it was obvious that Mervyn could not be guilty, clear that

208

Lex had to be lying. I said this to myself at the time, made these logical steps and came to the only correct solution. Lex was a monstrous liar and Mervyn a man unjustly accused. I acted to protect my friend Mervyn and by doing so, made it easy for the school to go on untroubled – made it easy for Mervyn. I'd missed the double meaning, failed to put all the parts of the clue together properly. Lex lied about many things, but he didn't lie about Mervyn.

That last night in Mervyn's rooms with Charlie lilting on his bony lap, changed everything. My lie led to that scene, led to it all. A memory long buried, suddenly now and forever alive. 'It's hard, it's hard.' I'd involved myself, acted to protect someone close to me, became personally entangled and it ended up with a drunken, twisted man preying on the vulnerable. Janice flashed into my mind. Could I help her, or was that a silly romantic notion, doomed to failure? She was a complication I should avoid, another tangle not to toy with. I'd done all right the last ten years, keeping out of things, of people. That was the whole point of politics, policy not people. It made sense to me. I should have avoided the village, Janice and her friends. I should never have come back to Bannock House. It was dead, all dead.

The Land Rover started. I heard the cough and splutter of the engine and the gravel grind. 'Hey,' I shouted as I ran down the slope to cut off the car. 'Wait!' I rushed out onto the drive just as it burst past and accelerated away, leaving me squinting in its wake.

Dust prickled my eyes. I had come to lay old ghosts to rest, or to kill them, but they had escaped me once more. Who would help me now?

'Can I help you?' A woman asked in a faded but still recognisable Canadian accent, sharp and straightforward.

I spun around. The frames of her glasses had grown bigger and bulkier and her waist had thickened. She still wore purple but her once blonde hair was now grey completely. 'Fran,' I said. 'It's me.'

She peered, like I was an ant crawling across her kitchen table. 'Who are you?'

'James. James Trefoil,' I said as I stepped towards her.

I saw the bright gleam of recognition in her eyes the moment before she slapped me hard across the face. 'Liar,' she said as she did so.

*

'Fire,' I cried into the phone. 'Ambulance. Police.'

'Where are you, son?'

I'd smashed off the feeble lock on the school's only telephone and stood with the receiver pressed against my ear, gabbling the address. I didn't have to pretend to sound upset. Although I was tall for my age, at nearly thirteen my voice still hadn't broken and I guessed the operator must have been convinced. The outside world was coming.

Someone yanked open the cupboard door. Fran looked at me, bemused. 'James? Who are you calling?'

'Hurry,' I said into the phone then ripped the wire from its housing.

She bent to look at the broken telephone while I pushed past her out into the hall. 'What are you playing at?' she called after me as I took the stairs two at a time. 'You know you'll have to fix this.'

The wah-wah claxon of a fire engine echoed down the valley soon after, followed by the blue blush of the lights as it skidded onto the gravel. I waited, out of sight, obscured by bushes at the edge of the football pitch. Most of the school spilled out from the Big House and their various dorms, attracted by the noise and light show – so rarely did we see representatives of the normal world, that when they did appear it was like a freak show. Fran stepped forward to one of the fireman, another of whom looked around him and spat. An ambulance lurched into view. A gang of Eagles wandered over from the carriages, Keith and Lone among them, holding hands, Raymond nowhere to be seen.

One of the firemen spoke to Fran and he walked up to the ambulance driver and waived him on. 'A bloody hoax,' he shouted over the siren. The words barely carried to my hiding place. Finally, what I had been waiting for – the boxy shape and flashing lights of a small police car pulled up next to the engine. A man and woman got out and the man joined Fran. The two firemen got back into their cab, their heavy trousers like flags pinned by a strong wind. The fire engine coughed into life and slowly rolled across the gravel towards me, its headlights strobing the bushes, before it arced abruptly down the drive.

The policewomen stood by her car, one hand on the top of the open door. I edged towards her, the ice-crystalled ground crackling under my feet, the smell of burnt plastic in my nostrils still. She turned to me, her face pink and pudgy, her eyes milk-cow kind. 'Can I help you, son?' she said.

I told her that my maths teacher Mervyn had been abusing me for the last year. I told her where he touched me. I told her of all the time we spent together alone in his rooms. I even told her that if she went to his rooms right now, she'd find my come-stained boxer shorts, still wedged in the bottom of Mervyn's cricket bag from the summer before. They had my nametag sown into the elastic waistband. I told her that no one at the school knew anything, that Mervyn was a bad man who needed to be dealt with.

Fran hadn't seen me at first, busy persuading the policeman not to enquire too deeply into who might have perpetrated the fake call. But as I went on talking, she saw me and I could see in the way she moved her head to the side that she sensed something was wrong, like a mother on the look-out for her baby's distress. She broke away from her conversation and walked towards us. I couldn't make out her face clearly, now the fire engine had gone, but her silhouette was stark against the windows of the Big House. She called out. 'James?'

The policewoman put her hand on my shoulder and stepped forward, as if to stop Fran coming any closer, shielding me. 'Is there somewhere we can go?' she said, her mild Scottish lilt elongating the final o.

Fran stooped towards me, her palms splayed upwards, reaching out. 'What have you done?'

'I'm saving the school,' I replied.

*

'You destroyed the school,' Fran said ten years later. She'd stepped back from me, as surprised as I was by her slap. 'You ruined Mervyn.'

I shook my head. 'It wasn't like that.'

'Are you telling me Mervyn abused you?'

Tiny whorls of dust twisted about my scuffing feet. Fran held out one hand towards me, her palm held upwards and I felt twelve again as if ten years of education, a different life, didn't yawn between then and now. She waited for her answer but this time, I didn't have a policewoman by my side to shield me, this time I couldn't stop the past and present colliding. 'No,' I said.

She flung her arms up in the air in a sudden burst of energy. 'I knew it. I knew you were lying. You hated everything we stood for from the very beginning, you bided your time and then you destroyed us with your lies.' She took a deep breath, set her jaw, composed herself. 'Now would you please leave? This is private property.'

'I just thought…'

'What did you think?' she said, sharply. But then all the animation when out of her. Her jowls sagged. 'It's all over, James.'

'Over?'

She gestured to the Big House. 'This place has been sold. The trust finally collapsed. No doubt that makes you happy. It's what you always wanted.' The sun flashed off her large glasses. She brought her hand up to her eyes and stared at me, her head on one side. 'There's nothing here now.' She pivoted

212

slowly and trudged away from me, her long grey hair wound in a plait hanging down her neck, her shoulders stooped.

'Maybe I can help?' I ran around in front of her. She came to a tired halt and watched as I gabled on. 'I'm going to get a job with New Labour, I'm in the party.'

'Why doesn't that surprise me?'

'They'll be lots of money for schools, new ideas. I don't know…'

She shook her head. 'For a smart kid, you still don't get it do you? There'll be no funding for schools like Bannock House. They're going to set down exactly what to teach the kids then test the hell out of them, that's the big idea. Oh, I know.' She raised her hand to stop my interruption. 'They'll be better than the Tories. I believe that – at least they'll spend the cash, give the poor a decent shot for a change. But it's not what we had here.'

'But we – the party – believe in education, like you. It's the number one priority. Personal responsibility, community, equality – all the Bannock House values. We believe in education.' I repeated.

'What's the point, James? You've got the buzzword, I get it. Education, education, education? But what do you think that means? What do you think education is really about?'

I hesitated. 'Equality of opportunity. Academic achievement. It's about preparing people for society, for the world of work.'

She squeezed her hands together, working the bones. 'That's not the game we were in, not at all. Happy kids, James, that's what we wanted. Happy, fulfilled children have a better chance of being happy and fulfilled adults. It's simple really. Bannock House was about the generation of happiness, the sole object of education or something like that. I can't remember the exact quote but you get the idea. The generation of happiness.'

'But I needed exams to make me happy,' I said, feeling younger by the moment. 'I needed to succeed.'

'You would always have succeeded academically, James. That was never your problem. You're an A student anywhere. But it's not just about the A students, is it? We all have a responsibility to help everyone as best as we can. Did you ever think of the others? What kind of society would it be if we were all out for number one? If no one else mattered.'

'I really didn't mean to hurt the school,' I pleaded. 'I liked it. It taught me how to learn. You wouldn't believe the kids I've met since who were sick of school, sick of learning. I'll always be hungry, Bannock House gave me that – not the times table or the date of the coronation. That's what stays with you. I understand that now. I didn't mean to ruin anything.'

She'd waited while I gave my speech but then shook her head again. Stray wisps of hair fell over her rumpled brow. 'What did you expect to happen, when you came up with your pack of lies?'

'I retracted at the trial.'

Fran sighed and began her measured tread once more, away from the gravel and alongside the overgrown football pitch. 'The school couldn't take that kind of publicity, you know that. We barely survived another term after you left. Especially without your dad's money.'

'My dad?'

She brushed the question aside with a waved hand. Two bangles chimed as she continued, with me a step behind. 'Don't play the dumb ingénue with me. I knew you when you were eleven, remember? I don't have time for this. Once, we'd have a discussion about it and I'd pretend to take your opinion into consideration and we'd all marvel about how civilised we were. But Bannock House is dead, James. Okay? It's over, it's all over,' as she said these last words she drew to a slow halt.

A breeze ruffled the trees above us. A small dust devil whirled for an instant and then disappeared. 'I saw him on the bus,' I said. She flinched but I went on. 'They said he lives in Dalry.'

'He didn't have any place else to go. Not once you ruined his life.' Her lips thinned and pulled her mouth tight in a regretful curl. 'That was the part I never understood. He was your friend. I know he drank too much but why did you do that to him? Why didn't you just leave?'

The wind dropped. For a moment, she looked uncertain, a doubt sounding in her heart, like an echo. Her shoulders sagged, as if she'd heard that echo often. But then her face closed and her chin set, a middle-aged woman all alone. She needed confirmation, the black and white validation of a long clung-to view, not the sickening greys of the truth, not the facts. They wouldn't help anyone.

'I can't remember,' I said at last. 'It seems so long ago. Maybe I was a spiteful kid.'

She shook her head and looked out over the meadow off to our right. 'That field's flooded each of the last three years, and now they are going build a golf course on it.' She squinted towards the way we'd come, back to the old gravestone grey Big House. 'This'll be a hotel. A centre of economic regeneration for the area, they say. That'll mean the kids from Dungowan can get jobs as busboys or chambermaids. Good job they got their O Grades.' Then she looked straight at me, ever the teacher still. 'I used to like you, James. Don't waste your life being spiteful, connect with people. Learn to be happy. The rest is nothing but detail.'

'Janice!' I banged on the back door of the house in Dungowan.

Her head appeared from the upstairs window, hair askew and puffy eyes pinched in annoyance. 'Zip it,' she hissed. 'I'll come down'.

I waited by the door. Fran's words sat heavy on my shoulders, confusing everything I'd ever thought, my mind raking through the past, catching on the tangles. Fran said to connect to people, maybe the present could make up for the past.

Janice glanced behind her and soft-shutted the door. 'My dad's asleep. What do you want?'

Her eyes darted, sharp and wary, not what I was expecting. 'A drink of water,' I said, suddenly nervy.

She scowled. 'Wait up there.'

A minute later, she tottered up the side of the grass bank with a scaly pint glass full to the brim. I gulped it down. 'You don't have to be afraid,' I said at last.

'Afraid of what?'

I drew my hand across my mouth and sat down on the ground. Janice stayed standing. 'I know what you're going through. With your dad and now Tam. It's a cycle. People get used to abuse.'

'What are you talking about?'

'The bruises on your arm, your dad, Tam. You don't have to lie about it to me.'

'Lie about what? You calling me a liar? Who do you think you are?' Her cheeks reddened, her eyes widened. 'Archie's a fucking drunk but he doesnae hit me, he's never hit me. Not that it's any of your business.'

'What about those,' I said pointing to the dark blooms on her pale arms.

'That's Tam, aye,' she said. 'But that's just sex. Me and him, on off. Christ James, I thought you were a nice lad. Manners, cute, lovely voice. Posh totty. But you're as bad as those wasters in the pub.' Her head tilted, her birthmark jutting. 'You don't know much about sex, do you?'

I looked away but nodded slightly, my face hot, my hand twisting in the pocket of my trousers.

She sat down beside me on the grassy bank with a sigh of disappointment. 'You were one of those boys, weren't you?' she said in a softer voice. 'I knew it. You were abused at that school, by the weirdo from Dalry. Is that why you see it everywhere?'

'No, I mean. God, I thought I could help,' I muttered into my chest and pulled at the grass with my free hand. It came away in simple clumps, easily, tired, ready to give in. 'I thought I knew what you were going through, that's all.'

'You can get therapy and that, you know. If you feel bad.'

'You don't understand. He never abused me. Mervyn, the guy on the bus, never abused me. I was never abused.'

'Oh, right. But, I don't get it.'

'I lied. I was the boy in the news, I was the kid who was "abused" but I lied. He never touched me.'

Janice sucked air through her teeth. She went to speak but stopped, then started again. 'That's terrible.' She stood up and patted clean her jeans. 'That's really, really bad. You shouldnae lie about something like that.'

'It's not what you think.'

She tilted her face away, back to her house. 'Tam was right about you – another rich kid who thinks the world owes him a living. You cannae treat people like that, you cannae use them. Aren't you happy enough with your money and your fancy education? Why are you here, anyway?'

'I can explain.'

'I don't care, alright? Why should I care, I just met you yesterday.' She folded her arms across her chest. 'I thought you were somebody else. I'm going to go back inside now. If I were you, by the way, I would apologise to that poor man from the bus. People round here think he's a paedophile. It's shameless.'

She padded down the slope and went into her house without looking at me again. All my plans had gone awry. Connecting to people wasn't that easy.

I couldn't see Mervyn's caravan from the road. It had taken me three hours to walk to Dalry. I put my rucksack on the verge and opened the gate, fastened by garish orange twine, frayed at the end. The small white caravan had a faded red door set between two head high oblong windows, curtains drawn. It sat at an uncomfortable angle, like it had been dredged up, for it only had wheels at one end: the tow-hook lay buried in the mud. Two small birds stood sentry on the roof. 'He lives oot past the hollow on the Kinlock road,' the old woman in the Dalry shop had said, eyeing me with distaste. 'But I don't know what you'd be wanting there.'

There was no sign of any power or telephone lines, or of any life even, other than the birds. I wondered, as I stood twenty yards away, if I'd come on the day of Mervyn's death. Then I heard a crash and the thin metal wall of the caravan quivered. From inside a burst of bellowed nonsense pursued the two birds as they fluttered up and away from their perch, into the mild white-blue sky.

I'd flown too. What could I possibly say on my return? Should I thank him for giving me the numbers and words, the wings to make it all the way to Oxford? Or was Fran right, would I have got there anyway? If indeed it even mattered. Maybe I should apologise, like Janice said, but that didn't feel right either. If I started apologising, I wouldn't know where to stop. I didn't move, couldn't take another step towards the hollow caravan. Fran's words twisted and turned in my mind, tangling with my memories, making sense. But I wasn't thinking about her, or Janice or even Mervyn. I was thinking of Charlie.

My first, my only ever, best friend.

*

I ran through the cold, clear November night, away from the cackling Sparrows, the burning plastic, Charlie lilting on his lap, away from the dark and poisoned man. All was plain: Mervyn's guilt and my complicity in it, the watch, the hand on Lex's back, 'It's hard, it's hard.' Charlie's shy questions 'Is it okay?' he'd said. 'What do you and Mervyn do?' 'Is it okay, is it okay, is it okay.'

'James,' Charlie shouted after me. 'Wait!'

I careered on, up the path along the football pitch in front of the Big House. Away from Mervyn's rooms, anywhere but there, never again, I ran pursued by the sound of Charlie's heavy breaths.

'Oomph,' he cried. I turned to see his dark shape stretched out in the gloom, face down on the stone-studded path. 'I tripped.' He held out his hand.

I hauled him to his feet and, in the scant light I made out his pale cheeks bunching. He smiled at me full in the face, almost as if it were me that made him happy, though this time his eyes didn't smile. I looked away, towards the Big House, its windows pinpricks against the darkness. Giant trees bubbled around it, swallowing the building like the smoke of a funeral pyre, black complete.

'It's okay,' he said. 'Don't freak out.'

I couldn't meet his eye, couldn't move.

'Don't be jealous.'

'I'm not jealous, it's just, just –' I tailed off, like an inarticulate child. I grasped the inner pocket of my trousers with a futile fist.

Charlie sounded strangely adult when he spoke, like he was tired. 'It's not as bad as you think. Honestly.'

'Don't go back there.' I turned to him. 'Go to supper, don't go back.'

'Okay,' he said.

'Stop saying that, it's not okay.' My eyes prickled. 'It's all wrong, wrong wrong.'

'It's easier,' he said. I wanted to cover my ears but he kept talking. 'Mervyn's lonely, that's all. It's nothing. He needs friends. You said yourself how important he is to the school.'

'I didn't mean,' I gasped. 'Not that you should…'

'Better me than you. Really, James, it's okay, it's not as bad as you think.'

A hard wind chilled my tear-wet cheeks. My head thrummed. 'NO,' I shouted in his face. 'I'm telling Fran. I'm telling her right now.'

I turned towards the house but Charlie grabbed my arm, an urgency in his voice for the first time. 'Don't,' he said, panicked. 'You can't tell. My dad would never recover. Please.' His fingers dug into the flesh of my bicep, then released. 'If you were ever my friend, please don't.'

He didn't follow me. I took off, towards the Big House but veered past it, beyond it and deep into the darkness of the Tangle. I tore through the undergrowth by the light of Jenny's bike lamp. I cut my hands and face on the thick thorns. I cried.

I shouted. Finally, I reached my hut and drew in deep lungfuls of air until my breathing slowed. I lay on my back inside and swung fitful torch beams across the cobwebbed boards that made up the roof, illuminating nothing.

The torch flickered and died. Without it, I couldn't see the hand in front of my face. But I knew the way back. I knew I had to halt the foulness at the heart of the school as soon as possible, to save it, to pull out the knots with the only means at my disposal. I headed back to the Big House, to the telephone cupboard, to my role as the accuser, and to my new life, a different childhood from the one that seemed so certain only hours before.

I didn't save Bannock House. Had I been anything other than a kid, I would have been able to predict this. My parents collected me from the police station the next day and we stayed in a hotel. After all the official interviews, we went home and I never came back. Like river ice trodden on by foolish children, the school collapsed under the weight of bad publicity. Suddenly it was gone, taken by the currents while I swam into a whole other life, memories of Bannock House jettisoned from my mind.

When they send you off to school, your parents tell you that you'll make friends, as if that's a good thing. They don't tell you the flip side; the duties it entails, the tangles you get into. They don't tell you how friends come and go, regardless of what's right or fitting or just. They don't tell you how to spot the bad ones from the good. You have to work all that out for yourself.

It took me ten years but I worked it out in the end, as I stood there on the edge of a Dalry field and sensed Mervyn's movements from the quivering walls of his caravan. I realised the last time I was truly happy: It wasn't my exam results, wasn't the letter of acceptance on the Corpus Christi letterhead, nor the chanting and cheering of election victory six weeks ago. It wasn't when I first cracked *The Times* crossword alone, or won the Webb Medley Prize. The last time I was truly happy was my first year at Bannock House, Charlie by my side, scavenging, dancing, climbing trees; poking fun at school democracy, cooking, painting, writing terrible poetry; learning by the by, while life went on; and simply going to bed at night excited for the morning, eager for the start of one more day. That all ended on the edge of the Tangle when we chased after Mervyn, when I chose him over Charlie, over the school. But I didn't need to know how to solve crossword clues, when to integrate or differentiate, or even how to calculate the length of the hypotenuse. I would have learnt all that anyway, it was easy, it was detail. If only I'd kept hold of the right strands, clung on to what made me happy, kept connected. But I didn't and it all unravelled, Lex, Charlie, Bannock House, lost. We all lost.

Mervyn's door swung open and banged against the side of the caravan. The empty space yawned dark but he did not appear, a magic trick gone wrong. Somewhere off to my left, free birds sang. I picked up my bag. I didn't need to talk to him, didn't need to apologise or understand or even indulge in a pointless confrontation. I hitched my rucksack tight and set off along the road, away from Mervyn forever, my education finally complete

Acknowledgements:

This book started out in the creative writing workshop at UEA. I'd like to thank my fellow students, and my tutors: in particular, Rob Magnusson Smith and DW Wilson from the former camp, and Trezza Azzopardi, Andrew Cowan and Giles Foden from the latter. I'd also like to thank those other patient readers who provided invaluable comments and encouragement: especially Andrew O'Hagan and Julia Caithness as well as my family, in particular my brother Tom who put me on the right track whenever I erred.

A short story featuring some of the elements of the novel also appeared in The Fiction Desk's first anthology, *Various Authors*, and I'd like to thank publisher Rob Redman for giving James and Mervyn their first chance in print.

I can't finish these acknowledgments without thanking my parents Sally and David, for providing me with a beautiful childhood as unlike James' as it is possible to imagine. I could not have wished for a happier upbringing.

Finally, and most importantly, I'd like to thank Annalise Davis for everything – for encouragement, humour, insight and more – and for our two little wrigglers, with us any day now.

About the Author:

Ben attended a succession of eccentric institutions known
as 'free' schools, where he couldn't have been happier.
He's worked in the film industry for the last fifteen years,
while also completing an MA in creative writing at UEA
and subsequently a PhD in Film and Television. He lives
in South London with his partner. *Terms* is his first novel.

Lightning Source UK Ltd.
Milton Keynes UK
UKOW04f1217080915

258276UK00002B/13/P